Angel in autumn

Agnes Carmichael knew a long-kept secret about her next door neighbours which made them of vital interest to her.

There was Bill Turner, a novelist, the lovely, vulnerable Stella (Bill's daughter?), her small son, Bruce, a nanny, and a lanky, guitar-playing youth, Rick (Bruce's father?).

And on the fringes of this strange ménage, the sinister, manipulative Hebe.

But it wasn't until little Bruce disappeared (or did he?) that Agnes, an ex-nurse in comfortable retirement, became involved both practically and emotionally in a complicated case of origin and descent – and summary justice.

Agnes's disquieting exultation in secret knowledge and its consequent power, now recorded in over twelve 'Nurse Carmichael' novels, makes her a unique character in present-day crime fiction.

*Previous books by Anthea Cohen,
featuring Agnes Carmichael*

Angel without mercy (1982)
Angel of vengeance (1982)
Angel of death (1983)
Fallen angel (1984)
Guardian angel (1985)
Hell's angel (1986)
Ministering angel (1987)
Destroying angel (1988)
Angel dust (1989)
Recording angel (1991)
Angel in action (1992)
Angel in love (1993)

ANGEL IN AUTUMN
Anthea Cohen

Constable · London

First published in Great Britain 1995
by Constable & Company Ltd
3 The Lanchesters, 162 Fulham Palace Road
London W6 9ER
Copyright © 1995 by Anthea Cohen
The right of Anthea Cohen to be
identified as the author of this work
has been asserted by her in accordance
with the Copyright, Designs and Patents Act 1988
ISBN 0 09 474400 9
Set in Palatino 10 pt by
Pure Tech Corporation, Pondicherry
Printed and bound in Great Britain by
Hartnolls Ltd., Bodmin, Cornwall

A CIP catalogue record of this book
is available from the British Library

PROLOGUE

The two nurses lowered the old lady into a chair. 'Do you want a rug over you, dear?' The patient shook her head and eased herself more comfortably into the chair. It was her first time up after having had her hip replaced.

'All right, then?' The second nurse seemed anxious to get on with the next job and was about to move away.

'No, it's not all right. I've got an ulcer.' The old lady looked accusingly at her.

'Where?' The nurse stopped short. 'I didn't know you had an ulcer, nobody told me. Where is it, on your leg?'

'No, stupid.' The patient put up a blue-veined, brown-spotted hand and removed her lower dentures, opening her mouth wide and pointing to her lower gum.

'Oh well, dear, we'll see to that later. Put them in for now.'

'No, I'll put a bit of tissue on them. I know how to do it. Give me the box.'

The nurse handed over a box of tissues to the old lady. She took one out and proceeded to tear off a neat strip, folded it into a small oblong, then put it into her mouth and wet it. She then removed it from her tongue and put it across the offending part of the denture and popped it back into her mouth, closing her upper and lower dentures firmly.

'That's better,' she said and smiled triumphantly at the departing nurses.

'God, I'll try and keep my teeth,' said Nurse Bennet when they were out of the old lady's hearing.

They proceeded up the ward, did one or two more jobs, then they were due for a cup of coffee. They were arguing.

'She's forty, I tell you. Sister Jensen is forty.'

Her companion, Nurse Carmichael, shook her head without much interest or conviction. 'Thirty-six or thirty-five, that's what I heard.'

'Forty! I know she's forty.'

'How do you know?' Nurse Carmichael asked rather irritably.

'I heard her say she was born in 1935. Now it's 1975 and her birthday, so . . .' She pointed a finger at Carmichael and wagged it, '. . . she must be forty, see?'

Carmichael shrugged. 'What does it matter, for goodness sake? I don't want coffee. I'll go straight to the men's ward.'

'OK. I'm thirsty and I want to sit down anyway. My shoes hurt.'

Nurse Bennet and Nurse Carmichael parted.

The entrance to the men's orthopaedic ward was directly opposite to that of the women's ward. The two were divided by a small tiled hall with a counter and chairs, which acted as a nursing station.

Sister Jensen looked up as Carmichael passed. She was just replacing the telephone; her brow was creased in a frown.

'Oh good. You finished in there?' Carmichael nodded. 'There's a road traffic accident in Casualty. The man's not too bad, been knocked out though, so he's being admitted for observation. His wife . . .' She didn't finish the sentence, but sucked the end of her biro and then wrote something down.

'Is she coming into the women's ward?'

Sister Jensen looked up again; she was still frowning. 'What? Oh, the wife? No, she's pregnant and she's on support. Query brain dead. Going to theatre for a Caesarean section. They're going to try to save the baby.'

Again Carmichael felt the familiar thrill – it was drama indeed. The poor man was to be admitted. Did he know, had they told him that his wife was brain dead maybe? And the baby . . . She was well aware that as a second-year nurse she would not be able to mention it, nor was she permitted to enquire about it – it was not her place. Certainly not her place to talk about it – it might get back to the patient. One had to preserve complete privacy for the patient. That was something that ranked very highly in Carmichael's estimation. Still, it was nice to know something so important and which the person in this case might know nothing about. It was a good feeling. Poor man, she would do her best for him. Secret knowledge always pleased her.

She went into the ward to draw the curtains round the bed that Sister Jensen had indicated, near the door, fold back the bedclothes and get the bed ready for his admission.

Bill Turner didn't know what they were doing to him. He could feel them moving about, but he felt dizzy, faint, muddled. He'd had a knock on the head, he knew that. There was a nurse touching his arm, giving him an injection. He felt the slight prick of the needle, but it didn't hurt – not much anyway. He tried to look at her, but her face disappeared in a mist – that was that.

There were a lot of people moving around him and he was moving now along a corridor. The lights flashed above him – one, two three – and he realized mistily that they weren't flashing but that he was passing under them – four, five, six – then sideways. Now he was being lifted. He felt more comfortable and he saw a man in a white coat – it might be a doctor. There was something hanging round his neck, a stethoscope? Why didn't he speak? Why didn't he say anything? And then, blank.

Some time later, Bill had no idea how long, he opened his eyes. Again he could see little. He wondered if he was blind and that was why they had brought him in – he had gone blind all of a sudden. Strange. Had he thought that before?

There was a nurse, another one. She said something like, 'All right, Mr Turner?' He couldn't imagine what she meant. Of course he was all right! He tried to move his arm, but it hurt.

'Don't move, just lie still. You're all right. Have you got a headache?' she asked.

He answered and said something foolish – something like, 'Yes, please.' He had meant to say, 'Yes, I am, thank you,' or at least that's what he thought he meant to say. He was very confused. Was he drunk? Drunk! He felt again the taste of wine on his tongue. That had been a good one – claret. Well, the Edwards always served a good wine; good wine, not plonk. Estelle had drunk it, too. Estelle! Where was she, what was going on? He relaxed into what seemed to be a sleep.

Later – how much later was this? – there was no one near his bed. He just lay there. The ward was lighted. There was a nurse walking about – he could hear her and see her momentarily as she passed by a bed on the opposite side of the ward. Ah, things were making sense. He was in a ward – that's where he was, he was in a ward. He'd had a bang on the head – and then there was the claret. Of course!

His mind went backwards. It was as if he was sitting in a cinema and could see what was happening on the screen – what was happening to him and Estelle. It was, he supposed, his memory, that screen.

When they had come out of the house . . . yes, they had hardly spoken all the evening. Why had they gone to the party? Well, because Estelle had wanted to; she said she was sick of being in the house. She should not have had anything to drink – but she had drunk the claret, he could remember that. They'd had something to eat, but she should not have drunk – not as she was nearly ready to be delivered of their bastard child. Ah, that was something else!

The bastard child, not his baby! No, the doctor – another doctor – way back (or it seemed way back) had told him that he was incapable of producing a child, his sperm count had shown this. Sperm count; yes, he was incapable of producing a child. They had been married six years. In love? No, they could not have been, not for Estelle to. . . .

She had been teaching at a public school – she was a good teacher and it was a good school. It had not been difficult for her. She was a beautiful, attractive, bedworthy woman and one of the pupils had fallen for her. Well, it was this pupil's baby – she had told him, she had been so honest. Honest? Did she know how it had broken him up? The very thought of someone else's child, a beardless boy's child, inside her? What could he say? He was not capable.

She had shown him the boy, pointed him out – not out of cruelty – and told him there could be nothing else, just the baby, that was all she wanted. She was not even going to tell the boy she was pregnant, so there was no question of an affair. It would look, she explained with pleading eyes, it would look as if it were their baby, there was nothing to worry about. She was sure the boy would never tell. How did she know that? She had pointed out the boy just so that he himself knew. He was tall, slender, young, virile and able to supply the sperm – the active, searching sperm that had given them the baby she so wanted.

The boy had not been good-looking, not particularly attractive. He had one strange feature, though – a streak of white growing through the luxurious brown waving hair; a family trait, perhaps? He had seen it once before, long ago at school. They had laughed at that boy and teased him about his white hair and the boy had tried to dye it. However, this one just combed it back and it lay across his head, a streak of white. Perhaps Estelle had found it attractive. He didn't know and he didn't care. The boy did not see him.

He had tried to blot it out as she grew bigger and bigger and her body became more and more distorted and, to him, more revolting. He had also tried to blot out the picture of the young man, but he could not, it was like a photograph in his mind. The cinema reeled on.

They had left the party. They had hardly spoken during the whole of her pregnancy. The relationship had been cold, accepting – and yet not accepting.

That night they had both got into the car and waved goodbye to the Edwards. He had not been fit to drive, but then neither had she. He had done all right, though, getting out of the drive easily, deftly, thinking he could drive better when he'd had a few. How many people think that?

A country lane on the way home had been deserted. He remembered Estelle slumping over towards him, asleep, snoring slightly, and her head had touched his shoulder. He had pushed her away. Once, when she had been undressing in the bedroom just a night or two before the party, revealing her big, swollen belly, he had seen the baby move – seen a slight ripple under her skin – and he had gone to the bathroom and been sick and she had heard him. He had made some excuse that he had eaten something at lunch that had disagreed with and by the time he had come back her body was covered with her nightdress.

Now – the hospital bed, the flashing lights, the corridor, the lifting. Oh, of course, he'd crashed the car! He smiled a little and turned his head on the pillow. Someone said, someone beside him said, 'Try to lie still, Mr Turner. Try to rest.'

He didn't bother to open his eyes to find out who had said that; he wanted to see the rest of the programme on his private screen. Crash! The tinkling of glass; the funny tipping feeling as the car turned over. Yes, he remembered that. How had it happened? Why? A tree. He remembered distinctly swerving. Was it when he had pushed her away from him after her head had touched his shoulder? Was it then? He remembered the big round trunk of the tree looming up, looking grey and rough in the headlights. And then . . . that's when the glass began to tinkle around him and the car had turned over. After that – nothing.

The screen clocked off in his head and he began to swim to the surface. As he came up and up he saw the nurse again standing beside him and he wondered about Estelle. Where was she? In a women's ward, perhaps?

'Where's my wife?' He said it almost abruptly, not fondly as the nurse would probably expect; not with anxiety and love, just abruptly.

'Oh . . . We'll tell you about her later. You rest now.' The nurse had hurried away as if to get someone else. Well, there was nothing he could do about it. Estelle was probably... He wondered if her face had been injured – she'd hate that. And the baby? Well, the baby, it was nearly due to emerge, to come into life, to look around and say, 'I'm Me. I'm nothing to do with you. I'm just Me.' The thoughts stopped again and he slid back into half-sleep, half-unconsciousness.

It was not until the next morning that they told him. The doctor and Sister Jensen went to his bedside and drew the curtains round them, leaving no gaps. Nurse Carmichael listened outside, but the voices were so low and guarded that she couldn't hear exactly what they were saying, only little bits. But she did hear the patient almost shout, 'Oh my God! She hasn't...' Then more low murmurings and the doctor at last emerged from behind the curtains. He looked at Carmichael, made a little grimace, shrugged his shoulders and then walked out of the ward.

Off duty Carmichael crossed the lawn towards the nurses' home, her red-lined nurses' cloak (a garment of which she was very proud) flapping about her. Many of the other nurses put their cloaks on anyhow, clutching them round them when it was cold, looking like bundles of navy material. Carmichael always put hers on properly, did up the hook at the neck and took the trouble to cross the red straps over her breast and button them behind neatly.

Now as she walked her thoughts were with the man who had said so loudly, 'Oh my God! She hasn't...' She supposed he meant, She hasn't died, or something. The woman had died on the theatre table. What a shock – one minute to have a wife pregnant, looking forward to perhaps their first child. Then Bang.

The car had been a write-off, apparently. Now he had no wife, only a baby daughter. Well, that was better than nothing, wasn't it?

She sighed and pushed open the door to the nurses' home. Split duty, off from 2 to 5 p.m. She would wash her hair, go to the canteen for tea then back on duty. She hated split duty. One day soon, they said, it would be done away with. That's what they said – but when? Probably after she had finished her training. She'd be thirty then. Thirty! Most of the nurses were young, eighteen or nineteen when they started, but she had been late for all sorts of reasons she would rather not think about.

She opened the door of her room and closed it behind her, went over to the window and looked across the lawn to the trees. Through them she could see the road and cars rushing by. A red one passed, faster then the rest. It made her think of the man in the ward. Had he been driving fast? She thought of him lying there staring at the ceiling; the gash across his forehead was already turning blue. He hadn't looked sad. As she had passed the bed he had looked angry, fierce. She would speak to him when she got back at five o'clock. He must feel strange – lonely, perhaps. Well, she was an expert on loneliness.

She turned from the window, opened the door of the little cupboard where she kept the bottle of shampoo.

When she went back on duty she was suffering her usual problem of keeping on her paper cap, always difficult when she had just shampooed her hair, which was fine and silky. In spite of three bobby pins it slipped sideways as she entered the nursing station. Sister Jensen, just going off duty, made a sarcastic remark as she went by. Carmichael paused as she entered the men's ward and stopped by the first bed, one bobby pin in her mouth as she tried to secure her headgear.

The car crash man – Bill Turner, his name was – spoke as he watched her, his eyes half-closed; the gash over one eye, the right one, was badly swollen now as well as blue.

'Can I have a drink?' he asked and then added, 'Please.'

Carmichael checked that he was allowed a drink and then gave him one. He drank thirstily from a straw, turning his head away from the tissue that Carmichael had produced from his bedside locker. She was going to wipe his mouth, but he obviously didn't want her to. She was at a loss what to say to him, in spite of her resolution made in the nurses' home.

Whilst she stood there the staff nurse, in charge whilst Sister Jensen was off duty, paused at the foot of the bed, smiling brightly. 'I've seen your little daughter. She's lovely and doing ever so well.'

There was no response from the man, so she passed on down the ward. Carmichael, stiffly holding the tissue, stood silent.

He looked up at her. 'She's not my beautiful – daughter, she's someone else's daughter. She's nothing to do with me. She's the child of my wife and her lover.' His voice was low and tense; the eyes looking up at Carmichael were rational and he looked as if what he was saying hurt him. Carmichael drew back as if she didn't want to hear. 'I couldn't produce a baby, but she got her another way – see?'

'Oh, come now, Mr Turner, please don't say that.' Carmichael made the remark almost automatically. She was not experienced enough to know exactly what to say in reply to such a communication and her reluctance must have shown, for he spoke again after a little pause, his head turning to and fro on the pillow.

'I shouldn't have told you that; maybe I shouldn't have told anyone. I don't quite see that it matters, but I shouldn't have told you. It's not the child's fault.' He closed his eyes wearily, then opened them again. 'Don't ever tell anyone I said that, will you? Don't ever tell anyone.'

Carmichael made an unusual gesture for her – she put her hand in his. 'No, Mr Turner, of course I won't tell anyone – I'm a nurse, you know.' She said it and as she did so she felt proud.

'Thanks – thanks, it's good of you,' he said.

Carmichael walked away from the bed, still feeling the pride that she had felt at his bedside – pride in the fact that he could confide in her and that it would go no further. She would not mention it to anyone; it was just between her and that poor man, her patient. She would put it out of her head, forget it. Well, perhaps not forget it, but never speak about it, never tell. And for many, many years she kept her promise.

1

Agnes Carmichael was hanging a picture in the sitting-room, above the fireplace. She stood back and looked at her effort critically. Was it a good place for that particular picture? She thought it was. The picture was a print by Louis Wain. She had picked it up some time ago at an auction and she loved it. She'd had it reframed. Louis Wain's cats were wild, humorous, benign and evil, and they were all depicted in this picture.

The first six weeks in her new home had been busy. It seemed ages since she had lived in a road. She had found much to do and arrange. The death of Ti Ling, her beloved cat, and the memories haunting the small village in Leicestershire in which she had been living for some time, had motivated her to move. She had found this grey stone early Victorian house after a troublesome search. She had lived close to a river once long ago, but this time she had chosen somewhere completely different – an island – and the house was in a road that ran down to the sea front on the Isle of Wight.

She knew no one here, nor did she know the Island itself. She had been here once on a day trip long, long ago when she was a child at the orphanage; forty years ago at least. She planned to explore every bit of it.

Several of the new books she had recently put in her bookcase were about the Island, past and present; so far, however, she had been too busy to go anywhere. The decorating, the installation of the telephone, the putting up of the TV aerial on the roof, the rewiring of the house, the carpet layers, interviewing the gardener and the daily – sometimes they came when they said they would, sometimes they didn't – it had all meant staying in the house waiting for them.

Her next-door neighbour, the one to her right, had left a card – very formally, so Agnes thought – but she had had no time up to now to acknowledge it. The house on the other side had made no attempt to get in touch with her, though in her less occupied moments she had seen a grey-haired, rather handsome man walk down the drive and a fair-haired girl with a dark, rather loose-limbed boy. Usually they went out together. Sometimes they got into an old car that was parked outside in the road. There was a toddler, too, whom she had often seen being pushed out in a pushchair, not by the fair-haired girl but by a shorter, fatter young woman. She seemed to complete the family, but what relationship one had to the other Agnes had so far no idea.

One afternoon Agnes had a telephone call from her right-hand neighbour asking if she would care to come for coffee at ten thirty the next morning, an invitation she at once accepted.

Next morning, as she walked up the pathway, she noticed and looked with envy at the neat, beautifully cut lawn – no sign of moss or dandelions. The rose bed in the centre was perfect, not a weed in sight, and the roses were blooming and budding with no black spot. Agnes noticed all this as she went by. Peace, though, was not a favourite rose of Agnes's and it seemed to dominate the collection.

The door was opened by a white-haired lady in a blue linen dress.

'Mrs Timpson?'

'Miss Carmichael. How nice, do come in.'

Seated in a rather pleasantly decorated sitting-room waiting for her hostess to bring in the coffee, Agnes had time to look round. The house was similar to her own, though this room was larger. The french windows opened on to a well-kept pretty back garden. The flowers were drilled into neat rows, not to Agnes's taste. Her crowded herbaceous border would perhaps not have suited Mrs Timpson, who clearly liked neatness and order. It was obvious in the house and in the garden.

A pile of rather expensive magazines occupied part of the coffee table in front of Agnes – *Country Life*, *House and Garden*, *Vogue*, *Interiors* – the title of each magazine visible, rather like a dentist's waiting-room.

'There we are.' Mrs Timpson came in with the tray containing pretty cups and saucers, matching cream jug and sugar bowl, silver apostle spoons and a plate of biscuits. She sat down beside Agnes. The sound of the Hoover came from upstairs. Mrs Timpson did not remark on the noise. A hedge similar to Agnes's in the front of the house did much to dull the sound of the traffic going by.

'Do you know the Island well, Miss Carmichael?' her hostess asked, looking at Agnes as she handed her the coffee.

Agnes shook her head. The coffee had the fresh aroma of 'real' coffee.

Mrs Timpson went on. How was Agnes liking her house? Had she found a suitable gardener? How did she find the shops and did she know that Hansfords would deliver groceries if asked, et cetera, et cetera.

It was some time before the next but one neighbours were referred to. Their name, Agnes learned, was Turner. That Mrs Timpson was in almost equal measures a snob and a gossip had already become apparent to Agnes.

'Yes, the Turners. It's a very strange household, neglected garden. He's an author, hardly literary – murders, detective books, not my type of reading. Have you seen the curtains?'

Agnes had to admit she had not and used her extreme busyness and preoccupation with the moving as an excuse for her lack of observation.

'My dear Miss Carmichael, they are a disgrace to the road... And that boy! His hair! I'm not particularly against long hair if it is clean, though none of my family...' She rambled on, pouring Agnes another cup of excellent coffee.

When at last Agnes rose to leave, thanking Mrs Timpson profusely for her hospitality, she knew quite a bit about the people in the road. Before she left, Mrs Timpson put what appeared to be a very important question to Agnes.

'Do you play bridge, Miss Carmichael?'

Agnes's rather firm, 'No, I don't, Mrs Timpson,' obviously disappointed her.

'That's a pity,' she said. 'I believe the Pitmans – that's at number 41 – do play, but they're not quite what one... I'm sure you know what I mean.'

Agnes assured her that she knew exactly what she meant and beat a hasty retreat as Mrs Timpson closed the front door. As Agnes made her way down the neat garden path and round to her own house, she felt that she would not be terribly anxious to make a friend of that next-door neighbour.

Three weeks went by – rather a long three weeks for Agnes. She had now started her exploration of the Island, and she had so far found the place quite beautiful. She shopped at the big supermarket, went to Newport to have her hair done weekly, spent quite some time at the Needles on a rather rough day watching the spray breaking over them – she had enjoyed that.

Still, it had been lonely. Osborne House and the Galleries had all been enjoyable, but she needed someone to chat to.

She watched television practically every evening and found herself drifting more and more into a hermit-like existence, which did not please her.

Rather in desperation she asked Mrs Timpson to coffee and did not find much more to like about her, although this time she did leave out the gossip. Instead she talked endlessly about her son, who lived in Melton Mowbray, was an accountant and, according to her, quite brilliant. He had no children and had just divorced his wife who, according to Mrs Timpson, had been both unfaithful and a dreadful spendthrift!

All this did little to relieve Agnes's boredom and she was very glad when Mrs Timpson left at one fifteen – a thoroughly uncivilized time when asked to coffee, Agnes thought, and not before she had accepted the offer of a gin and tonic.

'Only a tiny one, Miss Carmichael, even though I'm not driving.' She had laughed self-consciously.

Agnes in the kitchen had poured herself a double and for her guest, after all she had asked for it, a very small one. Agnes did not feel like wasting expensive drink on her.

As she left, with Agnes standing politely at the door watching her neighbour walk down the path, Agnes nearly sighed with relief – the woman had been a strain!

Life at the moment felt a burden, but the next day it was to be relieved in a rather dramatic way.

The morning was overcast. Agnes was rapidly getting into a routine, Wednesday being the day she went to Tesco's to stock up her freezer. She was toying – only toying – with the idea of buying a dog. A small dog, perhaps one from the local dogs' home. She was no dog or cat snob. She would have liked a cat, but felt that the road was too busy and she would not even think of putting a cat at such a risk. As to the dogs' home, anything that wanted a loving home most and was the least likely to get it, she knew she would fall for. But then a pedigree puppy from a shop! She might go up to London to Harrods. After all, even if it was a pedigree it needed love and a good home just as much. She was torn two ways – mongrel or well bred. She decided to give the matter more thought.

She was preoccupied with this as she locked her front door; the door had a mortice lock as well as the Yale and she always locked both. When she turned to go to the garage to get out her Porsche she had quite a shock – stumbling along her drive on short fat legs, teetering slightly, was a toddler. She judged him to be about three. Dressed in blue denim dungarees, with an incongruous baseball cap perched on his brown curls, he stood and looked at her, wide-eyed and silent; strangely silent in the circumstances. One leg of his dungarees was torn and the jagged hole showed his knee to be scratched and bloodied, a little of the blood staining the lower part of the tear. It looked a recent injury and painful.

As Agnes and the child faced each other the small boy's reaction became more normal – tears were already wetting his cheeks, but now he let out a wail. Agnes was not sure whether he was demonstrating pain or fright, maybe both.

She put down her bag and car keys and went towards the child, who promptly made to turn and run, but fell flat on the gravel. Agnes bent down and picked him up. He struggled to stand on his feet and she let him. She believed she was looking at the child she had seen being wheeled out from the next-door house in a buggy several times. She was not entirely sure, though. She would take the little one there and check.

After returning for her bag and keys she took the child's hand, grasping it firmly, and started the (for him) long walk past the screening hedge, along the pavement and up the weedy path of her next-door neighbours.

As she looked down at the child she noticed a bruise just above the left eye – not a recent bruise, she judged, as the edges were already turning orange and discoloration was obviously dying away.

The front door of the house was ajar. The bell push on the left-hand side was not working: there was no sound when Agnes pressed it. She tried again – still nothing. She knocked and as nobody came to the door she pushed it open and led the child inside. He had stopped wailing now and was pulling at his torn denim-clad leg. Agnes took his hand away from the injured area.

'Don't touch it,' she said and led the child forward into what appeared to be the sitting-room. The french windows were open to the garden; maybe the child had gone through them and round to the front of her house. A pretty hazardous journey, she thought, from the sitting-room, round the house and through to the road and then into her drive.

Both the sitting-room and the back garden were empty. Agnes then led the little boy out of the room and back into the hall, feeling completely at a loss. A noise suddenly startled her, coming from behind the closed door of a room on the left-hand side. She listened and could hear a typewriter clicking away.

She knocked. Someone, a man's voice, called, 'What?'

Agnes opened the door. The rather handsome grey-haired man she had occasionally seen leaving the house faced her. He was sitting in front of a typewriter, his forehead creased in a frown.

'Who are . . .?' His eyes travelled down to the child. 'Oh no, I forgot him. What's he done?' He did not seem to be particularly concerned.

Agnes explained.

'Came round to your house? All that way in the road? He could have been run over, killed. They're out and his nanny has got the day off.'

Agnes said icily, 'I see. Is there anywhere I could clean up the child's knee and dress it? As you may notice, he has had a fall.'

'Oh yes, of course.' He jumped to his feet.

They left the small room with the typewriter, word processor and fax machine. The floor was scattered with screwed-up paper.

'It's Miss Carmichael, isn't it?' Agnes nodded. 'I'm Bill, Bill Turner.' He picked up the crying child and carried him up to the bathroom. Once there he opened the bathroom cabinet.

'I'll dress it,' Agnes said. She felt annoyed with the man and yet did not want to say too much in front of the child.

He handed her a small tin box with a red cross on its corner. Inside were some sterile dressings, a small ancient-looking bottle of iodine, some Band Aid, a new roll of cotton wool and another of lint.

Agnes was surprised when Bill Turner took a pair of small scissors from the cabinet and cut neatly round the leg of the dungarees from the tear in the knee round to the back, raising the small leg to do so. The child watched him, not crying now, eyes wide and tear-filled but silent. Bill Turner drew the piece of denim quite gently down the leg and over the shoe and threw it on to the floor. He looked at Agnes with a brief smile.

'Easier than pulling the suit off the sore place,' he said.

Agnes gently washed the graze on the leg with wet cotton wool, then opened one of the dressings and put it on, holding it in place gently.

'Have you a bandage?' she asked, then noticed one in the box – another ancient relic, bound with blue paper. It looked clean, though, and she wound the bandage expertly round the small knee. The man stood watching her.

When she had finished he picked up the child and left the bathroom, leaving Agnes looking rather blankly at a litter of bloody cotton wool and odd bits of paper. Who would clear it up? she wondered. She washed her hands, dried them on a grubby towel and followed the two downstairs.

In the hall he thanked Agnes. 'I write novels – murders. I get preoccupied when I'm plotting and don't think of anything else. They went out, my daughter and her friend, and I was supposed to be in charge.' He looked at the child with some dislike, put him down and held him firmly by the hand. 'I forgot about him. He was asleep on the sofa and I thought . . . I'm no good with children.'

'Well, I wouldn't let him get out of the house again.' Agnes felt her stiff manner, which had rather relaxed in the bathroom, return. She walked through the front door.

'Miss Carmichael . . .' The man called after her quite loudly.

She turned and it was then, at that moment, that she recognised him. Bill Turner! Of course, of course – the man in the car crash, the patient of long ago, the man who had confided in her, told her that the child was not his daughter. The memory came flooding back. The face on the pillow, the bruised forehead – it was there, in front of her! No bruise on the forehead now, but the child he held by the hand had a similar abrasion. Strange.

'I'm glad I was there. I was just going out,' she said and turned quickly in case he should see the recognition in her eyes.

Back in her own house she decided to abandon her shopping expedition until the following day. She felt quite shaken up by the events – the child appearing so suddenly, and then the recognition. Bill Turner . . . at first the name had meant nothing to her, it was so long ago. She pictured herself then; wispy hair, red-tipped nose. Her nose had always been dripping with hay fever, she had been continally wiping it and her eyes had been red. When the pollen count had been high it had been awful, but now it had disappeared.

She crossed the hall and looked into the mirror hanging on her wall – beautifully cut hair, make-up well applied, the well-cut green suit (green had always been her favourite colour) flattering her rather thin figure. No wonder the recognition had not been mutual.

It gave her the usual strange feeling that knowledge – secret knowledge – always did. Was it the child of the girl who was born after the car crash almost of a dead mother, or at least a brain-dead mother? Was it Bill Turner's grandchild – and the fair-haired girl she had seen, had he told her she was not his daughter? Or had he brought her up to think...? And the boy, that lanky boy, was he the father of the baby? A family that was not a family; a grandfather, a daughter and a grandchild without the same blood flowing in their veins. And was she the only one who knew?

Not much of a secret, perhaps, but what a coincidence. A secret enough to dull the edge of Agnes's growing boredom. She must find out more. It had reminded her of herself – how she had been then, how she was now. It was a strange, half-nostalgic, half-regretful feeling, reminding her of what she had had and what she had missed.

Agnes watched with more interest than before the comings and goings of the Turner household. The next morning she saw the little boy – Bruce, his grandfather had called him – being pushed out in the buggy by the plump short girl who, she presumed, was the one Bill Turner had referred to as the nanny.

The thin, lanky boy went off and she heard the harsh roar of the old car starting up and driving off. No one else appeared.

Agnes might have missed some of the comings and goings in the morning when she had been in the kitchen and shopping. She had made an early start and gone to Tesco's and then been busy in the kitchen putting away the purchases.

She had noticed, when she had seen the little boy going out, that he had on a pair of loose black trousers, she presumed over his still-bandaged leg, and a white T-shirt, but was still wearing the baseball cap that seemed to be his permanent headgear. Something, she was not sure what, made her feel sorry for the child – which was probably, she told herself, a stupid thing to feel. The little boy was well nourished, well grown. Perhaps it was the complete lack of emotion shown by his so-called grandfather in the remark, 'Oh God, I forgot him,' which had hardly been loving or caring. He had not attempted to reassure or comfort the child, and indeed the little boy did not appear to expect it. Agnes wondered what his attitude had been after she had left them alone together.

She was just thinking of pouring herself a pre-lunch gin and tonic when the front door bell rang. She put down the glass, shut the refrigerator door and went out into the hall.

'Oh good, I thought you were out. Sometimes you shut your

garage door when you go out in the car, don't you?' It was the fair-haired girl who, she presumed, was the mother of Bruce.

Agnes opened the door wider. 'Won't you come in?' she said, to which the girl replied, 'Yes, I will.'

The girl was taller than Agnes. She was dressed in the usual jeans and sloppy jumper, but even that did not hide her almost perfect figure or detract from her posture and walk, which reminded Agnes of the models she had seen on the catwalk at dress shows.

Agnes gave her ten out of ten for grace; as she sank down on Agnes's rather low soft-cushioned settee, her movement was still full of grace.

'I'm Stella, Stella Turner – you probably know?' Agnes nodded. 'I called to thank you for rescuing Bruce – he might have been run over, as Dad said. It was decent of you.' She played with the edge of her jumper, pulling out a stray piece of wool, her plucking fingers revealing that she was not quite as composed as she would like to appear. Agnes noticed, too, the bitten fingernails.

'I must admit I was glad I was here, but all was well except for the knee.'

'Yes . . . Miss Carmichael, you must think us a funny lot.' Stella looked up at Agnes with amazingly dark-lashed brown eyes.

'Why should I think that, Stella? And please, my name is Agnes.'

'Well, the fact that Bruce was out in the road and Dad the only one there. The garden's a mess and our cleaning woman has left us, too. I think it's because she couldn't stand Rick's noise – playing the guitar, I mean. Another thing, Dad won't have her Hoover when he's dictating. It's all a bit mad.'

'Would you like a drink, a gin and tonic? I've just given myself one.'

Stella shook her head. 'No, I don't drink.'

'An orange juice, then?'

'All right.'

Stella's manners were hardly attractive, Agnes thought, as she went into the kitchen. When she returned the girl was standing by the small table near the fireplace, looking closely at the little silver frame in her hand. It was a picture of Fluffy, the blind cat which Agnes had rescued long ago; she had, in consequence, received the considerable fortune which had made her secure and comfortable for life.

As she put the drinks down on the coffee table Stella asked,

'Are you into cats then, Agnes?' She replaced the frame on the table and came over and sat down again on the settee. 'You haven't got one, have you?'

Agnes shook her head. 'Yes, I am, as you say, into cats, but that particular cat was rather special.' She was conscious of Stella's eyes, wide and beautiful, fixed on her full of curiosity and interest.

'You're attractive and dress beautifully, Agnes. Ever been married?'

Agnes shook her head, but gave no other answer.

'Lovers, perhaps?' Stella, her eyes fixed on Agnes's face, did not relax her stare. The questions, so directly put, amused and complimented Agnes.

She replied, 'Yes, a lover.'

Stella, her chin resting on her hand, nodded slowly. Agnes smiled almost secretly to herself. She was glad she was able to say, 'Yes, one lover.'

The girl put her hand up and pushed the strand of hair behind her ear.

'Bruce's father – I only slept with him once. I was only fifteen. He doesn't know he gave me a baby, but he was everything I'd ever dreamed of in a man. It was my first time with him and . . . Then we were together for three weeks. Daddy didn't know.' She looked suddenly defensive. 'He wasn't married or anything. He was older, quite a bit older than me, I mean. I told him I was seventeen and on the pill . . . all lies.' She paused and looked vaguely round the room. 'Funny how you lie when you want something. I'm not a liar, not usually. But then, do you know what I mean?' She looked again fixedly at Agnes.

'Yes, I think I do.' Agnes answered her so pointedly, the sentence sounded so full of meaning, that the girl smiled.

'Yes, you do – you do know, don't you?' She got up and reached for her orange juice and went on. 'Bruce is a bore. I can't go anywhere when the nanny has got a night off; can't go to a movie or anything.' Her shining hair fell forward again. 'Not that I want anything to happen to him, but . . .'

'You were very young. Why didn't you get him adopted or . . . ?'

Stella shrugged. 'I don't want to talk about it any more.'

Agnes felt a surge of understanding and almost affection for the girl sitting beside her. 'Well, let's talk about something else if you want to.'

'No. I must go, but thanks.'

She got up and left the room and Agnes followed her to the

door. Once there Stella turned, her face flushed, and she looked as if she could easily shed tears. 'I really do mean Thanks, Agnes. I'm not the maternal type. I want...' She stopped, moved forward and, taking Agnes completely by surprise, kissed her on the cheek. Agnes put her hands lightly on the girl's shoulders.

'Can I come again? I mean, just for a talk?'

Agnes watched Stella walk down the drive with her lovely model's walk. At the end of the drive she turned and raised her hand in farewell. Her hair blew back from her face, streaming out over her shoulders. She was a beautiful thing and Agnes felt a surge of envy. A girl so young, so full of beauty and yet so vulnerable. She had not even mentioned Rick, how he had figured in her life or why. Did she know that the man who wrote the books, Agnes surmised to keep them going, to keep the wolf from the door, was not really her father? Had he decided to keep the girl in complete ignorance of the fact? Stella referred to him as Daddy, but that didn't mean a lot. Perhaps in the age of Christian names, if he had told her that he was not her real father, then she might have called him Bill? Anyway, it was not a point that could be deduced on such a short acquaintanceship.

She went back into the house feeling much less lonely, much less isolated from the world outside. Perhaps she would ask them all to drinks, Stella, the boy Rick and Bill Turner. She went into her sitting-room just to check the drinks cupboard – plenty of gin, whisky, Cinzano, sherry. In the refrigerator she knew she had tonic, lemon and soda. Good.

Since Stella's departure, fine rain had started to fall and outside it looked damp and slightly dreary. Agnes poured herself another gin and tonic and switched on the news. First she saw the local news. The Isle of Wight was mentioned and for the first time since she had moved here she felt she belonged, she was interested. This was her world now, her area. She thought again of the sea beating against the rocks at Freshwater Bay. She was going to like it here. She began at last to understand why Jane Austen had made one of her characters call it 'The Island'.

The weather had been changeable for a few days. The summer was turning to autumn, but Agnes was able to go to Ventnor and Totland. She discovered a place in Shanklin that served a good lunch and on leaving to return home she decided she would take Stella out to lunch if she would accept her invitation. As she drove along she wondered if she would, if she liked that kind of thing, going out to lunch with another woman.

The traffic was decreasing now. School holidays had finished and the parents were going home to get their offspring ready for school. It made driving more pleasant. She noticed that there were still several coaches on the roads, probably late holiday-makers.

What about Rick, though? Should she ask him, too? Just what was the relationship between the two young ones? By the time she had arrived home and put the car away she had decided it would be better to ask Stella alone after all. She had not appeared to be particularly fond of the boy – but then she seemed only casually attached to her so-called father, her baby and the nanny. She interested Agnes, and for some reason she liked the girl. Perhaps, she told herself, it was because she knew her past – that little dramatic piece of her past, that small contact with Bill Turner. She wondered whether the girl looked like and maybe reminded Bill Turner bitterly of his unfaithful wife. He apparently had not remarried, so perhaps it had embittered him for life. Who could tell?

That evening Agnes rang Stella and asked if she would like to have lunch with her at the Rose Garden in Shanklin.

The girl's reply was so typical. 'The Rose Garden? Sounds posh. Yes, OK.' Then a belated, 'Thanks, I'd like that. Just me?'

Agnes hesitated. 'Yes, unless you would like to bring Rick.'

'God forbid.' This was said with a laugh.

The time and day were fixed and Agnes put the telephone down, wondering if she had done the right thing, yet looking forward to getting to know the girl a bit better. It would be nicer than lunching alone, anyway.

She decided to wear slacks and a jumper to allay the term 'posh' regarding the venue.

On the day of the lunch Agnes drew up outside the house next door. It had a name over the door, Stafford House, whilst hers had no name, just a number. She hoped Stella would not keep her waiting as she had booked the table for one o'clock and given herself just time for driving there and parking.

She need not have worried. Stella came out of the front door leaving it open behind her. She had on a white linen dress, short and severely straight with a low V-neck and around that neck a string of flat red beads matching the red belt at her waist. On her stockingless feet she wore white flip-flops. She carried an extremely small handbag, which Agnes thought would hold hardly more than a lipstick and handkerchief. This was slung over her shoulder, held by a thin strap. She got into the car as gracefully as she did everything else and a man passing by glanced at her legs with appreciation. Stella looked at him, banging the car door with rather more force than Agnes approved of, and smiled at her.

'Dirty old git,' she said and laughed. 'I hope you like the dress. I got it from Packs. Dad went ape when I told him how much it was. I didn't have enough to run to shoes.' She stuck her feet out so that Agnes could get a better view of her flip-flops. 'Sorry about these. Do you think anyone will notice? I did varnish my toenails.' She gave her familiar, rather rueful laugh.

Agnes laughed too and was suddenly reminded of *Pygmalion* – 'I washed my hands and face before I came' – but she only said, 'I think you look very nice, Stella,' and, glancing in her side mirror, drew away from the kerb.

Stella settled back in the car, stroking the upholstery with her hand. 'Smooth job this, Agnes,' she said. 'I'd love it. I hope Rick and Dad saw you glide away, though they've seen the Porsche before of course, but not with me in it.' She had curled her hair at the ends slightly and it made her look younger.

She threw a backward glance at her house as they drove away, but no one was to be seen at the window or at the open front door.

Inside Stafford House feelings about Stella's departure were mixed. Bill Turner was pleased. She didn't get out much, and by the trouble she had taken with her clothes and appearance it was probably somewhere more civilized than the places she usually frequented when she went out with Rick.

Nanny didn't care one way or the other – if Stella was out or in. She rarely came into the so-called nursery to see Bruce and they were off to the park anyway.

There was a new cleaning lady, who was wandering around with a duster looking rather lost. It was her first morning in the house and Stella had gone off out. Mr Turner had shut himself in the study and was typing, so Nanny decided to show the woman where the Hoover and cleaning things were. She was to be there from twelve until two – a stupid time, Nanny thought. Still, she felt sorry for her. She could hear Rick's guitar strumnming in the sitting-room, it always was. She could turn him out and let Mrs Whatsit vacuum in there. After all, he was only the lodger. She mustn't be too tough on him, though. If he wasn't there to pay the rent they might not be able to pay her. Anyway, he was behind with his rent, she knew that – two weeks. She knew more about the household than they realized. She didn't like any of them except Bruce, dear little Brucey.

'Come on – Mrs Brookes, isn't it? You can do the sitting-room first. I'll show you.' Then, as the woman looked a bit tired, she relented. 'What about a cup of coffee first, before you get started?'

The woman nodded, her expression grateful. 'Thanks. I've done Duttons, the pork butchers, this morning already. Their floor is so greasy it takes a lot of cleaning and wears me out.'

Nanny put the kettle on and for the moment the strumming went on undisturbed.

In the sitting-room Rick was not giving his mind to his composing. He was thinking of Agnes Carmichael – bloody woman with her Porsche. Rich, if her car was anything to go by. Stella would get a good lunch. She wouldn't go to a Macdonald's or Chinese; wouldn't have to make do with beans on toast or something like that. He couldn't go out and buy anything, he hadn't got enough money. He stretched his long, lean body and surveyed himself in the small overmantel mirror.

'Blast!' He had a spot on his chin, left side, red and sore to touch. No yellow head so he couldn't burst it. Once burst he could clear it, make it go away. It would disappear pretty quickly, that is if he could get into Stella's room without her seeing him and put a quick dab of her perfume on it – not too much or he'd smell like a fairy, just a small dab; it was magic.

Smell like a fairy – that sent his thoughts in another direction. Was he homosexual? He couldn't make up his mind. Girls turned him down and men didn't, so he thought he could be. Rick rather resented this in a way. Still, to be a fruit was, after all, rather in. You got more notice than when you were straight. Straight could be boring. Of course here, in this house, he acted straight. He wasn't sure that Bill Turner would tolerate him if he acted bent, and this room they rented him here was cheap, cheaper than a Social Security room, so he could fiddle it a bit, and he knew Bill needed the money.

He had met Stella at a disco. He had been sleeping in a park –

not too bad really in the summer, but in the winter – ugh ... another story.

He left the mirror, deciding against an exploratory squeeze. About to sit down again and pick up the guitar, he paused and looked at his watch – ten to one. Hebe would be in the pub now, perhaps with the others. His hand dived into his pocket – £3.04. Well, he could have a pint and maybe a sandwich. Suddenly he noticed Stella's handbag in the armchair. There was no purse in it, but he felt around and found two 10ps, two 2ps and a pound coin. Great! He pocketed that and lounged out of the room. He would prefer to drive to the pub, but the tank was empty. It was Stella's car anyway, and he hadn't the money for petrol.

At the pub Rick peered round the door before going in. Hebe was sitting in the corner at a table, an empty glass in front of him. He looked depressed and he was alone. Rick hesitated. He admired Hebe. He seemed to him to be a free spirit – did what he liked, never short of bread. He did a quick calculation. If he used the money to buy beer for both of them it might be a good idea. It would make Hebe think he wasn't always short of loot and today, if he missed lunch, he could run to a couple of pints. He threw back his shoulders, pulled down his denim jacket, put a hand up and finger-combed his long hair and swaggered in.

He made straight for Hebe's table. The place wasn't too full; it was a night watering hole rather than a lunchtime one. 'Hi, Hebe.' Hebe looked up at him, then looked down, uninterested. Rick felt his cheeks redden. It was terribly important that Hebe liked him. Rick grabbed the empty tankard in front of Hebe. 'Pint, Hebe?' he asked. Hebe looked slightly surprised, then amused.

'Yeah, OK. OK,' he said.

Rick went to the bar and came back with two brimming tankards. He noticed Hebe's smart trousers, well-cut jacket, black shirt with polo collar, silk? It looked like it. His hair was dark, slicked back into a short pony tail. Hebe looked down at the drink, then looked up, his eyes narrowing and his thin lips unsmiling. The skin of his face was unnaturally white. 'What's with this, then?'

Rick looked embarrassed. 'Don't usually have the bread,' he said, taking a small pull at his drink. 'Like to treat sometimes.'

Hebe took a long pull at his and licked the froth from his lips. 'Come into some, then?' he asked, but didn't wait for a reply. 'Gotta job yet?'

Rick shook his head. 'Don't want one. I want to get a group

together, rock and stuff, you know.' He felt embarrassed again. Why did Hebe make him feel like this? They drank in what Rick liked to feel was companionable silence. Hebe eyed him at first, then appeared to lose interest and watched the people coming and going.

'You doing all right, Hebe?' Rick broke the silence at last.

'Me? Fine, Rick. You still living with that book writer chap?' He poured the rest of his beer down his throat, apparently without swallowing. His Adam's apple didn't move, it appeared to remain still.

Rick grabbed the empty glass, went back to the bar and returned with another pint for Hebe – his own was only half finished. As he put the tankard down Hebe looked at him with a peculiar half-smile. 'What's the girl's name, the bint at your place?'

'Stella?' Rick looked at his companion, puzzled.

'Ah, Stella. She still got the kid you talked about?'

'Yeah.' Rick drank a little more beer.

'How old is it?'

'I dunno. About three, I think, but maybe more. Why?'

'Oh, nothing. You skint, Rick?'

His manner, his questions, had somehow deflated Rick – even the two beers hadn't deceived him. He couldn't tell if he was taking the mick.

'Yeah, I'm always skint, Hebe,' he answered, suddenly miserable. He finished his beer and became aware that as he'd put his tankard back on the table Hebe had stood up and was leaving. On the table by his empty tankard were two £20 notes.

'What's this for?' Rick asked, completely baffled.

'Just a pres. May ask a favour of you later,' and he pushed his way round the table.

Rick picked up the notes. 'Thanks, Hebe. I owe you.'

'Sure you owe me.' Hebe touched him lightly on the shoulder. 'And don't worry, I'll collect. See you.' He was gone.

Rick made his way home after enjoying a hotpot and another pint. He was preoccupied, though, and he had eaten the food almost without tasting it. Was he queer? Was this payment for future services? Rick felt a sudden surge of fear. He knew at that moment he wasn't bent, he was straight. He liked girls, for God's sake. Hebe mustn't think . . . Perhaps he ought to give him back the money? Well, he couldn't quite, he had already broken into it with the grub and another pint. What did that mean – when he replied, 'Sure you owe me one and I'll collect.'? Wasn't it something like that he had said? Could it mean sex?

28

When Rick had finished the hotpot in the pub something else had come into his mind: he had mentioned Stella. Rick wouldn't have thought Hebe would even have remembered that there was a kid or Stella. Oh well, he was a strange bloke. Maybe he just liked him. Liked him for . . . well . . . gave him £40 just because he knew he was skint, being friendly like. Well, he'd taken it now!

When he'd left the pub and walked home he had wondered and wondered now who he could trust. Not Hebe. Well, perhaps he could. Anyway, he'd give Bill Turner one of the notes off his rent, he owed two weeks. He felt curiously uncomfortable with the money in his pocket, as if he'd sold something he shouldn't. He walked fast on the way home, telling himself he was a nut case, £40 was better than nothing.

As he entered the door Nanny was pushing Bruce out of the house in his buggy. Again the words came back to him. 'How old is the kid now?' Why the hell should he have asked that? Why the hell?

Anyway, on the whole Rick was pleased. He was in with Hebe again and he'd got money now. He'd go down to The Feathers again tonight. Maybe his mates would be there as well as Hebe. One, Lenno he was called, was a drummer. They did a lot of practising. Hebe lived over a garage and nobody cared about the noise. Rick had joined them a couple of times with his guitar, but they never asked him to take part in a gig – just the odd session at Hebe's place. Perhaps now they were into drugs – that's where Hebe had got his money, the hard stuff, shit and all that.

They had never offered him anything, only grass. Hard stuff was really too expensive. Still, on the whole he felt well satisfied with his morning's encounter. Whatever they were in he'd like to be in it too. Stella wasn't getting all the breaks for once. He patted the money in his pocket and his feeling of discomfort about it disappeared; he smiled to himself.

Agnes was enjoying Stella's company. She told stories, some funny, about her father's adventures with agents and publishers. Once, she said, he had gone up to London to meet a publisher who had turned out to be a madly smart woman, black-suited, high heels, perfect make-up – 'Made Daddy feel terribly rustic, he'd only gone up in his tweed jacket and flannels. Well anyway, they went by taxi to this madly grand restaurant. By this time Daddy was feeling a real hick. Then, getting out of the taxi, this women stumbled and her wig flew off, plus the small black hat she was wearing.' Stella laughed, putting her head back. Her laughter made people at the other tables turn and smile and she put up her hand and covered her unlipsticked lips. 'Daddy felt so much better then, he said. He enjoyed the lunch and the booze and the woman soon got over it.'

Agnes learned more about Bruce, but not more about the father. Indeed, nothing about the man at all. A little more about the pregnancy, how good her father had been to her. She had gone to her doctor determined to have an abortion and he had told her to go away for a week and think about it. She had discovered that she was really dead scared of having an abortion. A friend of hers had died after one. 'I might die the same as Della, so I decided not to, I couldn't go through with it. She got septic, Della did.'

She didn't appear stressed, she ate well and obviously enjoyed the food. After the sweet she looked up suddenly. 'You asked me why I didn't get him adopted.' She looked down at her coffee cup and took a long time stirring in two heaped teaspoonfuls of brown sugar. 'He's deaf, Bruce. We found out pretty soon, the doctors did. He's seen all sorts of people.' She looked up at Agnes. 'No one would have him, you know, and somehow I couldn't let him go then. I felt it was my fault – well, it might have been something I did. I tried to get rid of him early on when I first realized. Do you think I did it to him?'

Agnes shook her head. 'I don't think so, Stella. I was a nurse and I don't think you could have made him deaf.' As Agnes said this her nursing career seemed a thousand years away.

Stella's mood changed. 'Daddy said you acted like a nurse, or as if you had done first aid, when you did Bruce's knee so beautifully.'

'Yes, I was, long ago. I was a sister and a private nurse – all sorts.'

'Do you miss it, looking after people?'

Agnes thought before she answered. 'Yes, I suppose I do. But most of all I miss being in charge, authority, knowledge.' She looked across the table at Stella, then, 'Deaf!' she said. 'I never realized. Of course, he was crying most of the time I was with him.'

They drove back home to Queen's Road, almost in silence. Stella seemed locked in her own thoughts. They drew up outside the drive. Stella opened the door of the Porsche and swung her long legs out.

'Thanks for a lovely lunch and for listening.' Then, as she was about to close the door, she bent down a little and leaned towards Agnes. 'It was wonderful, those times with him, Agnes. Not just the sex – and it wasn't only once – but he was, still is, everything I ever wanted in a man.' Her eyes were misty with tears. 'There will never be anyone else like him.'

Agnes looked at her, compassion and yet disbelief on her face. 'You're very young, Stella, you'll find someone else.'

The girl shook her head. 'I don't think so, Agnes. Compared to him all the men and boys I meet mean nothing.' Then her mood changed again, her face lit up. 'Be my friend, Agnes,' she said.

'Indeed I will. I am already.' Agnes's voice was warm and friendly, rather uncharacteristically. She had to admit she meant every word she said.

The Porsche door was slammed. Stella ran up the path and banged the front door shut behind her, not looking back.

When Stella got in she ran straight upstairs to her son's room. He was playing with a plastic train, putting the trucks on the train, his small fingers deft. He did not turn round as Stella entered the room. Nanny came in with a cup of tea and some orange juice for him. She looked slightly surprised, as Stella didn't often visit Bruce.

'We've been to the park and he kicked a ball about with another little boy. He was quite good. We'll make a footballer of him yet.'

The child took the red plastic beaker and drank thirstily. His brown, round eyes were fixed on his mother, then he threw the cup across the room. A little juice dripped on to the floor. 'Gr . . .' He made the noise lustily and continued to look at Stella, but he did not smile or hold out his hands like he did to Nanny.

Stella thought, He hates me – well, he dislikes me. There's nothing of his father in him, not even his eyes. His father's eyes had been very gentle, his lovemaking had taken her again and again to the world of sensation that seemed to have no relation to the brown-eyed, unsmiling child. She turned, nodded to Nanny and left the room, slamming the door behind her. It didn't matter, only Nanny would hear the bang the door made.

She ran downstairs and went in to see her father. She could tell him all about the lunch, persuade him to ask Agnes in for drinks. As she came down the stairs she remembered that the new cleaning woman was supposed to have come today. Had she been? She must ask Nanny or Rick. Daddy wouldn't know.

'Come,' a familiar voice commanded as she knocked on his door. She went in and told him about the food and Agnes and the lovely car. There was no mention of Bruce or his father, or of having told Agnes about him.

After that she went into the sitting-room. She felt restless now, unable to settle down. Rick was stretched out on the sofa, reading. He looked up as she came in. He looked unusually cheerful.

'Had lunch?' she asked.

'Yes, ta, down The Feathers. Hotpot. Good.'

Nanny put her head round the sitting-room door. 'Mrs Brookes came.'

'Mrs Brookes? Who's she?' Stella's face was blank.

'The new cleaner. It was her first day.' Nanny Linda looked faintly disapproving.

Stella got the message. 'Oh, I know. I remember. I forgot all about her coming, though. Anyway, I expect you coped. Was she OK?'

Linda switched off the disapproval. She liked her job, loved Brucey and didn't want to lose either so thought she'd be pleasant.

'Thanks, Linda, for smoothing it out. Do you think she'll stay?'

'Well, I gave her coffee and Mr Turner didn't stop her Hoovering.'

Stella smiled at her with a rare comradeship. 'Good. What about your lunch?'

'I did some for me and your father. Cold chicken and chips. All right?'

'Great, I'll do something for tonight.'

Stella left the room. Her time with Agnes had made her feel relaxed and genial. She thrust her head round the study door.

'Dad, we ought to ask Agnes for drinks or snacks or something.'

Bill Turner looked up from his typewriter. 'Who?'

'Agnes. Agnes Carmichael, who I've just been out to lunch with.'

'All right. Get it organized. Get some food and drinks, whatever. Money?' He felt in his pocket. 'Need some?'

Stella nodded and he took out a wallet and extracted some notes. 'Enough, do you think?' he asked.

She counted the notes – £50. 'Yes, that'll do.' Stella shut the door and his typing started again.

Now, when and what to get? Tonight's supper, I'll think of that first, then I'll have to do the drinks thing. I suppose I'll have to do it all. Stella sighed, but admitted to herself even as she sighed that it would be nice to have Agnes in as a guest.

When during an afternoon of weeding in the garden Agnes thought over the lunch it was with pleasure. She always enjoyed the company of young ones. Their problems and enthusiasms were interesting to her. The fact that Bruce was deaf had come as a surprise. Of course, as she thought back now to her contact with him, it consisted mostly of a little boy wailing and watching her with those big brown eyes. Mr Turner had said nothing about the child's affliction. But then, as she recalled now with a little grimace, she had hardly been easy to communicate with. Her attitude had been full of censure at the child being allowed to wander out of the house. Then she had, of course, demanded something with which to clean up the knee; after she had finished, she had left the house showing how she felt. She had hardly given the man time to confide the child's affliction.

Stella obviously was not fond of her little boy. Did she really find him such an encumbrance as she made out? After all, the girl's home life was constricted even with a nanny in residence.

Agnes made her way to the compost heap to throw on the weeds. She was glad she had taken the girl out. The lunch had been a success, she felt. Whether more would come of the acquaintance she didn't know. The girl's remark, 'Be my friend, Agnes,' had been appealing, but maybe it was just the spontaneous reaction of a young person in need of a little attention. She would see, time would tell, but Agnes felt decidedly less lonely.

Her mind was distracted from her own minor problems. She wondered why the child was deaf. Her nurse's mind wandered round the diagnosis. She imagined that ear, nose and throat specialists would have seen the child. He would probably need special education. Was his father deaf? Why was Stella so adamant in her secrecy about the child's father? What had she said? That he was older than her and not married. Why then had she not contacted him, told him she was pregnant? Agnes couldn't get at any of these answers, but she felt that one day the girl might tell her. It seemed to Agnes to be a family or household of intriguing secrets and she would love to know more.

2

Bill Turner opened the envelope. Before doing so he saw where it had come from – the bank. He unfolded the statement. Thank God, he was not in the red. His account was low though, dangerously low. His final payment on his last book was due, but his publishers never seemed to hurry themselves, get on with things. Rick owed two weeks' rent – God knows, he charged him little enough. He thought he had some royalties as well. No Public Lending Rights until next February.

He sighed and reached for the gin bottle behind the word processor and took a swig. He must give up gin, but not today. At first neat gin had disgusted him, but now he was used to it.

He wondered briefly about Rick – was the boy on drugs? Sometimes he seemed half asleep, wandering round the house, gazing out of the windows, sleeping a lot and rousing himself with difficulty, strumming on the guitar. Another time he would be as high as a kite, laughing and dancing about to the radio, sometimes with Stella, sometimes alone. Stella didn't bother about Rick all that much, said he was a slob to his face sometimes when she was in one of her tempers. He had asked her about drugs with regard to Rick one day. 'Do you think Rick is into drugs, Stella?'

She had just shrugged her shoulders. 'No, Dad. Don't think so. You need money for that and he never seems to have any.'

His so-called daughter Stella was a strange girl. Her mother, his wife, had been quite lovely – dark hair, long and curling. True, she'd always been at the hairdresser's, it had cost him a fortune, but Estelle's hair had been beautiful. Her lover's hair, Stella's father, had been dark, too, with that white streak across the front.

He drank a little more gin, pushing the memory of his wife's lover out of his mind, or trying to. Stella took after neither of them. She was taller than her mother, with fair hair, and her eyes were beautiful. She was a lovely girl and would probably at twenty-four or twenty-five be truly beautiful, a truly beautiful woman. Would she marry? Her pregnancy had come as a great shock to him – a little deaf child. He felt nothing for him. Would he have felt more if he had been the child's real grandfather? He didn't know. As it was ... Stella seemed indifferent to her little boy and would never tell, was completely silent, about who was his father. Thank goodness Nanny seemed really devoted to the little one. In a way Bill felt sorry for the kid, but still he fed him, clothed him.

He got up and stretched. That woman Agnes next door. Agnes – what was it? Agnes Carmichael. She had been so furious with him for letting the child run out. Well, it had been pretty poor. He had forgotten all about him, forgotten he was supposed to be in charge of him. She'd been crisp with him, though. A bit of a martinet, he thought.

He went back to his desk. He'd got to get on, grind the next book out. What a life, he thought. Sometimes Bill wondered if he had a real novel in him, a novel really saying something to the world, not just this facile trash – he probably hadn't, and anyway, he had no time to write it, his publisher expected at least one novel a year.

The typewriter began to click again.

Agnes's thoughts were still Stella the next morning as she made her early morning tea. She had not slept well, so had allowed herself to lie in until eight thirty. As she poured boiling water into the teapot the telephone rang. She heard the telephone click as the caller pressed the button and realized at once that someone was calling her from a call box.

'Miss Carmichael?' The voice was quiet, almost furtive.

'Yes?'

'It's Rick here, from next door. Stella's friend. I'm sorry to trouble you, but ... I want to see you. If you would ...' He hesitated, fumbling for words.

What on earth was this all about? Why should Rick want to see her? Agnes was puzzled, but her curiosity was aroused.

'If you want to see me, I'm in this morning.'

'Oh no,' Rick broke in quickly. 'I don't want Stella or Bill or anyone to know. I need to ... Please could we meet in a café? I know one.'

Agnes hesitated then made up her mind. There was something rather pitiful about the boy in a way. 'Very well, which café?'

'The little dark one off the High Street. It's called Miranda's. Saves you getting your car out. It's only a short walk away. Could you . . .?'

'All right. I'll meet you there in an hour,' she said.

'Thanks,' he answered.

When Agnes arrived at the little café he was sitting at a table in the darkest corner. He looked completely out of place surrounded by dried flowers in coloured baskets. The place was almost empty. Two white-haired, tightly-permed ladies chatted in low voices over coffee near the front window.

Rick was well mannered enough to get to his feet as Agnes went up to his table. He looked as if he had not slept for a few nights. His eyes were red and as they sat down he rubbed his left eye with fingers that shook a little.

A waitress appeared. 'Two coffees,' Agnes ordered after a glance at Rick, who was picking at a fingernail and not even looking up. 'I've ordered coffee for you as well. Is that all right?'

He did look up then. 'What? Oh thanks. I should have . . .'

'Never mind. Tell me what's the matter. Why do you want to see me?'

He looked at her, arms folded on the table, back slumped. Agnes felt that had he been a young male nurse under her supervision she would have said, 'Sit up straight, for goodness sake, and take your arms off the table.' However, she said nothing and waited for his reply.

He unfolded his arms and with one forefinger, the nail of which was dirty, scraped at a spot on the gingham tablecloth.

The waitress put down their coffee in front of them and Rick waited until she had gone, then: 'I want your help, Miss Carmichael. Life's got me sewed up, just sewed up and I don't know what to do. If I could get away to the US or even Italy . . . but I haven't any money.'

Agnes found it difficult to assess the boy. 'What exactly do you want of me – just to talk?'

'No. I wondered if you would lend me some money.' He looked up at her, his rather thick brows drawn together. 'I don't like to ask, but what with your car and all – I mean, you've got a Porsche.' His voice was pleading. 'I wondered if you would lend me a bit – you know, £500 or even £1,000. I could at least get away, join a group in America or anywhere. I'd pay it back – well, try to sometime.'

Agnes shook her head almost immediately. 'I'm sorry, Rick, I could not. I would not even think of lending you money, certainly not that much.' She suddenly asked, 'Do you use drugs, Rick?'

He nodded, but quickly denied the habit. 'I could give it up tomorrow, Miss Carmichael, especially in a new place.'

Agnes shook her head again. 'I've heard that story so many times, Rick. My answer is no. Can't you get a job? Do you try?'

He did not let her go on. 'Well, thanks for nothing. You're just the same as the rest. Once you're rich you're OK. Come off drugs, get a job. Do you know what it's like?' He spoke in a hoarse whisper. 'I'd ask Bill, but he's always skint, as skint as I am – and he's got Stella and Bruce to keep and Nanny to pay.' He got up and banged the table with his hip as he left, overturning the small china sugar basin.

The waitress appeared, eyebrows raised. 'All right, miss? More coffee?' she asked, righting the basin and sweeping up the spilled sugar.

Agnes smiled at her. 'Thank you, I think I will have another one.' She felt slightly shaken by the young man's outburst, but it made no difference to her answer to his request.

She certainly enjoyed the second cup of coffee better than she had the first, and left the café feeling she had had her morning wasted by a stupid and, to her, completely irrational request. What little pity she had felt for the youth evaporated.

Bill Turner was walking along the sands, unusual for him as he did not like walking. His own car, an old Rover, was his favourite means of transport, but this morning he felt the need to walk, to stretch his legs and to try and shake off this constant feeling of being near the edge of financial disaster.

Since that awful car crash, the death of his wife and the entrance into his life of Stella, her daughter, he had, he reflected, acted completely irresponsibly: giving up his job – a fairly lucrative one – selling his house and with the resultant funds moving with Stella, who was then so little, into a small flat. He engaged a fully trained nanny and spent much of his time out drinking, playing bridge, playing golf – no other woman had interested him. Oh, he had bought one or two, even confided in one or two friendly prostitutes. It was easier to try and relieve his heartache with them. Once he had left them they would forget; it was like talking to a man on a train.

Walking along today, watching the waves gently slide along the sand towards him, carrying now a condom, now half an orange, now a plastic bag – flotsam, bits – he felt lost.

His household was weird, he thought. Not many visitors, that Carmichael woman, she looked a cold fish. Stella seemed to have taken to her, though; she had been more cheerful since that lunch date. Stella seemed to have no friends of her own age, though she went to disco dances, or whatever you called them these days.

He stopped and lit a cigarette with some difficulty in the breeze, then paced on. He was out of touch with the young. His new book featured a teenager and he was not at all sure he had been wise to try and describe one, in spite of the fact that he lived with two – three really, counting Nanny, but she hardly counted as a personality at all.

A man approached him along the beach, a dog frolicking round his heels, a black, rough-coated dog. The man, fairly late middle-aged, threw a stick for the dog just into the water and the animal barked, rushed into the wavelets, retrieved the stick and brought it back. By this time the two men were level. Bill stopped and watched the dog, who refused to give up the piece of stick, so the man gave up trying and smiled at Bill. 'Not a bad day,' he said. Bill nodded in agreement.

'My wife will be furious if I take her home with wet feet.' He caressed the dog's head. 'I'll have to walk on the grass up there. That dries her off a bit.' He turned and started to walk over the shingle to the steps that led to the promenade, which was bordered with grass verges, and the dog followed.

'I think I've had enough, too,' and Bill followed.

The man held out a hand. 'I'm Bryn Jones. You live in Ryde?'

'Yes, Queen's Road.'

The man's handshake was warm and firm. 'I was a local doctor, but I'm retired. I had a couple of heart attacks and decided to call it a day and try to live a bit longer.'

Bill went up the steps. The dog bounded up second and the man came up a little more slowly. Bill had time to look at him more closely. He was rather older than Bill had at first thought. His pleasant, rather brown face was not short of wrinkles; his abundant white hair was crisp and wavy and did not blow about in the wind as Bill's rather sparse crop did. He had a small military-type moustache as white as his hair. He stumbled slightly at the top of the steps. The dog dropped the stick. She was no longer interested; it was as if she knew the game was over for the time being. The two men walked on, the dog following at heel.

'Come in for a beer?' Bryn said as they were passing a pub.

'Yes, OK. I'll get them,' Bill said. 'Lager?' and Bryn nodded.

They went in, glad to get out of the now rising wind. There were quite a few men and one or two women sitting at tables or standing at the bar. Bill glanced at his watch – twelve o'clock. This was pleasant, he thought, as he stood at the bar waiting to be served while his new acquaintance went and found a table.

The barman took his time and Bill's thoughts wandered. It was ages since he had been in a pub. They had lived in London until Stella was fifteen. He had managed, although money was getting short, to send her to a decent school. Decent? She'd managed to get pregnant, though. He should never have let her go on that skiing holiday with her friend's family. By the sound of it the supervision of the youngsters had been pretty slack . . . *Après-ski* . . .

'What's it to be, sir?'

He jumped. His thoughts had blacked out the barman's request. 'Oh, two halves of lager, please.'

He carried the two drinks across to the table, unaware that the barman was following him until he spoke. 'There you are, then.' He was speaking to the dog and placed a drinking bowl of water down. The dog lapped thirstily. 'Always has to have her tipple as well.' The man smiled, returned to the bar, and the dog lay down, head on paws.

'You're a regular, then?' Bill asked.

The man opposite him nodded. 'Usually come in after a walk. Nice pub, this.'

Bill's thoughts at the bar rather precipitated his next question. 'Do you have children, Dr Jones?'

'Bryn, please. Yes, I have two sons, both doctors. Didn't know whether to say silly devils or well done, boys.'

'I expect you said, or thought, the latter!'

Bryn nodded. 'Yes, I did. One is a consultant paediatrician in Australia and the other is a GP in Goole, so we don't manage to see much of either. We've got three grandchildren, but I'll spare you the photographs and their unbelievedly clever sayings.' Both men laughed and Bill felt more relaxed than he had for ages. 'And you?' Bryn asked.

'Oh, just a daughter and one grandchild.' He didn't feel like giving any more information at the moment and his companion didn't press the matter. Another drink was bought by Bryn Jones and the conversation became general – chat about the town and the surroundings. Bill learned a little about Island politics and found it quite interesting. In spite of what he had said, Bryn did refer once again to his grandchildren. 'I'm grateful that they're all OK. One had a slight problem, webbed toes, but it's been attended to and apart from a little scarring he's OK.'

Bill was silent for a few moments and downed the last of his second half-pint, then spoke almost abruptly. 'My grandchild is deaf, stone deaf. He's just over three.'

Bryn Jones frowned. 'Oh, hard luck.'

Bill named the surgeon he had seen and the tests that had been done.

'How about his mother and father – your daughter, did you say?'

'Yes, my daughter. She was fifteen when he was conceived.'

'I see. The father's not deaf, though, or ill?'

Bill moved his empty glass to and fro before he answered. 'My daughter has elected to keep the father's name from me, so we don't know.' He felt suddenly embarrassed. 'I don't know why I'm telling you all this,' and he rose to leave.

'Do you take a stroll along the beach often?' The retired doctor's manner was friendly and matter of fact. 'Come on, Merc.' The dog got up, shook herself, smelled the water and decided she didn't want any more. Bill picked up the dish and took it back to the bar.

'Oh, thanks.'

The two men reached the door. 'Maybe I'll see you tomorrow or the day after – repeat the prescription, eh?'

'I'd like that.'

They parted in front of the pub and Bill patted Merc's head. 'Why Merc?' he asked.

'It's short for Mercedes. She's a lady, is Merc. We've always wanted a Mercedes car, then decided it was ridiculous, such a big, fast car on the Island. Mercedes is a girl's name, you know. It was my son's idea. Some of his ideas are a bit way out, but the name stuck and Merc it is.'

'Right, I've learned something. See you, may be tomorrow or some time.'

'Sure. 'Bye.'

Bryn Jones walked off and Bill watched him go with a trace of envy – retired, wife, two sons both done well, no need for him to work any more. Oh well...He made for home, his mind automatically clicking back like a computer into his latest story line.

As he passed, his new next-door neighbour was just walking out of her drive. She paused to let him go by, smiling. She was wearing what Stella rather rudely called the Island uniform. Her well-cut navy slacks topped by a navy V-necked jumper were covered by a short red coat. The coat gave more colour to her face, which was well and discreetly made up. Her perfume reached him as she walked by. She looked pretty good, he thought.

He rather wished his daughter Stella would give up the torn jeans, the lumpy trainers and great giant woollies and dress with a little more care. But then this well-dressed woman next door was old enough to be Stella's mother. Stella had said something about asking her in for drinks. Well, maybe he would try and be a little more enthusiastic about the idea. He could still smell that perfume. What was it? he wondered. He would ask Stella.

He opened his house door and was greeted by the roaring toddler in a tantrum and Nanny's conciliatory voice trying to calm him – and, of course, the inevitable strumming guitar. He sighed, shut the front door, went into his study and shut that door purposefully behind him.

Agnes Carmichael's immediate refusal to lend Rick money had not had a particularly strong effect on him. After all, this was not the first time by a long way that he had tried to touch someone for a loan and he thought philosophically that it would not be the last. Sometimes he was lucky, sometimes unlucky, but he had thought the new next-door dame might have coughed up. What would a couple of thou mean to her? After all, that Porsche must have cost – and it was a new one, not a second-hand job.

He was still strumming away. He thought he was near completing the tune, but the end part just wouldn't tail off in the way he wanted. It seemed to melt away into nothing, not slowly die out as it should. He was even having a go at the beginning again and then going right through, but it didn't come. 'Heat Up The Past' was to be the title. All about a girl who thought she could reheat the embers of love if she could only date her boyfriend once more. 'Silly cow,' he suddenly said aloud, then he put down the guitar beside him. 'You have to mean what you're saying, mean what you write or it won't jell.' That's what Mike, one of the group he was trying to join, had said, and he had in a way published – well, cut a disc. It had not done much, actually it hadn't done anything, but that's what he had said and probably he was right.

Sincerity, that was the stuff. He got up. 'Heat Up The Past' would have to wait a bit, he couldn't do any more. It was one thing seeing himself there on *Top of the Pops*, lights flashing and cascading over his leather-clad body, backing singers, three lovely girls swinging behind him, their gorgeous bodies moving to the rhythm of his music. Sometimes he could almost hear it. He must have a rest from it. 'Going out,' he yelled. No one replied. He crossed the hall to the kitchen. Stella was in there cooking supper, the eternal spaghetti. He was sick of that, too. 'Going out. Won't be in for supper,' he said.

'You might have told me before. It's almost ready.' Stella peered into the pan containing the spaghetti; the mince was burning slightly and she pushed it on to the back burner. 'Want me to save some for you?' she asked.

'No thanks. I'll grab a bite with Hebe.'

Stella did not reply or even look at him again. He closed the kitchen door on her and left the house. 'Fat lot anyone cares,' he muttered.

The same pub, the same table, but this time at nine thirty at night the place was partly full and Hebe was not alone, he was surrounded by his mates. Elbow the saxophonist, Misty the girl Hebe slept with and who wanted to consolidate herself as their backing singer, or even a soloist, but Hebe didn't seem to catch on. Rick thought that she wasn't really good enough, not to grab the mike and belt out one or two numbers that Hebe had had a go at writing. She often sulked, but she hung around Hebe, wouldn't let him brush her off. Any other girl around and she was like a tigress. Maybe Hebe was keen on her, it was hard to say. Hebe was an enigmatic sort of bloke, at least that's how Rick judged him, and he was a bit in awe of him.

He made his way over to the table with a certain amount of diffidence. There was no vacant chair, but much to his surprise Hebe pulled a chair from a little way away towards him, told the chap next to him to move up and make room for Rick.

'Hi, Rick. How's it going?' he asked.

Rick was quite overcome. Never had he been greeted like this, especially by Hebe. He was usually tolerated, just a chap on the fringe, kept out.

'Thanks, Hebe.' He sank his long, lean form into the chair provided for him.

Hebe looked up at Elbow and gave him a nod. Whatever the nod meant, a pint of bitter was soon placed in front of Rick. He felt warm and grateful. He was 'in' – he felt that they had at last accepted him. But why so suddenly? He couldn't imagine. Anyway, his feeling of warmth and gratitude persisted; his initiation was maybe over. He thanked Hebe almost shyly and Hebe touched him on the shoulder. Then the conversation surged around him – he was one of them, not just lonely, isolated Rick any more.

He drank his beer and smiled at them, smiled at all of them – though the others didn't seem quite so enthusiastic to have him there as Hebe had been. But, he reasoned, Hebe was the leader, the boss – what he said went. He didn't bother with them, he concentrated on Hebe.

Elbow, so called because he was always nudging people, ignored him.

Hebe bought Rick another drink. They were all talking about the music scene and Rick put in his two bits about 'Heat Up The Past'. Most of them had heard it and were bored by the very title, but again Hebe appeared to be much more interested than he usually was. He concentrated on Rick.

'It's a good title, Rick. Try and get the end sorted out and we'll try it one night, really have a go at it.' He looked round the table.

'Yeah, all right, when it's finished,' Elbow answered and wandered off, bored, by the look of him.

But Hebe took no notice of this attitude. 'Good on you, Rick. You work on it,' he said.

One more beer and the group split up, Rick going his way alone, the others moving off in the opposite direction – where to and what to Rick didn't know, as he wasn't asked to join them. He felt mellow, though; four pints of beer was an unusual amount for him. He had a suspicion they were off to shoot up. Speed or LSD, that was fashionable again now. Anyway, he wasn't asked to join them and this time he didn't mind too much. He wasn't much of a user, drugs frightened him a little, especially crack.

As he walked away only a few yards from the crowd he heard a step behind him. He turned round. It was Hebe. 'Listen, Rick,

I've got a bit of a proposition for you. Can we have a meet some time, soon as possible?'

'About the song, Hebe?' Rick felt a surge of excitement. Here was Hebe, Hebe the Great, Hebe the Wonderful, asking him for a meet. 'Where? When? Shall I bring the guitar? Will the others –?'

Hebe interrupted him. 'Well no, Rick, just you. The pub on the hill, the Niagara Falls, do you know it?' His eyes were fixed on Rick, he drew heavily on his cigarette.

Rick knew it, full of old men mostly. Not Hebe's scene, he would have thought, but he instantly agreed. Whatever or wherever Hebe wanted he would agree.

'Wednesday, about nine o'clock. If I'm not there wait for me. OK?'

Rick agreed, his head nodding violently. 'Yes, OK. Whatever you say, Hebe.'

'Right, be there.' Hebe gave him a friendly thump on the arm and turned and walked rapidly away to join the others.

Rick continued his walk home. The house was in darkness, but even in the hall he could smell the spicy smell of spaghetti bolognese and wished suddenly that he had asked Stella to save him some. He went into the kitchen where on a saucepan of water on a very low light was a plate of spag. bol., as Stella called it. It was a bit dried up round the edges, but in his complacent and rather elated mood it was heaven. He turned off the gas, put the plate on the kitchen table, grabbed a fork and waded into the food.

'Decent of Stella,' he said aloud and found himself almost crying with the goodness of people. He knew he was a bit maudlin with the drink, but he didn't care. He felt like crying at that moment. Life was lonely, even here living in this house it was lonely, but now maybe things would improve.

After the food he took himself off to bed, but for a long time he couldn't sleep. What was Hebe's proposition? He felt sure it was something to do with the group. That made him sweat a little – was he good enough? Was his playing good enough? 'Heat Up The Past'. He was immensely proud of that title but very unsure of the tune. Was it good enough, specially the ending? He worried about the ending. He sweated a little more and turned restlessly in his bed. Should he get up now and try to get it right? No – that would wake up the damned house, of course he couldn't do that. He tried to hum the tune, to remember it. He couldn't. His thoughts turned again to Hebe.

Hebe was everything he wanted to be – tough, self-confident, well-dressed. He'd tried once to do his hair like Hebe's. It didn't look too bad, but he hadn't the nerve to go out and let the others see it, see he was copying Hebe. No way. Oh well, he'd have to wait till nine o'clock Wednesday, the Niagara Falls – funny place to have a meet, specially with Hebe. Still, in a way Hebe was a funny bloke – but great.

Anything Hebe wanted him to do he'd do, no danger. He couldn't sleep, he'd have to get up and have a leak. Four pints, that's what it was. He crept to the bathroom – not a sound in the house – then back in bed he began to calm down, to feel drowsy, and was soon asleep.

In spite of Rick's care Stella had been awakened by the noise: one of the floorboards had creaked on his way to the loo. He was in, then – she needn't bother about the meal heating downstairs, he would have eaten it. She turned off the light. She knew Rick, always hungry. It was Nanny's night off, too. She got up after she had heard Rick's bedroom door close and padded on bare feet to the nursery to check on the sleeping child. He was in the deep, maybe dreamless, sleep of childhood. He had kicked the covers off and she replaced them. He murmured in his sleep and turned his head on his pillow. He wouldn't hear her.

His deafness had been a shock to Stella when they had first found out. Yet, as she leaned over the cot looking at the sleeping child in the dim nursery light, she wondered at her own lack of feeling, of thought. After all, she had created him. 'Some women have no maternal instinct,' she'd heard that said. She had loved his father – or had she been too young to know what the rapture she had felt was? It had been so sure, so . . . He was older than her, more than twice as old. She had told him she was seventeen and he had believed her.

That holiday, that space in the white mountains of snow, flying – yes, it seemed like flying – over the slopes together. And the nights – the stealing away to his room and lying in his arms.

She had told him she was on the pill, another lie. It had been a relationship built on lies. Then the parting, the tearful goodbyes, she could almost feel again the snow crunching crisp and white under her feet. He had gone, waving, waving. She was afraid he would find out how old she actually was and she was afraid that would get him into trouble. Anyway, they had parted.

Then Dad had taken her away from London and they had made the move down here. After the skiing holiday she had gone back to the convent. She had not told the nuns, not told even her friends, that she was pregnant and at first the nuns had not noticed.

It was the next holiday at home when everything was revealed. It was too late to get rid of him and here he was, her child, Bruce.

Stella was used to his deafness now. Dad had been good, he'd seen every kind of specialist and they had said, 'Maybe a hearing aid, later.' She wondered whether it had been a punishment for all her lying and the things she had done to get rid of him. Sometimes she thought it was stupid to think that and at other times she wasn't so sure. She hadn't wanted him. The stuff hadn't worked – the ergot, or whatever it was. She'd drunk loads of gin, it had all proved useless. Had that made him deaf? She couldn't love him because in a way he had come between her and that wonderful romantic love up there in the snowy mountains. He would not have wanted a child – and a deaf child born of a fifteen-year-old mother! No, she was sure he wouldn't have wanted that and she had never got in touch with him, never told anybody his name.

But she had got Bruce for ever and ever and ever; he would probably always cling to her because of his affliction. That was terrible to think of – someone you didn't love clinging to you for ever. Adoption. They had thought of it, but who would want to adopt a deaf child? They hadn't even tried.

Sometimes she felt like running away, leaving it all – leaving Dad and the child and the house and Rick and Nanny. Poor Dad, what would he do bringing up a child, or trying to? That had always held her back. No, she was chained to this house and to this sleeping child.

She felt cold, the night air was chilly. Again she drew the little duvet up closer round the child's shoulders and left him to his dreams and went back to her own room. The depression she felt was wrapped round her like a familiar cloak.

3

Rick turned up at the Niagara Falls at ten to nine. He was afraid to arrive late – afraid that if he kept him waiting Hebe could turn nasty, and anyway he wasn't used to this pub. It was small and dark and almost empty compared with The Feathers, which at this hour of the night would be heavy with smoke, heaving with talk and the television on over the corner of the bar so that the drinkers would watch the football if they wanted to, or maybe the athletics.

Here there were about six or seven old men at the bar talking quietly. Two were seated at a table in the far corner of the room with their wives, fat, white-haired old tits, Rick thought. One was smoking, the cigarette stuck in her mouth, which was heavily coated with a bright scarlet lipstick. Every now and again she let out a screech of laughter and slapped the man beside her on the arm or shoulder as if he had come out with the world's greatest witticism.

Rick turned away: he hated old people and couldn't cope with them. His own parents . . . well, they weren't so old – not as old as that quartet in the corner – but their thoughts were different from his. Their ideas seemed to him sort of bizarre – 'Why don't you find yourself a nice girl?' 'It's time you settled down.' 'What are you going to do when you're older?' These questions poured from them like tea from a teapot. When he said that he wanted to be part of a group, a band, they had sighed and looked at each other, so he'd left and eventually ended up in his present lodgings. Glad to be rid of them.

He ordered a beer and sat down at the only other table that the little bar boasted, in the corner furthest away from the screeching lady and her companions. The table had once been polished, but by the look of it the barman now gave it only a cursory wipe; the round marks made by the glasses remained and the table was still wet – horrid, Rick thought.

Rick sipped his beer and waited. At nine twenty Hebe appeared. Rick had just about given him up, but he made no sign that he thought he was late, nor did Hebe apologize. Rick would have been astonished had he done so.

'Oh good, you're here.' He went first to the bar, then came over to the table carrying what looked like a double whisky. He downed it in one go.

'Bloody hell, I needed that,' he said, wiping his lips.

'Been working, Hebe?' Rick ventured. It didn't do to enquire into anything Hebe had been doing.

'You could say that.' Hebe went back to the bar and ordered the same again, but this time the same for Rick, two double whiskies. Hebe planted the two glasses down on the table.

'Oh thanks, Hebe.' The smell of the whisky was pleasant to Rick, who was always too skint to indulge himself in such expensive booze.

'You'll need it, maybe.' Hebe sipped his own drink, then leant back and glanced round the little bar; obviously he wanted privacy for what he was about to say.

Rick began to feel nervous. Hebe had a reputation for pushing– maybe using and obtaining dope with some ease – that wasn't very healthy. Rick took some more of his whisky. He was not about to get involved in dope, it was too dangerous, too . . .

'Want to earn five grand, Rick?' he asked casually, pushing his glass gently to and fro on the table. Rick thought, it is dope; well, he wouldn't . . .

Hebe laughed, obviously noting Rick's expression. 'Don't take fright, man. Five thousand for one night. One thing, just one thing for you to do and the five thou is yours.'

Rick dare not say, 'Not dope, Hebe.' He might offend him and that was the last thing he wanted to do. After all, Hebe was his friend, his mate. He waited. Hebe leaned forward. Rick noticed that his hands were particularly white, the nails beautifully manicured, polished slightly. Hebe's eyes narrowed calculatingly, watching Rick. He put up a hand and brushed his immaculate hair.

'Tell me, Hebe, what is it you want me to do?'

Hebe's eyes did not leave Rick's face. 'Kidnap a child, Rick.'

The words did not sink in at first. Rick's face remained blank, not understanding; the words seemed to mean nothing, fall through his mind.

Hebe repeated the words. 'Kidnap a kid, Rick. Pass him on to me for five thou. You could take off for the States with that.'

Rick very slowly came to life. His mouth, which had fallen open, closed. 'K-k-k kidnap who?' His mouth had gone dry. He could hardly speak.

Hebe's voice was quiet. 'Your Stella's little boy. Bruce, isn't it? You talked about him, you said –'

Rick broke in. 'I couldn't do it, Hebe, I couldn't. How could I? I live there!'

'Sure you live there. Nanny has a day off and a night, right? Wednesdays. I'll let you have some dope – won't hurt the kid, just knock him out.' He waited, his white fingers drumming on the table.

Rick shook his head again. 'But –'

Hebe didn't let him continue. 'No buts, Rick. You bring him

out to me. I'll have the car parked just outside – 3 a.m. next Wednesday.'

'But the police, you know –'

'No worries, the child will be far away that night. He will go to a really nice family. You told me that Stella bint can't even look after him and the old man never takes any notice of him. It's only the Nanny who seems to like the poor little bleeder. That's what you said, Rick, and think of 5,000 nicker.'

Rick was almost paralysed with fear and incredulity. 'How did you know all this? I told you Nanny's night off and all that, but how did you know the rest?'

Hebe shook his head dismissively. 'Never mind that – will you do it?'

Rick put his head in his hands. £5,000! 'How do I know Bruce will be all right? How do I know everything will be as you say? How do I know?'

'He's going to a rich family. They've adopted one little girl already through my contacts, see? They're considered too old to adopt through the proper channels and they're desperate for another child, a boy.' Hebe spoke with quiet urgency. Then he got up and went to the bar for two more whiskies.

Rick tried to pull his chaotic thoughts together. They'll go berserk when they find Bruce has gone. But would they really care? he wondered. Hebe was right, Stella did think the child was a drag, she always hated Nanny's night and day off. Bill Turner looked and spoke to the kid as little as possible. Was Hebe speaking the truth about the wonderful home the child was going to?

Suddenly another bomb burst in Rick's head, the little boy's deafness. Did Hebe know, had he ever mentioned it to him? Had he . . . ? Rick couldn't remember that he had. Would it make any difference to the would-be parents? Should he tell Hebe now? He realized that the very fact that he was debating whether or not to tell Hebe and worrying about how the would-be parents would react meant that he intended to do it, to do this awful deed. He went cold at the very thought.

It was such a mess, to be without money to enable him to offer the talent he knew he possessed. You must have bread even to cut a disc. £5,000! No, he'd say nothing about the kid's problems.

Hebe was talking to the barman, drinking a whisky, perhaps giving him time to think. Yes, Hebe was like that, slow like a cat, like a panther, walking slowly then springing. He'd come back to the table and say, 'Well, Rick?' or something like that and expect an answer.

That was exactly what he did and what he said – well, almost. Glass in hand, he stood looking down at Rick, eyes narrowed. 'Well, what about it, Rick? Next Wednesday 3 a.m? I'll be outside, behind that hedge, in my car. We'll have a meet here, Wednesday lunchtime. I'll give you the pills for the kid. Right?' Rick found himself fastened to his chair. He couldn't move or speak. He had heard of people, what was it, 'freezing with fear'. He found his voice again after what seemed to be ages, but Hebe seemed not to notice any pause. 'Will the pills hurt him?'

Hebe shook his head. 'No, they act pretty quickly, knock him out. What does he have at night, cornflakes?'

Rick couldn't think. 'Nanny gets it. Milk – Ovaltine – I don't know.'

'Not on that night, stupid, it'll be the girl, Stella, the kid's mother. You just drop the pills in when she's not looking: he must have something to drink before he goes to bed, all kids do.'

'Supposing she sees?' Rick knew he was being feeble, not strong and resolute as a mate of Hebe's should be.

Hebe looked forward and put the palms of his hands on the table. Standing, he seemed taller – his face miles above Rick, who was still seated. His white face looked like a mask, his lips were red and moist, his hair shone, as did the gold ear-ring, in the rather dim light of the bar.

'Do you think you'd get five grand for nothing? You do your bit. If anything goes wrong I won't even know you, right?'

Rick nodded and Hebe lifted his hand and patted Rick on the cheek, like a child, like a grown-up child, patronizing. For a second Rick hated this, but only for a second. He went to get up; Hebe pushed him down, one hand on his shoulder, gently, without force, but Rick obeyed.

'Stay there, I'll go first. See you Wednesday next, lunchtime.' He was gone. The swing door rattled behind him.

Rick did not move for a moment or two. He felt sick, slightly drunk, and his mind was swinging from thinking it was a wonderful opportunity to get away, to vamoose, to leave all this behind him – in the United States anything could happen – to the fear of doing such a risky thing, of being caught.

He left the pub and started to walk home; as he paced along the road, his mind changed again. Five thousand wasn't all that much – and supposing he wasn't a success over there, 'Heat Up

The Past' was no good, rubbish? Sometimes he felt it was no good, just a dream.

As if in answer to his thoughts a car radio boomed at him: 'If I can make it there I'll make it anywhere! New York, New York, New York!' He felt suddenly elated as if he was on a high, had taken a pill, an upper. But he hadn't and in a moment or two the high left him.

The kid's deafness. Hebe may have been able to get to know the comings and goings of the household, Nanny's night off and all that, but did he know the kid was deaf? He tried to remember again if he had ever mentioned it, but he didn't think he had – after all, why should he, why should such a fact interest Hebe? No, he was pretty sure he hadn't. But then, the kid – how would the new, wonderful parents take it?

'Oh God!' He stumped up the weedy, gravel drive, head down, fingers stuck in the pockets of his jeans. Five thousand – could he make it on that? Yes, he could. Plane tickets to the US, especially one-way, were cheap these days and this would be his only chance. The kid would be better off. Could he trust Hebe about that, though? Next Wednesday. Well, he had a week to make up his mind, that was something, but he knew in fear and trembling that his mind was already made up. He would do it.

'That you, Rick?' Stella called out.

'Yes, it's me,' he answered and strode across the hall up the stairs and into his own room, shutting the door firmly behind him. He switched on his radio – he didn't want to think.

4

At Stella's invitation Agnes went in to have coffee with the girl. The fleeting thought crossed her mind that it was a little unusual for an eighteen-year-old to be asking her in to have coffee with her. Usually it was women of about her own age who got together in the mornings to talk about hair-dos, the price of goods or clothes or anything that interested their age group. However, Agnes suspected that Stella was lonely and, after all, her background was not similar to others of her own age. The child, the nanny, her father who needed quiet and the rather strange young man Rick. What a queer group for a young girl to be part of, to have to cook for, look after.

On the whole, though, Agnes detected a change in the household next door. She couldn't put it down to anything that Stella had confided to her – that she was worried about her father, that he was irritable and had formed the habit of taking himself off in the mornings walking!

'But really, it's a healthy habit, Stella.' Agnes sipped the rather turbid drink; she was sure that Stella had put too much instant coffee in the cups.

'Daddy walking! But he hates walking. I think he just wants to get away from us all, that's why he goes out now and I can't blame him for that.'

'Oh surely not, Stella. He probably enjoys it and it does him good to get away from his typewriter.'

The girl looked sceptical, but went on. 'Then Rick. I really worry about him, too. I think sometimes that he's going odd, Agnes, really I do. He's been so strange for the last few days, as if he hardly knows what he's doing.'

'Have you spoken to him; asked him if there's anything the matter?'

'Not really – not really talked to him, I mean. I did ask if there was something wrong, but he just said he couldn't get his head together.'

Agnes kept her thoughts to herself – for an eighteen-year-old Stella had got enough on her plate. Agnes did wonder if Rick was using or pushing drugs. Yet he seemed to be without money – but if he had any he would probably spend it on his habit. Money in and money out, a vicious circle!

At that moment Rick walked into the room. 'Oh sorry, I thought...'

Stella got up at once. 'Come in, Rick. I'll make you some coffee.' She disappeared kitchenwards.

Rick threw himself down in a chair. He looked awful, Agnes thought, white, drawn, distracted. He didn't look directly at her, but began to pick at his nails, the lank hair falling forward and almost hiding his face. There was a tension about him, the dangling foot twitched and when he took the cup of coffee that Stella was offering he nearly dropped it.

'Careful, Rick.'

He nodded, mumbled, 'Sorry,' then looked up at Stella. 'What day is it, Stell?' he asked.

'Tuesday, Rick, for goodness sake – losing your marbles?'

'Tuesday – yes, Tuesday, that's right.'

Stella looked at Agnes and shrugged. Agnes made a tiny

grimace in return. She thought that Rick certainly looked and sounded weird and anxious. He had already asked her for a loan. Was he so stuck for money, money he owed to someone who he knew would rough him up if he didn't repay? Was that it, she wondered, or was he on something?

The telephone rang. Stella got up to answer it, but Rick leapt out of his chair in a manner quite uncharacteristic for him. He shut the door of the sitting-room behind him and the telephone ceased ringing. A few minutes later he came back into the room.

'It was for Bill,' he said. This time he didn't stay, but went out of the room carrying his coffee cup and saucer with him.

'See what I mean? I don't know what's the matter with him, Agnes, but he's in a state about something.' Stella curled her long legs up on the settee and lit a cigarette, first offering one to Agnes, who refused.

'We're all in a state in this house.' She blew the smoke out in a long plume. 'Dad's in a state about money. Nanny's in a state because perhaps Dad won't be able to keep her on – she adores Bruce – and I'm in a state, too.' She took another heavy pull on her cigarette.

Agnes watched the girl and thought of herself at eighteen – timid, shy, frightened of offending, usually speechless in company, with a self-esteem that couldn't have been lower. Yet here was Stella, so lovely, articulate, not badly educated, but tied hand and foot – or she soon would be if Nanny had to go.

'What about your father's books, don't they –?' She was about to say earn enough money, but the girl forestalled her.

'No, authors don't get much, not unless they write a bestseller or turn out something like Jeffrey Archer. Dad doesn't earn much – £3,000 advance, and it takes about ten months to write a book. Who'd work for that money?'

'Even so, I should have thought . . .' Agnes hesitated.

'No, even with paperbacks and library fees it's not a large sum. If one of the books went on the telly it would help, but up to now he's had no luck there.' She drew again on her cigarette, then suddenly stubbed it out violently in the glass ashtray on the table in front of her.

'I'm worried about Nanny; she's upset because of Daddy saying he might have to sack her. I asked her to change her day out tomorrow so that I could go to . . .' Suddenly her eyes reddened and she hung her head forward. 'She wouldn't. I suppose she's fed up with us.' She raised her head and looked at

Agnes and suddenly grinned ashamedly. 'Sorry, Agnes. What an awful lot you must think us – and you're not wrong!'

Agnes shook her head. 'Why did you ask Nanny to change tomorrow?' she asked.

'Oh, nothing much. Well, one of the few friends I have made on the Island is going over to the mainland to the clothes show at Portsmouth College – design, you know. She's got a couple of tickets and I'd just love to see what the clothes are like. The girls, the undergraduates, design, make and model the clothes themselves. Some are pretty way out, as you can imagine, but they're fun. Some go on to make clothes for firms and get on awfully well, sell their designs. Great!'

Her pretty face was alight with enthusiasm. 'More coffee?' Agnes refused, but then seeing the disappointed look that replaced the girl's smiling expression she relented and Stella took the cups back into the kitchen.

Agnes got up and walked over to the french windows and looked out. She was still standing there when Stella came back into the room carrying the coffee.

'A mess, isn't it?' Stella was referring to the back garden, which fitted her description exactly – it was a mess. In the centre was a rose bed, but the earth was so full of weeds and columbines climbing up nearly to the top that one could hardly tell they were roses.

'Couldn't you and Rick do a little weeding or cut the grass?' she asked.

Stella shook her head. 'Agnes, do you mind?' she said, laughing. 'The lawn mower is broken and if I or Rick started on the job it would take every day, hours and hours, and I hate gardening just as much as I hate looking after children, even Bruce. Rick would die at the thought. Anyway, he's a lodger and we can't ask him to work.'

Agnes took the proffered cup and replied mildly enough, 'Well, you did tell me he couldn't pay the rent. Perhaps –'

She was surprised at the resultant outburst. 'Agnes, don't you start! I thought you wouldn't – wouldn't be a should-do-this, should-do-that sort of person. I want to do my own thing, not other people's. I don't care if the garden is a jungle or if the grass is waist-high!' Her voice rose to an hysterical scream as she burst into a torrent of tears.

Agnes was surprised at the outburst, but in a way understood it. She went close to the girl and put her arm round her shoulders; her problems must seem to her pretty insurmountable, and they would be if Nanny left or was sacked. The girl would be tied by the child, tied by the house, looking after her father, cooking, shopping . . .

'Supposing you got a job and paid Nanny?' she ventured.

'What job? I've got no qualifications, no work experience. I couldn't even get a job as a waitress. I'm an uneducated nit with a deaf child and an ageing father who can't even write a bestseller.' She looked up then and her tearful eyes met Agnes's. 'Sorry, that's a pretty rotten thing to say. Well, all I've said is rotten, full of self-pity.'

Agnes handed her her own handkerchief and her arm round the girl's shoulders tightened a little. Then she said something that rather surprised herself. 'Look, Stella, tomorrow I'll look after Bruce for you and get your father's lunch. You take the day off, go to the clothes show and just for a day forget all about everything here.' She stopped.

'Agnes, I couldn't ask you to do that.'

Agnes laughed. 'You haven't asked. Just put it down to the fact that I've been looking at *Neighbours* on television too long.' She said this with a rare touch of humour.

Stella gave her a quick, impulsive kiss on the cheek. 'Agnes, you're absolutely wonderful,' she said.

On the way back to her own house after the ecstatic agreement from Stella, Agnes was already thinking of what to prepare. It would have to be something cold. Perhaps she would cook the half-leg of lamb she had in the freezer, cook it tonight so that it would be ready for lunch tomorrow. The little boy could eat some of that and so could Stella's father and Rick.

She realized that this was a new role for her and the idea of the arrangement made her smile. It was the first time she had really felt needed since she had left Penny Stratton and come to the Isle of Wight.

She realized that Stella was unwise. She shouldn't have had unprotected sex at fifteen; she was apparently feckless and unreasonable, but she was so young. She thought, too, about Bruce. Did it make any difference that he had been conceived by a mother who was so young? She wondered who Bruce's father was, who it was that Stella had lusted after so much and who she had protected by her silence.

She opened the freezer, took out the lamb, placed it on a large platter in the kitchen and covered it with foil. It would take several hours to defrost. She would cook it tonight.

After suggesting that she should take over tomorrow she had

peeped into Stella's oven. The inside was brown and smelled of fat, even when cold. She would rather cook it here – her own oven was immaculate. She wondered if the little boy would eat meat and vegetables. Did Bill Turner like courgettes? Would Stella eat a meal when she got back? It was lovely, like having something she had never had – a family!

5

The following day was more enjoyable than Agnes had anticipated. It was very pleasant to see Stella, bright and smiling, depart with her friend to catch the nine o'clock ferry. She threw her arms round Agnes and kissed her cheek as she had yesterday. 'Thanks, thanks, Agnes. This really is a terrific treat.'

Agnes noticed that Stella did not even say goodbye to Bruce, who stood with his hand in hers, his big brown eyes looking up at the departing girl, hearing nothing. Agnes felt a pang of pity for the child in his silent world. Did it matter to him that his mother was off somewhere? If so he didn't show it, but turned with Agnes to start the day with her, eyes fixed on her face.

Rick disappeared before the meal, but Bill Turner appeared to enjoy the cold lunch Agnes took him and was profuse in his thanks to Agnes for giving Stella the day off. The child, too, enjoyed his lunch and ate everything, including a sweet which Agnes had made specially for him. He had a rest after lunch, then they went to the park, had a nursery tea and the day went by quietly and quickly.

At six thirty Agnes gave Bruce a bath and brought him down to the kitchen for a bedtime drink. To her surprise Rick was in the kitchen, just standing as if he was waiting for her and the child – perhaps to say goodnight to the little boy?

'Do you know what Bruce has before he goes to bed, Rick?'

'Yes, chocolate, hot chocolate,' Rick answered. He seemed brighter and more with it than normally. 'I'll make it for you.' He grabbed a small saucepan, poured milk into it and put it on the stove. Then he stood watching the liquid heat, not moving away from the stove.

'Thank you, Rick.' Agnes tried to keep the surprise out of her voice.

Bruce clambered on to the kitchen chair near the table and sat swinging his little fat legs, watching Agnes. She felt quite a growing affection for the little boy, he had been so co-operative all day. She had feared tantrums, perhaps due to the change in his routine or to his missing Nanny. But no, he had been good, and she wondered how he would take it if Nanny disappeared altogether from his life.

It was so very difficult to communicate with him. There was a picture book on the kitchen shelf. She took it down, searched through it and found a picture of a mug – just a mug, well illustrated against a blue background. She put the picture in front of him. He pointed at it, looked up at her and smiled, then banged the table leg once or twice with his small feet, his eyes going back to the picture.

Rick finished making the chocolate and, unseen by Agnes, slipped in the two pills. It was so easy with her bending over the child and the book. He added sugar and stirred it vigorously; this action Agnes could see and she thanked him again. 'Is it too hot for him?' she asked.

Rick nodded, took the milk bottle and added a little cold milk to the sweet-smelling chocolate, then stirred it again. The spoon going round and round seemed to fascinate Bruce. Rick put the cup in front of him and gave him the spoon. The child copied Rick and stirred some more, laughing, and Rick stood watching him.

'I must go out. Got a date,' he said suddenly.

'I was going to make some sandwiches with the rest of the lamb. If you –'

'No, no, thanks.' Rick seemed anxious to be gone. He paused just long enough to see the child drinking and then went.

Agnes took the little boy up to the bathroom, where he cleaned his teeth pretty efficiently, probably due to Nanny's tuition, Agnes thought. She put him in his bed and tucked him in. She stayed with him for ten minutes or so, but he fell asleep almost at once, more quickly than she had anticipated.

She went downstairs and proceeded to make the sandwiches. She put some on a small side plate, covering it with clingfilm, just in case Stella should want them when she came home. Then she put the larger plate of sandwiches and two smaller plates on a tray and took them into the sitting-room. She had heard Bill Turner come out of his study and then the sound of the television. He sprang up as she entered; he looked tired, but relaxed.

'I hope you won't mind eating lamb again,' she said, putting the tray down on the coffee table.

'No indeed. Thanks. I like lamb sandwiches, but just a minute.' He left the room and came back in a moment with two glasses and some wine. 'Not very chilled, I'm afraid,' he said, put the two glasses on the table beside the sandwiches and poured wine into them. His hand shook and he glanced at Agnes. 'I've been typing all day,' he said as if to excuse the tremor. 'I won't bore you again with thanks,' he said. 'These sandwiches are good.'

'Thank you. They'll have to do in place of your evening meal, I'm afraid.'

Bill laughed. 'Instead of the baked beans on toast, you mean. Stella is not much of a cook. She does try a roast meal now and again, but she's not overly successful.' He took another sandwich. 'Rick's out, I expect, so can we finish these off?'

Agnes nodded. 'Yes, he went out. Said he had a date.'

Agnes looked at him as he stared into the distance, munching away. He was not particularly good company, she thought, and she wondered what the effect on him would be if she said, 'I saw you long ago lying in bed and you told me a secret, which I have always kept.' She looked at her watch; it was twenty to nine. She was glad to hear a key put in the lock of the front door. It would be Stella.

She came into the sitting-room and took over the conversation entirely. Yes, she had eaten, the clothes had been mega, so way out. She described them, the hats, the waist-high tights with minimum hot pants and tunics – flowing coats and cloaks. 'Oh Dad, it was wonderful to be able to see them, to see what is going on. Nobody's wearing their hair like mine now, it's dead old-fashioned, I'm having it cut tomorrow.' She looked at Bill. 'Have we got any money, Dad?' she asked.

He shook his head. 'Haven't you anything to say to Agnes?' he said, rather brusquely.

Money in this house was a prickly subject, Agnes thought.

'Oh, of course I have. Thanks and thanks and thanks again, Agnes. You've been great too, really you have.' Not up to now had she mentioned the child, Agnes noted.

'Bruce has been a very good boy all day,' Agnes said, a little reproachfully perhaps.

Stella was at least honest. 'Oh yes, Bruce, I'd forgotten him. He's all right, is he?' Her tone flattened as if the thought of her son brought her down, down from the day's heights.

'Fast asleep, but we'll check on him before I go. There are some sandwiches in the kitchen if you want some.'

'No thanks, I don't. I feel too excited to eat, anyway, and we got eats at the show and a snack afterwards. Oh, it was great, Agnes.'

Bill Turner got up, grinned at Agnes and said, 'Good, I'll have them then,' and wandered off to the kitchen.

'Dad looked cheerful,' Stella remarked.

In the nursery the little boy did not stir, even when Agnes switched on the side light. He was in the same position as when she had put him in his bed, breathing evenly, his long lashes resting on his flushed cheeks. One small fist was near his mouth on the pillow.

'He usually kicks the covers off,' Stella said, 'but he hasn't tonight.'

'He was probably tired. I played with him quite a bit. He's been running about. We went to the park and fed the ducks.' Agnes felt it was rather like the old days, a day nurse giving a report to the night nurse. Stella did not attempt to kiss or even touch the boy, but looked down at him quite dispassionately. Then they left the nursery.

'Well thanks, Agnes. Dad looks more benign than usual – probably he was glad to see the back of me for a day.' She stood at the front door.

Agnes was in a way glad to leave. Although she sympathized with the girl, her attitude was so cold towards the child it was almost unnatural – particularly as she professed to have been in love with his father. Still, who could fathom people's emotions?

She let herself into her own house. People were so complicated that sometimes, as at this moment, she was glad to be alone. She was just in time for a television programme she particularly wanted to see. She went into her neat, well-ordered sitting-room, switched on the television and took the *Radio Times* from its normal place. She sat down thankfully in her armchair, dismissing thoughts of other people's problems and hang-ups completely from her mind.

6

Next door Rick had come back. He felt sick with nerves. Stella was rattling on about clothes, clothes, clothes to her father and saying if only she could go to college and design. She was sure she could, she had ideas, and clothes were her passion.

As Rick watched them both Bill seemed to be getting more and more irritated. He was hiding behind *The Times*. The television was on, but Rick could tell that Bill was neither watching nor reading. Suddenly he got to his feet and looked down at Stella. His face had not got its usual pleasant, preoccupied look; it was red, and he looked enraged.

'For God's sake, girl!' he said loudly. 'If you wanted to do all these things why did you go and get pregnant? You know very well it's no use talking like this to me now when we can no longer afford Nanny. Why even talk about going to college? The boy is your responsibility now – he's your son, not mine. Yours!' He flung the paper down.

Rick, who had sat down for a moment, stood up as if to leave the room, but Bill, now in a very bad mood, turned on him too. 'And you, Rick, owe me two – or is it three? – weeks' rent. I want it, all right? So get it!' He got up to leave the room, *The Times* screwed up in his hands, and he threw it down again as he reached the door.

'Phew!' Rick blew his lips out and Stella burst into a torrent of tears, all her lovely day ruined.

'Never mind, Stell,' he said. She took no notice, so he tried again. 'It'll be all right, you'll see, I promise you.' Suddenly he felt better. He had done his job with the pills and soon everything would be better for poor old Stella. The kid would be out of her hair. Of course, it would be awful for a bit, police and all that, but then she would be free and so would he. He'd have the money and she'd be able to go to college if she wanted. He felt suddenly like a Fixer. He went a bit cold when he thought about carrying the boy out to Hebe's car, but he had done the first bit, the pills, and apparently they had worked.

He went up and patted Stella's shoulder awkwardly. 'Listen to what I say, Stella. Everything is going to be all right. I know it is.'

She looked up at him, her eyes red. 'What do you mean, all right? How can it ever be all right?'

Rick withdrew his hand from Stella's shoulder. 'Well, I feel it will be. Somehow I feel it will be.'

'Oh, feelings. They're no good.' Stella got up. 'I'm going to bed, Rick,' she said, 'and for goodness sake rustle up the money for Dad.' She left the room, kicking the newspaper in front of her, and Rick heard her go up the stairs to bed.

He looked at the clock – only ten past ten. Should he go out or stay in? He didn't want to have any more confrontations with Bill Turner in his present temper. Five hours before he could take Bruce to Hebe. He shivered, but even Hebe had said it was a good home. The question was, could he trust Hebe? Well, he'd have to, he'd just have to. He would go up to his room and sit it out – well, sweat it out would be a better word.

He picked up *The Times*, straightened it out and took it upstairs to read. He knew full well he wouldn't sleep. 3 a.m. He longed for the time to come, yet dreaded it too. He wished it was over. The thought of putting that child into Hebe's car . . . Still, it had to be done. That instant, even imagining it made the sick feeling return.

He threw himself on his bed and opened the paper, but he couldn't read it. Time went on and on. Midnight – one o'clock – two o'clock – then the hands crept towards the dreaded time. Rick tried to control himself – keep his fear at bay.

3 a.m. And it was all so easy. Hebe was there outside. The child just murmured as he lifted him from the bed. He had never held him before and the small warm body, the quiet sleeping face, had a strange effect on him. 'Poor little bleeder,' he whispered to himself.

Outside, Hebe placed the child on the back seat of his car. There in the semi-darkness of the street Rick thought that Hebe looked sinister, heartless, cold. He closed the door of the car noiselessly, put his hand in his leather waistcoat pocket, drew out a fat, brown envelope and gave it to Rick. Rick wiped his hand down his trouser leg before he took it. Thirty pieces of silver, he thought – thirty pieces of silver. 'You'll look after him, Hebe?' he asked. 'You're sure he'll be OK?'

Hebe, just getting into the driver's seat, looked up at him. 'Getting paternal, man?' he said, a slight sneer twisting his mouth a little. 'Sure I'm sure he'll be all right.'

Rick shook his head, the car slid away and he was left standing, the brown packet still in his hand. At that moment he was wishing with all his heart that he had not done it – but it was too late now, too late for regret. He went back into the house, treading along the grass verge beside the drive, taking great care shutting the front door and gaining his room without hearing a sound in the house. There was nothing to warn them that the little boy had gone.

He put the envelope under his pillow and tried to think of New York and of his wonderful 'Heat Up The Past'; tried to think of its success – a gold disc, a platinum one – but even that thought didn't help him sleep. He lay there with one hand over the money and tried to convince himself that what he had done was worth it, but in his heart he felt it wasn't.

Then he had a brilliant idea, so brilliant that he sat up in bed to think about it. How about a new tune, a new lyric called 'Thirty Pieces Of Silver'? A guy that let his chick down, or made her sell her body – something like that. Great. Had it been done before? He didn't think so. He was so excited about the idea that for a moment at least the thought of the child was driven from his mind. He lay back on the pillows still thinking of the new tune, still thinking of a lyric that would fit it, and so he managed to relax a little – not to sleep, but at least to let his thoughts wander away from what he had just done and, instead, to think of what he might achieve.

In the children's home on the sea front just outside Ryde Theresa was having a grumble and reporting to the superintendent. 'Bugger that child, Ada, he's wandered off again.'

The superintendent raised her eyes heavenwards. 'Not Alfie again? When did he go?'

'I don't know – early this morning. I'd opened the garden door to let Gyp out, and of course off he goes. The other kids won't tell. All they'll say is that it was early. They won't say anything else.'

The superintendent went back to making out a kitchen lunch menu for the children. 'Well, have a good look round. If you remember, last time he went to Woolworths and pinched some sweets, so get someone to go to the town; look in the shops.'

Theresa frowned. 'We're short anyway – still, I'll go.'

The superintendent agreed. 'He's so small that people don't realize he's four or nearly five.'

'He's a little devil, Ada, that's what he is. He loves giving us a hard time. I hate that kid.'

The superintendent reacted to this more sharply. 'Maybe you'd be the same if your mother was HIV positive and an addict, not counting the booze. What do you expect of the child? She doesn't give a damn if he's dead or alive.'

'Yes, well . . . I suppose so,' Theresa agreed, and went off to search, as she had done on four or five previous occasions, for the same child.

All the girls in Woolworths smiled at Theresa when she asked them. 'No, not this morning. Wee Willie we call him, he's so little, isn't he?' Theresa nodded. Wee Willie was a real little demon at times. 'I think he pinched something when he came once before, didn't he? Something besides the sweets, I think, but I forget what it was.'

'Water wings, a pair of water wings, I remember, but you told me about his mother and his background and so we let him have them.'

'I'd forgotten that.' Theresa left Woolworths and searched along the High Street looking and getting more and more furious. If she had to go back without him they'd just have to let the police know and they wouldn't be very pleased. She hadn't got time to go looking for him – after all, she'd got too much to do already.

She turned and left the High Street, still looking into the shops as she went by, arriving back just in time to meet the superintendent coming out of her office.

'No sign of him?' she asked.

'No, no sign. Shall I ring the police?'

The superintendent shook her head. 'No, not yet. Give him a bit of time and he'll be back – he always appears when he's good and ready. Calling on the Old Bill gives the place a bad name. Leave it for a bit.'

7

Stella woke the next morning at quarter to eight. Her first thought was of the previous day. What fun it had been, being with her friend, watching everybody, seeing people of her own age, the clothes – the music that had blared out noisily as the girls, boys too, moved up and down the catwalk in the outrageous outfits.

Minuscule skirts in leather and plastic, the long tight trousers and the voluminous ones that looked like immense skirts. There had been one really fat model who had had fabulous clothes which she had designed herself for herself. She had looked great, pushing her rather large bum out each time she had turned, big breasts, the low cleavage, showing them off. She got more applause than some of the willowy ones.

Not a sound from Bruce – usually he gave her a hard time

when Nanny was off. Nanny should be back soon – she usually got back about ten in the morning and Bruce would hold out his arms as if she had been away for weeks and he was welcoming back his mother. Well, she wished Nanny was his mother and she could adopt him. Some hopes!

Stella yawned, stretched and got out of bed, shrugged into her dressing-gown, thrust her feet into rather worn-out mules and did up the belt of her gown. Still not a sound from the nursery. Probably Agnes had tired him out playing with him all day and taking him to the park. Stella felt really grateful to Agnes; what other friend would have offered? Still, she was a nurse and maybe that made a difference.

She sat on the side of her bed for a moment, not wanting to start the dreary, normal, routine day. Dress the child, give him his cornflakes, make breakfast for Dad and Rick, think about lunch. If Nanny went she would have the child every day, wash his clothes, get appropriate food for him at the superstore, see that he ate properly, went to the lavatory, walked in the park, went to bed at the right time. The thoughts loomed ahead of her – freedom never!

She sighed, got up and went to the bathroom. Bruce was still quiet. She would have a quick bath and pluck her eyebrows, then go and wake him. The longer he slept the nearer the time for Nanny's return.

She began to feel a bit more cheerful. Dad would sell a book to TV, perhaps; one would take off and be a bestseller. He had got so angry yesterday evening. Poor Dad. She had dropped him in it, too, having this baby. How could they ever get out? In a way it was all her fault and she knew it, but that didn't make any difference.

Rick lay in his bed sweating. He hadn't slept at all, not all night. He lay now, not daring to get up. Usually he liked lying in bed, getting up late, ignoring Stella's yells that breakfast was on the table. But this morning he did not get up. He heard Stella's bedroom door open. He shoved the sheet between his teeth to stop them chattering with fright. She would see the empty bed now, the empty room. He was surprised that she hadn't already. Evidently she thought Bruce was sleeping late.

The bathroom door opened and shut, the bath water began to run. Cripes, she was having a bath! He couldn't get up, just couldn't, not until she had discovered . . . He pulled the sheet up round his neck and lay staring at the door, waiting, waiting. Silly cow! Why didn't she at least go in and look at the child? Well, it showed how much she cared. He waited, it seemed like hours, but when at last he looked at the clock it was only eight twenty-five.

Then the bathroom door opened and closed again. He heard the soft pad of Stella's feet across the landing. The moment of discovery, of panic, of incredulity, had arrived. He turned on his side and feigned sleep just in case Stella should burst into his room, crying, carrying on, expecting him to do something about her discovery. But it wasn't like that at all; discovery or not, nothing happened.

He wondered, too, as he lay there, cringing at any noise, where was Bruce? Where was Hebe? Supposing he was lying and took the little boy and put him in a snuff movie, tortured him, killed him. Supposing, supposing . . .

He got up, he couldn't lie there any longer. Then it happened. Well, not quite as he had imagined, but more quietly, rather in a very ordinary way. Stella knocked on his door. 'Rick?' He didn't answer at first. 'Rick, is Bruce in there with you?'

Stella put her head round the door. 'He's wandered off again. I thought he might be in here.' She closed the door behind her.

Rick got up and started to dress. His hands were trembling so much he could hardly zip up his jeans or do up the buttons of his shirt. He felt sick again and was glad she wouldn't think of breakfast – not when she realized the boy was nowhere around.

Stella ran downstairs. She was furious with the child. He could get downstairs now, he was a bright child. After all, he had managed to get round to Agnes's house.

'Oh God,' she said aloud. She found the front door still locked. Thank goodness for that, he hadn't gone that way. Dad wasn't up yet. No sign of Bruce in any of the rooms – the kitchen, the sitting-room or Dad's study. Stella was getting more angry by the minute, but was not really alarmed as yet.

The back door leading to the garden was unlocked but shut. They often left it unlocked, foolish, but . . . Outside she began to call, 'Bruce, Bruce!' She ran round the garden, looking behind the large hydrangeas, in the shed (once he had hidden there). Why was she calling him? He couldn't hear her! Still, she couldn't stop calling his name. She came round the side of the house into the front garden – nothing. She was beginning to panic slightly now. Where was he? She sprinted round to Agnes's house; the upstairs curtains were still drawn.

The early morning traffic was building up now, cars going to Newport, others coming from Newport to Ryde, buses. An ambulance flashed by. Stella saw it, heard it and it frightened her. Had Bruce wandered into the road and been knocked down? Killed perhaps? Was he in hospital, injured? After all, he might have wakened at six o'clock, sometimes he did. He could have wandered anywhere. He had had two hours before she got out of bed.

Stella ran back to the house. She was really panicking now, heart thudding. She had some difficulty in riffling through the telephone directory to find the number of the hospital.

No, no little boy had been brought in this morning. Yes, they were quite sure, neither through Casualty nor into the children's ward. Yes, of course they would know if a child had been brought in, now or earlier in the morning.

'What's the matter, Stella?' Bill Turner came out of the kitchen sipping from a mug of tea. She had not heard him come downstairs or go into the kitchen.

'Bruce has gone,' she answered.

Bill stopped sipping his tea and rubbed his forehead as if he'd got a headache. 'Gone? What do you mean, gone?'

Stella put the telephone down. 'He's not in the hospital. He's wandered off, Daddy. You know how he did that day when you had him.'

'He went next door. Have you looked there?' He sipped more tea calmly.

'No, not properly. I will.'

Rick came down the stairs. He looked ill; even Bill Turner noticed it. 'You all right, Rick?' he asked, finishing his tea.

'Yes, but what's up?' Rick's voice was hoarse. He cleared his throat.

'Bruce has wandered away again. I'm going next door to see if he is in Agnes's.'

He wasn't. It was easy to see all over Agnes's neat garden. Agnes, still in an elegant dressing-gown, came to the back door and was helpful when she heard Stella's fears. 'Stella, he's only a little boy. He can't have gone far.' She, too, was drinking tea and offered Stella some. Stella, almost angrily, refused, then apologized. 'Sorry, Agnes, I just feel a bit rattled.'

'Of course. You'd better ring the police.'

Stella looked at her, wide-eyed. 'I can't, Agnes. What will they think? What will they think of me? I know he's wandered off before, I'll have to tell them that – I'll have to tell them that he came in here. I was in bed till eight o'clock and I didn't even go and see if he was all right, I thought he was asleep. What will they think?'

Agnes put her teacup down with an impatient tinkle of china. She was never at her best in the morning and Stella's attitude struck her as infantile and selfish, thinking first of what the police would think of her behaviour and not considering the child at all. She gestured towards the telephone. 'Of course you must phone.'

'Of course. May I use yours? What shall I say?'

'Well, just that he's gone missing. Give his description and age. They'll come to your house. Go on, Stella, get them notified.'

Stella picked up the telephone, dialled and then the conversation started. 'Well, he usually wakes about six thirty. I went into him about eight o'clock ... Well, I thought he was sleeping late ... Yes, he's three ... Yes, he can get downstairs ... All right. Thank you ... I will.' She put the telephone down. 'They sounded queer, Agnes.'

'Queer?' Agnes raised her eyebrows.

'Well, as if they were holding back something. I don't know.' She was very pale, as if the full implication of the boy being missing had only just got through to her. 'I rang the hospital earlier, but no child had been brought in.'

Agnes nodded in approval. 'That was sensible, Stella,' she said.

'I must go home now, the police are coming to the house.'

She left and Agnes made herself more tea and thought of the peaceful youngster she had put to bed last night. Surely at that age he couldn't wander far? But of course, the child was deaf and therefore dumb and he wouldn't hear anyone who spoke to him. No, he couldn't have gone far. There was probably some lane or small road nearby where he had gone and he would soon be found or come home himself.

She kept a watchful eye after she had seen the police car arrive.

Some time elapsed and then a policewoman left the next-door house and, to Agnes's surprise, came up her drive and rang the door bell. She was a pretty girl – young and with neat hair pulled back into a bun in the nape of her neck.

She looked serious and when Agnes opened the door said, 'Miss Carmichael, may I come in for a moment?'

'Of course,' Agnes led the girl into the sitting-room, but neither woman sat down. The girl looked upset. 'I've had to give Miss Turner very bad news, Miss Carmichael. Of course it may not be her son, but a young boy of his size and description has been found drowned under the pier this morning.'

Agnes did sit down then, rather suddenly, on the settee. 'When?'

'About seven o'clock this morning. Of course, it may not be Miss Turner's son, but...' The young policewoman sat down, too.

'Poor Stella. How could such a young child get that far?'

'It sounds almost impossible, but toddlers can walk quite a long way. We've found that out to our cost,' the young woman said.

'Did you want me for something?' Agnes was curious as to why the policewoman had visited her.

'Miss Turner will have to come to the mortuary to see the child and she asked if you would go with her. You need not go in and see the little boy, it's only her, the mother – that is, at least, if he is her son.' She blinked and suddenly looked young and embarrassed as the tears came into eyes. 'Sorry.' She took a handkerchief from her jacket pocket. 'I'm not supposed to get emotional or involved.'

Agnes touched her arm sympathetically. 'I know,' she said. 'I was a nurse and you're not supposed to get involved then – but sometimes you just can't help it.'

'I suggested perhaps her father might go with her, but she wanted you.' The young woman smiled and nodded, then pressed the handkerchief back into her pocket. 'Will you go with her, Miss Carmichael?'

'Of course I will. Do you want us to go straight away?'

'The sooner the better, Miss Carmichael, if you will.'

Agnes nodded. 'I'll be round in ten minutes.'

The policewoman left and Agnes got herself ready for a task she felt she could well do without, but she could not refuse. She got dressed and checked her handbag for keys and purse.

8

Stella waited for Agnes. She herself had changed into a frock and looked older. She was terrified but dry-eyed.

Bill Turner was walking up and down the hall, smoking. 'How could he at his age get down to that pier?' He pulled hard on the cigarette and it glowed red. 'It's ridiculous. I just don't believe it. It's not him. I'm sure it's not him – you'll see, Stella.'

Stella shook her head. 'I don't know, Daddy. He's so active, I feel it is him – funny, isn't it? Like one of your books. Do you remember, the little boy they all searched for?'

Bill Turner waved his hand as if to drive away the thought and idea of the book, but Stella could see he did remember – only too well.

Rick came out of the kitchen – he, too, was drinking tea. Tea, tea, tea. Stella could have shouted at everyone to stop drinking tea; everybody, for God's sake. She realized she was beginning to get hysterical. She shook herself. Agnes would make her feel better, she was always so cool and composed. Even as she had that thought, Agnes's Porsche drew up at the gate.

'Where are you going?' Rick spoke for the first time since he'd left the kitchen. 'Where are you going, Stell?'

Bill answered for her. 'She's got to go to the morgue to identify a boy they've found drowned. A little boy of Bruce's age. It's not him, though, I'm sure.'

Rick almost dropped the mug, now empty, but caught it before it reached the floor. 'Morgue? What are you talking about? Bruce is all right, he's OK.'

'Maybe it's not him, but I've got to go,' Stella said.

Rick seemed almost beside himself. 'He's OK, OK. I know he is. Honest, I could swear it.'

'How can you swear it, Rick – you can't be sure. I, too, feel it's not Bruce, but of course I can't be really sure.' Bill sounded irritated.

Stella thought that Rick looked really weird. 'All right, he's OK. Maybe he is, that's what I hope and that's what I've got to go and find out.'

She was shaking as she made her way to the car – not outwardly but inside. Her own feelings were making her shake!

If it were Bruce when she got there and he was dead there would be no more ties, no more being a mother when she wasn't ready for such a responsibility. How could she think like this; how could she...? She tried to banish such thoughts, but couldn't.

'Bear up, it may not be Bruce.' Agnes's voice was quiet and kind, but Stella found herself resenting even that remark. How did she know what she was thinking – she with her money and without responsibilities? How did she know what it was like to be...? How did she know what she was thinking, and what would her thoughts be if she did know? She would despise her!

They did not speak again until they reached the town morgue. They drew in. The morgue was situated in a beautiful cemetery. The flowers were blooming and the green grass blowing softly in the breeze. 'Do you want me to come in with you?' Agnes asked.

Stella did not look directly at Agnes, but put up her hand and pushed the hair behind her ear in the familiar gesture. She looked strange, Agnes thought. She got out of the car, closed the door gently and stood still for a moment. She shook her head and then walked steadily up the short path and entered the door.

To Stella it smelled strange inside and after the morning sunshine it felt cold. A woman in a white overall came through the door to meet her. 'Mrs Stella Turner?' she asked, her voice low and mournful.

Stella had to clear her throat before she could speak and say, 'Yes.'

She heard another car draw up outside and the car door bang. The same two people, the policeman and policewoman, came in. All four went into a large white room. There were table-like slabs – six or eight, perhaps – spaced at regular intervals. On one a sheet covered a small figure. The policewoman approached with Stella, but stayed a little behind. The woman in the white overall folded back the sheet.

The little boy's face was white with blue mottling; the lips, too, were blue and were slightly parted, so that the teeth were just visible. Across the left side of the forehead was a large graze. The small chest was also very blue, the hands slightly clenched each side of the body.

Stella stood looking down at the little child. It was not Bruce, it was not her son. She neither spoke nor moved for almost a minute. The policewoman touched her arm. The white-clad woman put the sheet back over the face and shoulders again.

Stella turned and faced the policewoman. 'Yes, that is my son Bruce,' she said and walked, rather unsteadily, out of the morgue, the policewoman's arm supportingly across her waist at the back.

She was helped into the car. She did not look at Agnes as she sank back into the seat. First she let out a long sigh as if she had been holding her breath, then she spoke.

'It was Bruce,' she said.

'I'm so sorry, Stella.' Agnes put her hand out to touch Stella's, but the girl drew her hand away with a quick defensive gesture that Agnes took to be a manifestation of extra-sensitivity and grief. She was wrong! Stella was not now suffering from grief, but guilt. She had lied. When she had approached the table she had no idea what she was going to say. At a glance she had realized it was not Bruce. The lie had come almost involuntarily, without thought. Did she regret it? Not yet. At the moment she felt completely numb.

9

On the way home Agnes watched her companion. When they paused at the lights she looked with curiosity at Stella's profile. It was white and strangely set and purposeful, as if she had started on a course and intended to go through with it – as though she had banished tears.

At Agnes's further attempt at condolence Stella still did not look at her, but continued to stare ahead. At last she spoke. 'Well, Agnes, it's a blessing in one way. No more police, no searches, no enquiries. We know now where he is and what has happened to him. Better than continued uncertainty, then perhaps finding him murdered in some field or back street.' Her voice was flat and toneless.

Agnes wanted to say, 'But how much better if we could have found him alive and well.' She did murmur something of the kind, but Stella shook her head. 'No, they always find them dead somewhere, or sexually assaulted.' She shivered a little. 'I'm glad to know! They said there will have to be an autopsy and an inquest.'

Agnes could not help but think it was a strange way of taking the death of her child, but she kept quiet. She'd had too much experience in her hospital days of being constantly surprised at the different ways people took bereavement, from disbelief to anger to grief.

When they arrived at Stella's house Agnes was about to drive in and let Stella go into her house by herself, but the girl turned to her with great urgency. 'Please, Agnes, come in with me – please. I don't want to go in alone.'

Agnes agreed. 'I'll park the car in my drive and walk round, then I won't have to back out,' she suggested.

Backing out of the drive of either house on to the busy main road was never easy and Agnes avoided the manoeuvre whenever she could do so, backing her car into the drive and into the garage. She had perfected this routine with practice and now drew the Porsche up in front of her own garage. They got out and walked in silence round to Bill Turner's house.

The door opened when they were half-way up the drive. In the doorway stood Bill Turner and slightly behind him Nanny, red-eyed, the knuckles of her right hand to her mouth. Beside Bill stood Rick, who seemed completely composed – indeed there was a tiny grin on his face. They all then backed into the house to let Agnes and Stella in.

Bill was about to say something, but Nanny uttered a small wailing sound which might have been just anything. Rick forestalled them both. 'It wasn't him, was it, Stell? I just knew it couldn't be him!'

Stella turned to him first – maybe because he was sounding so positive, so confident. 'It was Bruce, Rick.' Then she turned to Nanny and Bill. 'It was Brucey, Daddy.' She used the word Brucey because of Nanny – it was her name for him. Stella never used it herself when speaking to or referring to the child normally.

Before anyone had time to respond there was a crash – Rick had fainted. He lay, his long lean body crumpled, his face like death. It was such a shock that for a moment nobody did anything; then Agnes knelt by the boy and felt his pulse. It was rapid but regular.

'Shall I get an ambulance?' Nanny asked, but Rick was already coming round. He raised his head and looked at the anxious faces around him.

'What is it?' He was confused, until his eyes fell on Stella. 'Stell, it's not him – it's not the boy, it's not Bruce. I know it's not, I do, I do.'

Stella stood quite still, her hands clenched at her sides. 'It is

Bruce, Rick. I saw him on the table thing at the morgue, dead, quite dead. He was drowned, they said, found by the pier.' Her voice was quite without emotion, as was her face.

Bill Turner put his arm round her shoulders for a few seconds, then the familiar gesture, threading with her forefinger the hair from her face to behind her ear. She looked first at Agnes then at Rick, who was now seated on the hall chair. Then she looked at Nanny.

'We won't be needing you any more, Nanny. You can go now.' She spoke like an automaton, in the same flat toneless voice she had used to Agnes in the car.

Linda burst into tears. Bill Turner looked at Stella, his expression shocked. 'Steady, Stella, not just now,' he said mildly.

Stella turned to him quite tearless. 'Oh yes, Daddy, it's better to get things straight. No point in putting things off.'

Agnes moved nearer to Stella, but she did not attempt to touch her. 'She's in shock, Bill,' she said. 'It's been a dreadful morning for her.'

'What now, then?' Bill asked. He, too, seemed shocked. Agnes looked at Stella, who said nothing as Agnes supplied the information. 'They said there would have to be a . . .' She paused, but Stella did not react at all. '. . . an autopsy and, of course, an inquest.' Stella moved away and then went upstairs.

'Shall I call her doctor, do you think? He did come once when Bruce was ill. I can't quite remember his name.' He looked at Nanny uncertainly.

'Stephenson, Dr Stephenson.' Nanny had ceased crying; perhaps Stella's extremely callous behaviour had cut short even her grief, Agnes thought.

'Yes, that's his name. I'll call him. Tell him what has happened and ask him to call.'

'Perhaps he'll give Stella a sedative – she needs one,' Agnes suggested.

She longed to get away. There was something so odd, so missing. A child had died and Rick, neither a relative nor, Agnes felt, someone close to the child, had been the most affected and Nanny Linda the most sorrowful.

She was about to make her excuses to Bill and disappear back to her own domain when Rick sprang to his feet. He still looked ill and distracted.

'I've got to go out, there's something wrong, I've got to see Hebe.' Then when he realized that Agnes, Linda and Bill were all regarding him with puzzled eyes, he seemed to collect himself. 'I mean, I've got to go out.' He made for the door and disappeared into the road. Agnes watched him running in the direction of a small side road where he parked the battered old car.

She then left. Bill, she saw, was making for the telephone; Linda was just standing, the tears running down her face again.

Agnes was glad when she was back in her own house. Why had Rick fainted like that? Why had the little boy's death been such a shock to him? He seemed to be absolutely unable to accept it. Stella's manner too ... Well ...

Agnes realized she had had no breakfast. She switched on the kettle, but she certainly did not feel like eating – a cup of coffee and a biscuit would be all she could cope with. She went into her sitting-room and saw the police car drawing into the next-door drive.

10

Rick raced across the road towards his car. He had never fainted before in his life and the brief moment of unconsciousness had left him sweating and clammy. Even as he ran in the sunny air it felt cold to him, though judging by the thin dresses worn by the women around it was obviously warm in the sunshine.

He turned the ignition key and for a change the elderly engine fired and roared into life. He paused for a moment. Where was he going? To find Hebe, that was the answer.

He drove to Hebe's flat about a mile and a half across the town. It was over a garage, a rather grotty place – one or two cars had a price tag – but others stood about disembowelled, their aged engines exposed, the smell of oil and petrol always there. Upstairs was better.

Rick had been to Hebe's flat twice before. He liked it. At the top of the steps was a glass-panelled door, which needed a lick of paint. Inside, Rick knew, the decor was dead modern. Smashing posters on the wall, stiff, glossy ones – Tina Turner, almost lifesize. A chair hung from the ceiling; it fascinated Rick. If ever he got a flat he intended to have one just like it – but would he ever get a flat?

But Bruce, Bruce. As he hammered on the door the child's face haunted him. He could see the puzzled brown eyes, the rather fat, pudgy, babyish face. Oh God! Why did Hebe have to do that – why did he kill him? How could he drown a kid? If only he'd never handed Bruce over to him.

Nobody answered his banging. At last he gave up and decided he would try the pub. In The Feathers the few drinkers looked up at him as he walked in. The barman recognized him and said, 'Hi.'

'Has Hebe Grant been in?' Rick asked, ordering half a bitter.

'Not yet today,' the barman said, uninterested. Rick downed the drink quickly. He didn't feel thirsty and didn't want the beer, but he was too shy just to walk into the pub, ask for Hebe and then walk out again.

'See you,' he said, got up and left the pub. He felt he must try the Niagara Falls, though he had thought when he had met Hebe there that it was hardly the sort of pub Hebe usually frequented – he preferred much posher places, with plenty of life in them.

At the Niagara Falls he drew another blank. No Hebe. Rick felt ill. Where was he? Why, why, why had he killed Bruce? Even if he found Hebe and demanded an explanation it wouldn't bring the little boy back to life. The poor little sod couldn't hear anything; couldn't hear what was being said to him. He wondered if Hebe had said anything when he was drowning him or taking him to the pier? Oh God! Oh God! Rick hated to go back to the house, but where else could he go? He felt as if he might pass out again.

He parked the car back in the old place, but didn't get out at once. He just sat there trying to think what to do. Stella had been so calm when she had told them what she had seen in the mortuary. No tears, no hysterics, and that awful way of telling Linda she was – well, redundant. That had been awful. Even Bill had said something to her. Miss Carmichael had looked a bit shocked, and she'd used that word to try and make it better for Stella. She had said Stella was in shock. Rick supposed she was right – she was in shock. After all, she'd just come from seeing her little boy on that slab.

Rick's thoughts overcame him. He leant his head on the steering wheel and began to cry. Never, never, never would he be able to forget what he had done – he had handed over a child to a murderer. He'd got to tell somebody – he'd got to talk to someone, get this terrible burden off his chest, share it. He couldn't tell Stella, nor Linda, nor Bill; after all, it was Bill's grandchild. He couldn't tell them that he had handed over Bruce to a killer – for money!

He got out of the car, walked away – then realized he'd left the keys in the ignition and the car unlocked. He was always very meticulous about that, but at the moment he felt so shaken. He was fond of the car, though it was really Stella's. He went back, took the keys out and locked the car door. He aware that he could hardly think, his preoccupation was so deep. He wandered across the road almost in front of a car. It hooted at him wildly and swerved, making him jump backwards on to the kerb.

As he did so the thought flashed through his mind that he wouldn't mind being killed – he just couldn't face himself. He crossed the road safely this time and reached the hedge dividing Bill's and Miss Carmichael's houses. Maybe Stella would be sleeping if the doctor had been and given her something to calm her down, though she seemed calm enough already. Still, perhaps that was shock, as Miss Carmichael had said.

Miss Carmichael – his tortured mind fixed on her name. He would go and talk to her, tell her the whole thing, the whole dreadful mess. She would tell him what to do, what to do about Hebe. To tell someone, to confess, seemed at the moment the essential relief that he wanted. He felt he would never again be able to lead a normal life until he had made some reparation for that poor little kid.

He dodged round the hedge and made his way up the neat drive, so different from where he lived next door. Even the neatness of the small lawn and the weedless roses comforted and reassured him. He rang the door bell, aware of his racing heart, dry mouth, sweating palms and the awful feeling of regret, sorrow and fear.

Agnes Carmichael, even late in the morning, was still bewildered by Stella's attitude after her visit to the morgue. Seeing your child, that you had made, carried and given birth to, lying dead, would surely have made more impact on you that it had on Stella. Poor child, she thought. No one seemed to be mourning the little boy – only Nanny who, although fond of Bruce, must be considered to have had a vested interest in him. He was her job, after all, and without him she would probably be unemployed. Rick's obvious horror, too, had been strange!

Her thoughts were interrupted by the front door bell. Rick stood there. He looked terrible; his eyes red, his face white, blotched with red marks.

'Rick!'

'I want to talk to you, Miss Carmichael. Please.' His manner was so desperate, so urgent, she felt she could do nothing else but let him in.

'Come in.' Agnes, having witnessed the boy's fainting and then rushing away, felt a certain pity for him – and curiosity. He was such a thin, white, half-starved-looking creature. It crossed her mind, could he possibly be the child's father? He had behaved like it.

They went into the kitchen. In spite of the warmth of the morning the boy seemed frozen. He sat down at the kitchen table and put his head in his hands. He seemed unable to speak. Agnes quietly left the kitchen and came back with a tot of neat brandy. 'Sip that, Rick.'

He looked up at her. 'Thanks', he said and picked up the small glass and sipped the liquid.

Agnes sat at the table opposite to him. 'Now, Rick, tell me what is the matter? Why are you so terribly upset? I know the death of a little child is always dreadful, but you . . . well, it just seemed to shatter you.'

'I killed him. It's my fault he died, Miss Carmichael – it's all my fault.'

Agnes was appalled as she listened to his story. If the boy really thought Hebe would be as good as his word and sell Bruce to this couple who were longing for a child and who were too old to adopt . . . But she was puzzled. She'd heard and read that thirty, forty or even a hundred thousand pounds could be earned by a person willing to supply a child; why then would Hebe destroy him? What had happened between Rick delivering the child to Hebe, and a few hours later, when the police had found him drowned? Why had he sacrificed the child and by so doing lost the final payment?

This appeared to baffle Rick, too. He rubbed his eyes constantly, making the lids red and inflamed; the whites of his eyes, too, were streaked with red. Agnes could see the carotid artery in the side of his neck pulsing far more rapidly than normal.

'What am I to do to make it better? What have I done?' It was the plea of a child. 'I only wanted the money so that I could get away to America and sell my songs. I know they're good. It's just that here . . .' He tailed off miserably. He looked at Agnes as if she had the answer and could solve it all.

She said nothing for a moment and the boy resumed his former position of head in hands, his hair falling forward. She was completely mystified by the story – and yet there was a thin thread of suspicion running through her feelings. She was not sure what the suspicion was about, but the people involved in this terrible business seemed to be acting out of character. Still, she'd not really known any of them long enough to rely on her own suspicion.

Hebe she had never met. But why had he committed that act? And Stella – her odd reaction when she had left the morgue. And then the almost cruel remark to Linda. And Hebe, obviously doing the whole thing for money – why had he opted out apparently so suddenly, only a few hours after he had snatched the child? Agnes was interested; she had a challenge in front of her thrown down by this boy. She wanted to find out, to know why. This did not mean she would tell or report anything she found out to anyone – that was not her way. But to solve the problem and keep it to herself – that was thrilling to her, like a breath of life. What had gone wrong with the whole scheme . . .?

'Where does this Hebe live, Rick?' she asked, half expecting him to refuse to answer, but he was so surprised by the question that he raised his head and told her the address without apparently thinking.

'You'll not tell him I've told you, will you, Miss Carmichael? He'll kill me if you do. He's like that, he's ruthless.'

Agnes shook her head. 'No, I won't tell him,' she said. 'Has he done this baby-selling before? Tell me the truth, Rick.'

Rick winced at the way she put it, but it was obvious now he had started to confess, to get the burden off his chest, that he couldn't stop. 'I don't know, Miss Carmichael, not really – but he did once say . . . Yes, I think he has. He's into drugs mostly. He lived in London, but he had to leave and come down here.'

'Where does he get the drugs? Do you know, Rick?'

Rick looked at her; his eyes were shifty now, veiled. He shook his head. 'No, I don't know. He goes over to the mainland on the ferry – the car ferry – quite a bit when . . .' He stopped.

'Do you take drugs, Rick – and Stella, does she?' Agnes asked.

He looked suddenly defiant. He leaned the chair back and then brought it forward with a bump before he answered. 'Yeah, but only sometimes. When Stella can get out at night we go to Hebe's rave and sometimes have an E. Makes you feel good. Pot too.'

'Makes you feel good?' Agnes asked.

'Well, relieved like, not caring about anything . . . Well, you know . . . No job, all that stuff – no bread, no chances, that's Stell and me, you know.'

Agnes shook her head. 'No, I don't know and I don't want to know, Rick.'

Rick suddenly changed his attitude. 'Well no, you wouldn't, would you? I mean, you don't have to get a job, try and make a chance for yourself. You've got it all. It's fine for you, not like me and Stella.'

Agnes let this outburst go by. In a way she felt the truth of it. 'What can I do, Rick, to help you?' she asked. 'Why have you told me all this?'

'No reason, I suppose, but I just had to tell someone. Do you know what worries me, that makes me feel so awful?' Agnes shook her head. 'Well, suppose the kid woke up and Hebe found out he was deaf. He could have, Miss Carmichael, and thought, This isn't any good; they won't pay for him, and then . . .' He began to rub his eyes again, this time to try to conceal the fact that he was crying.

Agnes had to admit there was some truth in this supposition – but could anyone be as vile as that? Then she thought of other things – snuff movies, child abuse . . . Yes, they could! Well, if that was what had happened, the child-seller, drug-pusher, Hebe – he would have to be punished, and not with a light punishment that some judge might pass on him. Oh no, that would be inadequate, very inadequate. Any sentence they gave him would be inadequate!

She thought of Bruce, the deaf child she had played with all day, fed, bathed and put to bed. She was no lover of small children, but Bruce had appealed to her, perhaps because of his imperfection, his handicap.

She put her hand across the table and pulled Rick's away from his face. 'What is Hebe's address and full name again, Rick?' she asked. He told her, unwillingly now. She felt a thrill of excitement go through her. She scribbled the information on her shopping list.

'You wouldn't do anything . . . ?' Rick looked at her with his red-rimmed eyes full of apprehension, fear, yet tinged with hope.

'No, I only wanted to know out of interest, Rick,' she said.

Suddenly Agnes wondered if she felt as the young felt just after they had taken, what did they call it? The big E... High – her boredom had fled out of the window.

11

The day of the child's cremation was warm and sunny. As Agnes drove into the grounds the beds of flowers were brilliant in the sunlight. The grass was green and well mown and tended, the edges of the lawns cut so neatly that they gave a slightly artificial look to the scene. One could not, in spite of the flowers, dissociate the gardens from the low glass-doored building which housed, or would soon house, the small white coffin.

She found it strange that she was here looking at a scene which Bruce would never see. He would never see the flowers round the strip of grass; never experience growing older, taller and going to school. Again, perhaps he would miss a lot of pain, frustration, injustice and anger, too.

She parked her car and sat for a moment preoccupied with her thoughts of the child. An untimely end. But there it was – nothing was as inevitable as death. She sighed and got out of her car.

While she was listening to the reassuring 'click' as she pressed the remote control switch, Bill Turner drove up in his old Rover. Stella, Rick and Nanny got out after him. Bill slammed the car door, not bothering to lock it. He turned to Agnes. 'Your car rather shows up my old bus, doesn't it!' He looked at the two cars without smiling. He was right; the pristine Porsche shone, well cleaned and well polished – the glass of the windows caught the sun and reflected it. Beside it the old Rover looked dull and uncared for. The wheel hubs were covered with dried mud and one wiper lay lopsided on the windscreen.

The thought went through Agnes's mind that Rick, who owed two weeks' or maybe more rent, could have given up his so-called 'composing' for a bit to concentrate on giving the old car a good wash and wax.

Bill Turner looked older, she thought. The lines round his nose and eyes, the creases each side of his mouth, all appeared deeper, accentuated. The time – nearly two weeks – they had had to wait before they could have Bruce's body returned to them had no doubt had its effect on him. Rick, too, Agnes thought, looked different. Since his confession to her he looked much as he had then but more so, broken down with guilt. He would not now look directly at her, but walked rapidly away towards the crematorium, avoiding contact with her as if any form of address between them would highlight their complicity. Agnes could understand his attitude but was rather contemptuous of it. He was a feeble lad and would never be anything else.

She had not as yet decided what action to take. She was not sure if Rick had managed to get in touch with Hebe and confront him with what he had done. Should she ask him after the ceremony? She was not sure. Of one thing she felt pretty certain – if Hebe was confronted by Rick he would hardly deny that he had either killed Bruce or at least had some hand in his death. His hold on Rick was obvious. Rick had kidnapped Bruce, and handed him over, which made him an accessory and accomplice to some crime which, admittedly, had brought 'accidental' death. But surely, if the actions prior to this had been exposed at the inquest, the verdict would have been different?

What to do? Wait a little while, perhaps until Rick and Hebe had met and talked? Rick she had a certain sympathy for, in spite of her contempt. He had, according to him, let Hebe have the child in good faith – if such a term could be used. A better home, loving parents. He was obviously a gullible lad and he had believed Hebe. Well, Hebe had lied, killed the boy, but why? That she would have to find out in her own way. But she would find out and if necessary cope with Hebe, also in her own way – not by reporting him or even making his crime public. No, she would deal with it in what she considered the right way and mete out what the act deserved – what justice she thought was right.

They all stood hesitantly in the small carpeted foyer. A soberly dressed young man came out from the chapel, closing the double doors behind him, but not before they'd seen three or four people, presumably mourners from the previous funeral, disappearing slowly out of the door on the left of the short aisle. 'Just a moment sir.' He addressed Bill Turner. 'Only a moment and we will be ready for . . .' He looked uncertainly at Agnes and then Stella. Rick turned his back on them, as if he wanted to separate himself, dissociate himself from the scene.

After a few minutes the doors were opened and they filed in. Bill Turner, Stella and Agnes sat in the front pew. Rick and Linda went in behind them and sat in the second pew. Linda knelt for a moment, hands clasped in front of her, head bowed, then sat back. She sniffed rather loudly and Agnes caught a quick look of distaste on Stella's face, otherwise she was composed.

They all sat quietly looking at the small white coffin, brass handles gleaming in the rather subdued light. A man's voice startled Agnes – a priest or vicar had taken his place at the side of the stage-like structure on which stood the coffin. His entrance through the side door had caused the heavy purple curtains to stir very slightly. His tone seemed curiously muffled, perhaps by the closeness of the purple curtains, which had now resumed their stillness.

'Suffer little children . . .' His voice droned on. ' . . . taken from us so early in his young life.' He finished, took off his glasses, folded them into the large book and left, glancing at the five people in the pews. He had gone, but this time the curtains parted and the small box began to move away, making a rumbling noise as it disappeared.

Linda let out a half-stifled sob and the curtains fell together with a swishing sound. Agnes looked at Stella, who was still gazing at the now unmoving curtains. Her expression was totally unreadable to Agnes – pale, wide-eyed, her mouth set in a thin straight line as if she was making sure she would not let a sound escape. Nor did she. She turned, looked at Agnes, then towards Bill. She signalled that she was ready to leave. They left the pews; the black-suited man appeared again and let them out of the chapel and through the door. They then found themselves in a short covered way. On the ledge on the left running the length of the covered way lay a few wreaths – a very few.

Slowly Bill led them along. The first wreath, of yellow chrysanthemums, was slightly away from the others. The card in the middle was easily readable: it was from Mrs Timpson. Agnes was a little surprised, but gave her neighbour credit for such a gesture. The next was a circle of white daisies, 'To my beloved Brucey'. The letters were printed in ink and it was of course from Linda – she was the only one who called the little boy Brucey. There was one from Bill, a cross with a little card concealed. Stella's was of white daisies again, but larger than those from Linda. The card Agnes thought strange: 'To a dear little boy' – the note was obviously typed by the florists.

Agnes watched Stella pause and look for some time at her own, a bunch of flowers. Agnes hated wreaths and she had sent a bunch of pink carnations and pink tulips, her card reading

'Loving memory of Bruce'. It struck her now, as she looked at it, as rather trite, but at the time it had been all she had been able to think of. The last wreath was, to Agnes, in rather bad taste. It was slightly more colourful than the others – one or two red carnations mixed in with green leaves and yellow daisies. Agnes wondered if it was from Rick, but the small sealed envelope had scribbled on it, with a felt pen by the look of it, the words 'For Stella'. Funny way for Rick to have addressed it, Agnes thought, and wondered again if Rick felt he meant more to Stella than he pretended. He could say more inside the little envelope. The child could, of course, not be his – almost surely wasn't – but was he in love with Stella?

She hurried a little to catch up with Rick, Bill and Linda, leaving Stella still standing at her own wreath, gazing at it with a very strange expression on her face and yet almost smiling.

Indeed Stella let her mouth twist into what was almost a grim smile as she read once again what she had instructed be put on the little card: 'To a dear little boy'. How could she possibly know that the small, rather stunted-looking child lying on the mortuary slab had been 'a dear little boy'? She had not been able to put the name 'Bruce' on the card; she had shied away from that. The twelve, or was it fourteen, days since she had identified the wrong child had been a nightmare. Every telephone call, every knock on the door, every car stopping outside her house had terrified her. Each knock, each ring, each person, had, in her imagination, been bringing news to say that Bruce had been found. Her lie would be found out, made immediately apparent. If they had found him dead the same thing would apply. But then in another moment she thought differently. Whoever they found, they couldn't say it was Bruce because she had already identified her son, so why would they approach her at all? No. At times she felt safe; at other times unsafe!

It haunted her. Who was the child she had identified – who was he? Who was it that the pathologist had examined, the inquest heard about, deliberated over? What would her father, Rick or Agnes think if they knew?

She arrived at the last wreath. She had liked Agnes's flowers – so like her, elegant and expensive. The last wreath, though, was odd-looking, red, yellow and green with a tiny envelope with 'For Stella'. Perhaps it was the cleaner – though surely not, she had been with them such a short time. She untied the thin yellow ribbon that attached the envelope. It was not well sealed and she opened it easily with her thumbnail, and extracted a small, plain card. At first she could not take in what she was reading, then the words seemed to come into focus and her brain grasped the meaning of what was printed in black biro:

WHOSE BODY IS IT IN THE COFFIN, STELLA?

She felt herself swaying and put out her hand to steady herself. She looked along at the few people with her. They were at the far end of the covered way facing the cars. Thank goodness, they were not looking back at her. She fought for control. Who had sent the wreath and the note? Someone who knew the truth; knew that the coffin did not hold her son, but another child! She put the card carefully back in the little envelope, the ribbon still attached to it, and thrust it into her handbag, opening the middle part where she kept her bank card, then zipped it up again. She was surprised at her own control. So someone knew! Why had he or she been so secretive about it! Why not expose her to everybody? Why do it this way? Because they wanted the secret kept, too – or was it a blackmailer? That thought calmed her, strangely enough – but who would blackmail her? What would they hope to gain . . . money? She had none. Blackmail her? It was almost funny!

She waited a little longer, aware that although she felt herself to be calm her legs were shaking so much she was afraid to walk. After a moment or two she joined her father, Rick, Linda and Agnes.

'Who sent the last wreath?' Bill asked, taking her arm. Stella looked at him blankly; her mind felt totally empty. 'Rick,' she said. It was the only name she could grab from her mind.

Agnes saw Rick's look of surprise. He was about to speak, but Agnes saw the wide-eyed pleading look that Stella gave him. 'Well, yes, I did,' he said, almost reluctantly.

'That was nice of you, Rick,' Bill said – but it was no use, Agnes knew that Stella and Rick had both lied. Rick had been taken by surprise, but had supported Stella; after the initial reaction, he had supported her. By the look of him he didn't even know why! What did the little envelope contain? Agnes's curiosity was roused. There was more to the whole situation than Rick had confessed to her – much more. But what? She left the others and made her way towards her car. She raised her hand to them.

They all had secrets; they were all burdened with guilt and secrets!

Agnes felt a thrill of excitement and anticipation, tinged with rejection and irritation. What a mystery – Bill and his secret, not being Stella's father at all; Rick's kidnapping; and now Stella, that look passing between her and Rick. Why? Who had sent that wreath? Rather a different-looking wreath – its colours a little... garish? And the sealed envelope. Strange. Not Rick, but who?

Agnes drove slowly out of the gates, gained the road, but turned in the opposite direction away from home, away from Ryde, and followed a country road. She drove into a lay-by and stopped the car, wound down the windows and gazed over the fields for a long time. Five or six sheep passed the gate near the lay-by. They stopped and looked at the car, then resumed their cropping. The sound of the grass being pulled and eaten was audible to her in the sunny silence – their look, their brown incurious eyes, met hers. Not one of them, she thought, was devious, deceiving or plotting anything – just living as much of their lives as we allowed them. Suddenly Agnes felt a hatred for Rick, Stella, Bill – and for many other humans, too, who had destroyed part of her life with their actions: the nuns at the orphanage, the night superintendent who had made her life a misery, Derek with his lies and deceit.

The sheep moved away as she switched on her engine, turned the car and made for home, feeling a little less repelled by the strange intrigues and undercurrents to which she knew she was returning.

As she drove, a plan was forming in her mind. She would wait a few days, giving Rick time to challenge Hebe with the murder of Bruce. Was it Hebe, she wondered, who had sent the wreath, and not Rick? She was pretty sure it had not been Rick – that cryptic glance which had passed between him and Stella had convinced her. Rick had assented only because he had known that that was what was wanted of him. But why? Did Stella know Hebe? Yes, of course, she must do; the disco, the rave-ups. And yet...

By the time Agnes arrived home and had garaged her car, the thought of how devious and false the human animal can be was receding a little and giving way to a more exhilarating feeling – curiosity. The wish to reveal, to uncover any part of the mystery of the little boy's kidnapping and subsequent killing was important to her . . . and she would do it, too!

12

Hebe sat at a table at The Feathers waiting for Rick; his expression was amused as he gazed about him. People amused him, the things they got up to, the chances they missed. His rather thin-lipped mouth was very slightly curved at the corners. He looked smug, pleased with himself. He wondered how his little note with the wreath had affected that girl Stella. Frightened the shit out of her, no doubt. Still, that was what he had intended to do. What a bitch to identify another kid as your own son!

He had received a very shaky telephone call from Rick asking for a meet. What a wanker that boy was. He was late for the meet, too, and that didn't please Hebe at all. When he asked people to jump they jumped and he wasn't used to waiting around for anyone. He felt relaxed though; his new suit, he stroked the lapel. He'd kicked at the price at first, but it had been worth it. He paid for dressing, he knew that. The jacket fitted so smoothly, lightweight and light in colour, almost a dull dove grey. He fingered his new gold ear-ring, eighteen carat – this child-adopting business was a money-maker. Why did wrinklies want kids? After all, the kids would be teenagers when they were old, crippled with arthritis, doubled up with age. Stupid fools – still, useful to him.

Bruce's new mum and dad, fifty, fifty-five. When the kid was twenty they'd be seventy-five. Still, no matter. Thirty thousand nicker was not to be sneezed at. He'd have to give Rick another five thou. He felt generous, he'd give him five. After all he already had another client lined up. They wanted a girl, about a year old. He already knew the bint who would supply the product, a sixteen-year-old. She had planned to keep the kid (all maternal devotion) when it was born, but now she was sick to death of it. Not able to get out, her mum and dad equally sick of baby-sitting the thing. Good-looking girl, so maybe the baby would be pretty too – pretty, that's what they wanted, a pretty child.

Hebe began to feel more irritated than ever by Rick's lateness.

The bar was nearly empty. His feeling of smugness disappeared. He took two uppers, only mild uppers, threw them into his mouth and washed them down with lager. At that moment the door opened and Rick came in, looked round anxiously, saw Hebe and came over.

'You took your bloody time,' Hebe said. 'I'll have a whisky, double.' Rick did not speak, but went straight to the bar, got the two whiskies and brought them back to the table. He pushed one glass towards Hebe.

'How could you do such a thing? Hebe, how could you? I trusted you, you said . . .' His voice was hoarse, his face distorted with disbelief and distress.

'How could I do what, Rick?' Hebe sipped the whisky, watching Rick with narrowed eyes.

'Kill Bruce. You said he would be all right. You promised, a loving family. I wouldn't have done it if I'd thought anything would happen to him.'

'Kill Bruce my arse! Get your head together, Rick. He's with his new doting parents. Oh, they took the deaf business very well, no thanks to you. You didn't tell me; it could have made all the difference.'

'Don't lie to me, Hebe, he's dead, he was drowned. Stella –'

Hebe raised his hand. 'Shut up, Rick.' Rick's voice had risen to an indiscreet loudness. People were looking at them. 'Shut up and listen. Whoever was cremated, it wasn't Bruce.'

Rick bent forward, his arms on the table. 'It was. Stella went to the morgue and identified him. She was gutted; we all were.'

Hebe leant back in his chair and took his time lighting a cigarette. 'Stella identified him, eh? I saw the report in the local rag. I could hardly believe it. Who was it, I thought? Certainly not Bruce.' He slipped the lighter back into his pocket and tapped the cigarette needlessly on the empty ashtray.

'I don't believe you. You killed him. You found out he was deaf and you drowned him.' Rick's husky voice was lowered.

Hebe leaned forward on the table, his face very close to Rick's. Rick could smell whisky on his breath and a faint smell of garlic. 'Listen, Dickie, your little friend Stella is lying in her teeth. That was not her son. Who the hell it was I don't know, but she's lying. I left a note for her on the wreath at the bloody funeral. Did she tell you? No, I bet she didn't.' He leant back and drew on his cigarette again. 'You said she didn't want the kid. Well, she's rid of it. She must be dead scared in case Brucey turns up dead or alive. But he hasn't, has he, because he can't, can he?' He took an envelope from his pocket. 'There's your money. Now get away somewhere and keep your mouth shut.'

Rick's mouth was open. 'But you took Bruce and if you didn't kill him you sold him. You're as much in this as I am,' he said.

Hebe looked at him almost with a touch of compassion. 'Don't be wetter than you need be, son!' he said. 'Bruce is dead and buried and was identified by his own mother. You and I are clear of everything. After all, who did we kidnap?' He put his head back and laughed. 'Relax, lad,' he said through his laughter. 'Let her do the worrying if she wants to, poor cow.'

'But if you didn't drown him, who was the . . .?'

Hebe slowed up, put his finger to the side of his nose and tapped it. 'Now you're asking, Rick – now you're asking!' He patted Rick's shoulder as he went past him – to Rick a patronizing gesture. The pub door slammed behind him and he was gone.

Rick left the pub soon after and drove down to the sea front. He felt as if his mind was whirling round like a wheel – Stella, Hebe, Stella, Hebe. He left the car and walked along the beach. There were very few people about, but the edge of the waves looked dirty to Rick, flotsam. A plastic cup bobbed about just out of the reach of the edge of the wavelet, half an orange, heavier and more stubborn, let the water run round it, looking like a giant orange pimple. A condom floated in almost to his feet.

Stella, Hebe, Stella, Hebe, who to believe? Stella, of course. Hebe was lying, of course he was lying. Stella had seen Bruce, her own child, at the mortuary. Of course she hadn't told him about Hebe's note. She knew Hebe – not as well as he did, but she knew Hebe's reputation; knew he was a bum, a pusher. She'd be frightened.

He wouldn't say a word about this meeting to Stella. Why upset her? What good would it do? He had the money now and he would go away. He began to feel better. Even the water at his feet looked cleaner. A breeze fanned his face and blew back his hair. America! If I can make it there I'll make it anywhere. Rick pulled back his shoulders. He'd finish with Hebe and Stella and Bruce and all of them. He would get shot of the lot and go his own way.

Once home he glanced into the sitting-room. Stella was standing by the french window looking out into the garden – she was perfectly still. There was a rigidity about her stance, as if she was frozen.

'You all right, Stell?' Rick felt compelled to ask her, to speak to her, to make her move. She looked like a statue. She jumped, turned round and looked at him. 'Yes, I'm all right, Rick. I was just wondering . . .'

'Wondering what, Stell?' Rick asked.

She shook her head and turned back to the garden. 'Nothing, Rick. I'm all right. Thank you for asking.'

Rick gave up; he felt the conversation was slightly insane. He left the room. Of course Hebe was lying, he was always lying. Stella would never do anything like Hebe had suggested – never, never. He began to think again as he had whilst walking along the beach. He didn't care any more, he was letting these people eat his talents away. They wouldn't let him think, let him just get on with his music. Bill, Stella, Nanny, Bruce, even Miss Carmichael. He had the loot now so stop thinking about what he had done to get it. Just prepare to leave, to fly away, fly away, leave, take off.

He ran up the stairs. He'd sort out his clothes, go to the travel agents. He was afraid of going, yet more afraid of staying. He slammed the door of his room, stood there for a few moments and then threw open his wardrobe door.

In the *Island Gazette* a certain short piece was, in some cases, read with only a slight amount of interest, in other cases almost ignored.

A small boy, aged four and a half, had disappeared from a local children's home. In spite of an intensive police search the boy had not been found. The police stated that after this interval of time there was little chance of finding the boy alive.

His mother, aged forty-four and mother of three other children, all of whom were in care, had assured them that he had not been with her, although she had taken him away from the home on several previous occasions. The police were continuing their search for the little boy, without much hope.

Several remarks were sparked off by this piece – 'I suppose all of these kids are being paid for out of our taxes,' or 'Why don't these women take some kind of precaution, the pill or something, if they want sex all the time?' Or, as a nurse remarked more succinctly, 'I'd sterilize the damn woman and all like her – save us a lot of trouble and a lot of money.' None of the children were apparently by the same father.

13

Agnes neither saw nor heard anything of her next-door neighbours for three days. On the fourth day she decided to telephone Stella and ask her if she would like a run to Godshill for tea.

'No, I really don't feel up to it, thank you, Agnes.' Stella's reply had been abrupt. It was so unlike her that Agnes wondered if something else had happened to upset the girl, or had the impact of all the recent events only just had its effect? Stella had been so controlled, so calm, Agnes felt that maybe she had now at last really broken down and was feeling the loss of the child. Agnes resolved to leave it for another day or two and then try again. She liked Stella and could excuse the blunt refusal, believing she knew how the girl felt.

The next day Agnes had a phone call and she half expected it to be from Stella, regretting her attitude of the previous day. But it was not, it was Madge Hillier, an old friend from her Penny Stratton days. She liked Madge, she was a cheery soul, and her invitation did a lot to cheer Agnes's spirits. The past few weeks seemed to have been full of death and deceit.

'Hello, Agnes, I'm off to London next week. I'm having my ears looked at, I'm getting deaf. Bernard's going on a golfing week to Scotland.'

Her suggestion was that she and Agnes should spend a few days or so in London at Durrants Hotel. 'We can do a show or a couple of shows, get up late and shop, shop, shop. What do you say?' Her rich laugh bubbled down the telephone.

Agnes was about to demur, to hesitate – it always took her some time to make up her mind to go away – but Madge gave her no chance. 'I've told Bernard I'm going to wear out a credit card and that I'm contacting you. I'm due for a fling. Marcia is looking after the dogs. By the way, she's divorced again – that's three!' This last statement was also followed by Madge's inimitable laugh. 'She's making a hobby of it, that's what I tell her.' Marcia was Madge's beautiful, elegant daughter.

'Right, right, Madge, I'd love to. What day do you go?' A delighted Madge gave her the time she would arrive – the day after tomorrow, Tuesday.

As Agnes put down the phone she felt, she told herself, several years younger. She went upstairs to choose the suit she would travel in and the clothes she would take with her. Dear Madge, and Bernard. When she had lived in Leicestershire the house had always been a joy to visit. It was a big house, always untidy, but warm when the weather was cold. The garden was untidy, too. The two black and white clumber spaniels climbed up on to the sofa when they felt like it, or lay upside down, paws in the air, on the rug in front of the fire. Agnes had often thought how she would love to own such a house, but she knew she wouldn't, couldn't, fit into it or let it be so; she would have to tidy it, mend the tear in the cretonne cover of the settee. She even remembered that tear, and the dog lead and the dog biscuits and the woollen glove in the beautiful rose bowl.

People's houses grew round them, or some did. She looked round her neat bedroom, everything in its place. The hand mirror on her dressing-table – if her cleaner put its handle to the left she would change it to its original position to the right. She had to, she couldn't bear things to be out of place. Agnes sighed; she was as she was and Madge Hillier was as she was and that could not be changed.

Did everyone want to be someone else? she wondered, as she put her suitcase on the bed ready for packing. Her thoughts turned almost obsessively to her neighbours. Stella, certainly, would like to be someone different . . . a clothes designer or a model. Bill, he would rather be a famous novelist, a bestseller or a playwright. Rick a pop star, writing his own music, while Nanny just wanted to be employed, an employed person rather than an unemployed. She thought then of Mrs Timpson, the next-door neighbour the other side; she seemed happy enough being herself – perhaps she was one of the few. That was why Agnes looked forward to being with Madge in London for a few days. Madge was so happy to be herself, with Bernard her husband and her beautiful daughter, whose divorces she seemed to ride over with ease, her dogs, her country house; everything about her was just Madge, warm, comfortable and right.

The day before her departure Agnes packed carefully. A dress suitable for the theatre or dinner, a suit slightly warmer than the one in which she was travelling in case the weather changed a little, perfume, toiletries, nightdress, a gown, underclothes, slippers. At last she closed the lid and went to the telephone to ring her hairdresser for an appointment and her cleaner to let her know she was going away.

*

In the taxi from Waterloo to Sloane Street Agnes suddenly wished she had not come – one of her familiar mood changes, but she was used to them. London looked the same, the pavements sunny and dirty, the crowds in Knightsbridge, the slow-moving, impotent-looking traffic honking – trying to go faster, but failing. The shop windows with their stiff sculptured models looking out at the crowd with mascaraed eyes, wearing clothes no one more than six stone could possibly get into. Then Harrods – Harrods cheered her up. In the bright afternoon all the windows were lit up. Madge had suggested, 'We'll breakfast at Harrods – I'd love to do that – and I want a new handbag, I'll get it there.'

The down mood surely enough began to disappear. The taxi drew up at Durrants Hotel, a place familiar to Agnes. She got out, paid the driver and walked in.

'Here you are, looking as trim and as slim as ever.' It was Madge, and from that moment Agnes was glad she had come. 'Got rooms next door to each other, first floor.' Madge looked as excited as a girl.

Agnes followed her plump figure across the hall of the hotel to register, then up to Madge's room, where she produced a bottle of brandy from her suitcase and a couple of small bottles of ginger ale from the room refrigerator. 'You like this tipple I know, Agnes – right?' She looked at her watch. 'Ten to six, just a swift one. Cheaper than going down to the bar, eh?' They both raised their glasses and started exchanging news from their now different parts of the world.

'You must come and visit me on the Island, Madge. It's so different from Leicestershire and even more different from Penny Stratton.'

Madge nodded in agreement. 'We'd like to. I believe Bernard sailed there before we were married, but I haven't been there for many years.' She laughed and poured them both a second brandy. 'I think I was five. We stayed in Shanklin, but I can hardly remember it.'

Agnes finished her drink and got to her feet. 'Do we change for dinner? Where do we have it?' she asked.

'I thought we'd eat here tonight and be more adventurous tomorrow. I'm going to change out of this.' She motioned to her grey London suit. Even that looked countrified on Madge. 'I'm going to see if I can squeeze into this little number.' She got a black dress out of the wardrobe, which she had already put on a hanger.

'Nice,' said Agnes.

'Nice maybe, but size sixteen I believe and I've a nasty feeling I'm coming up to eighteen. Anyway, if I hold my breath and put on my foundation garment I'll probably get through dinner.' She laughed again. Madge seemed to be always laughing. 'Then we're booked for a concert at the Barbican – culture plus, my dear and it's on me.'

'Oh, I couldn't.' Agnes was well aware of the price of tickets for anything in London.

'Don't worry. I've booked for *Show Me The Way* for the next night and that's on you – OK?'

Agnes felt she was being swept along by Madge as usual on her tide of enthusiasm, but she liked the feeling. Everything at Ryde was being pushed out of her mind, at least for the moment, and she was glad of it.

Two shows, three new frocks, four pairs of shoes, one new handbag later, they had the promised breakfast at Harrods. Madge seemed to enjoy it immensely, as did Agnes.

Madge's appointment with the ear, nose and throat surgeon, Sir Henry Rouse, was at three o'clock on the last day of their stay. The taxi drew up at the consulting room in Wimpole Street. Agnes looked at Madge, eyebrows raised. 'Posh,' she said, smiling.

Madge paid the taxi driver and as he drove away she clasped Agnes's arm. 'Whatever he says, I won't have a deaf aid. Bernard must just shout at me, make me hear.' Then she realized what Agnes had said. 'Oh, posh, yes. Bernard met Henry Rouse at Leicester, he was there at some meeting or other. Bernard found out what he did for a living and when he told me I thought it was a good reason for a London trip. Come on.'

They went up the four steps and rang the bell. A sombre-faced, middle-aged woman opened the door. She did not speak, but merely raised her eyebrows.

'Mrs Hillier. I have an appointment with Sir Henry Rouse.' Madge smiled her wide smile, but for once it had no effect and no smile was returned.

'This way, Mrs Hillier. In here, please.'

They were ushered into a high-ceilinged, richly carpeted room. The sombre lady shut the door without a sound behind them. They crossed the room, also soundlessly, on the thick carpet and sat down on a wooden-framed settee which looked to Agnes suspiciously like an antique. Taking up practically the whole of the centre of the room was a huge, beautifully polished table on which were neatly arranged magazines – hello! and, strangely, as well as some children's books.

Agnes looked round the room. There were three other occupants, all silent. One was a nun – she sat quietly, her eyes fixed on the net-curtained window, and seemed to be watching the traffic passing to and fro. There was also a depressed-looking man wearing a small deaf aid; he had his back to the window and did not look at them, but continued to thumb through a *Country Life*. An untidily dressed young man, legs stretched out and his creased jeans and grey jumper looking out of place in the chandelier-crowned room, opened his eyes, looked at them, then closed them again.

'Jolly,' Madge whispered. Her remark was audible, but none of the three reacted to it in any way. 'They're all deaf, poor souls,' Madge said, concealing her mouth with her gloved hand but not able to suppress a slight giggle, which caused the nun to glance at her then turn her attention back to the moving traffic outside the window. Madge gave a big sigh and looked at Agnes. 'Let's go – not bother,' she said.

Agnes smiled and patted her arm. 'Nonsense, Madge. Now you've made the appointment and are here you must see him.'

Only minutes passed before a young woman in a white coat opened the door. 'Mrs Hillier?' Madge got up, dropped her handbag, grimaced at Agnes, then followed the young woman out of the room.

Agnes guessed she might have some time to wait. Madge might have an audiogram to measure the extent of her deafness, as well as an examination by the great man. She got up, picked up the latest *Harpers* and returned to her seat. The large black clock on the mantelpiece ticked softly.

Suddenly the otherwise silent room was invaded. The solemn woman opened the door. 'Will you wait in here, Lady Preston.' A tall, good-looking woman of about fifty came in, holding the hand of a pretty little girl who Agnes guessed was about four. Her hair was fair and fell to her shoulders. A blue hairslide on the top of her head held the shiny curls back from her face.

Agnes was about to resume reading her magazine when she suddenly realized that someone else was entering the room behind the woman who, presumably, was Lady Preston. She was carrying a little boy. 'Sit over there, Nanny,' Lady Preston said, 'then the children can see the cars going by outside.'

Agnes looked up again. Then her eyes became riveted on the

second child that the Nanny was just lowering to the floor to follow the little girl. It was Bruce! She could hardly believe her own eyes. The group sat down, the mother picking Bruce up. The little boy sat for a moment, then struggled free and toddled over to the magazine table. He was just tall enough to reach one. Just as he was about to do so, his eyes met Agnes's. He looked at her steadily, his eyes not leaving her face, and then he smiled widely, stuck his forefinger in his mouth – a familiar gesture to Agnes – and came over to her. He stood in front of her, still smiling.

'I'm so sorry. Nanny, don't let Mark worry that lady.' Lady Preston sounded apologetic. The grey-haired nanny got up and came over to Bruce and gently took his hand. He went with her willingly back to Lady Preston, but he looked back at Agnes as he walked away from her, his finger still in his mouth.

'I am so sorry. Mark is deaf, I'm afraid. That's why we're here.' Agnes inclined her head. She found herself quite unable to speak. Bruce! But what was he doing here? He was dead, drowned, identified, but there he was in Sir Henry Rouse's waiting-room. No doubt he was a patient of the surgeon. He looked healthy and well dressed, as did the little girl. Lady Preston bent down, put her arm round the little boy and kissed his cheek. He turned, looked at her, then kissed her cheek. Agnes had never seen Stella kiss her son, not once.

She was aware that she felt almost disorientated by the appearance of the little boy who Stella had . . . But why? She stood up, went to the table and changed the magazine. In doing so she passed quite close to the children. The little girl was leaning against the nanny, who was turning the pages of a small picture book she had obviously brought with her. In spite of her rather severe dress she looked kind and leant down to the little girl, explaining the pictures. Bruce, now apparently Mark, was still encircled by his new mother's arm; she looked up as Agnes went by. Bruce's eyes again met Agnes's, then he turned his head away and snuggled into Lady Preston's lap in an attack of shyness. She picked him up and he sat on her lap, still keeping his face averted and pressing it against her breast. The woman smiled, then looked down at the child with an expression full of love.

How long had he been with her? Three weeks, or a month was it, since Rick . . .? At that moment the door opened and the girl in white and Madge came in.

'Lady Preston, will you bring Mark through?' Nanny restrained the little girl, who was about to follow.

Madge spoke. 'Can you bear it, Agnes? I haven't finished. I've had one test, then seen Him, but I've got to have a hearing test now.'

'Of course, I'm quite happy,' Agnes said.

'We'll go and have a super cream tea at Duffy's, it's just up the road,' said Madge and disappeared again, the door closing behind her.

The nun was summoned next, then almost at once the man with the small deaf aid. A few more minutes, and then the boy. Agnes was alone with the little girl and her nanny.

'What a dear little boy,' she remarked, wondering how the nanny would react to her speaking to her; she looked slightly forbidding.

'Yes, isn't he? It's a shame he's deaf, but perhaps Sir Henry will be able to do something for him; we certainly hope so.'

'Has he been deaf from birth?' Agnes asked casually, flicking the pages of her magazine. Did the nanny's expression become guarded? As she looked up Agnes couldn't be sure; the woman's eyes were still on the picture book.

'Oh yes, he's always been deaf. No, dear, that's an elephant and that's a donkey.' She did not look at Agnes. Was she hiding anything? How long had she been with Lady Preston? Agnes longed to ask, but of course she couldn't. She gave up asking any more questions; she felt it would be resented. Lady Preston looked over fifty. Old to be mother of the little girl, surely – yet the child had called her Mummy as they had come in the door. Had Lady Preston bought both children? She would venture another question. 'Have you had to come far?' she asked.

'From Scotland,' the nanny said. There was now definite hostility in the woman's voice.

'Oh, really?' Agnes feigned complete indifference and returned to her reading, determined not to speak another word to the woman. At least she knew more or less where they came from. Lady Preston of Scotland was something!

After a short wait Madge reappeared and beckoned to Agnes. 'Nearly done. So good of you to wait,' she said. 'No deaf aid. Let's go and have those cream cakes.' She was obviously pleased at the result of her examination and they walked down the steps and out into the busy street.

'What attractive children,' Madge said.

'Yes, they were,' Agnes replied.

'I should think that was their grandmother, wouldn't you?' Madge held Agnes back as a car whizzed by, and they crossed the road. Agnes did not reply to the last question.

'National Theatre tonight and home tomorrow. I have enjoyed it, Agnes, and I'm so glad you came.'

Agnes could not concentrate for some moments. It was only after they had arrived at the small exclusive teashop and the tea and cream cakes were ordered that she could drag her mind back from seeing Bruce and ask about Madge's visit to the surgeon.

Madge chatted on. 'Well, he said – is it Bellibel loss?'

Agnes corrected her. 'Decibel loss, Madge.'

Her companion went on, 'It's not yet bad enough for me to have an aid. He said it might come to that, but he took some wax out...' The cream cakes arrived; Madge took an éclair and bit into it with obvious enjoyment while Agnes poured the tea. Try as she would she still felt preoccupied. Not only were her thoughts with the child, but with Stella, too. Why had she said the child in the morgue was hers? Did she know that Bruce was adopted? Was Rick unaware that...? No, Rick's horror had been genuine enough!

'You're far away – penny for your thoughts, Agnes.'

'They're worth a lot more than that, Madge.'

Her companion looked at her intently. 'I believe it's that next-door neighbour of yours – Bill, isn't it?'

Madge's remark triggered a sudden response in her. She was drawn towards Bill because of his troubles – but was it just that? She felt the colour rise to her cheeks, much to Madge's delight.

'You've gone quite pink,' she said.

'It's the tea, and it's hot in here,' Agnes replied, but she couldn't keep her lips from smiling.

'See!' Madge said loudly. 'You're falling for him – good-oh. It's time you got married.'

'Madge!' Agnes laughed. But behind her protestations was a slight, slight thrill. Just supposing... Agnes sipped her tea. Bill was attractive to her, but was he attracted to her? If only – she might even – when she got back... She cut off her thoughts abruptly and looked at Madge. 'You're just an old matchmaker, Madge,' she said.

She helped herself to a cream cake and bit into it. 'Delicious,' she said, and as she sipped her tea she came to the conclusion that nothing could be done to solve the puzzle whilst she was here. But one bit of knowledge she did store in her memory – Lady Preston who lived in Scotland was where Bruce had eventually been delivered by Hebe. Abetted by Stella? And most of all, the drowned boy – who was he? Had his death been, as they had found at the inquest, just accidental?

Agnes and Madge shared a taxi the next morning, Agnes going to Waterloo and Madge to Euston. 'Let's meet again soon, Agnes,' Madge said as they stopped at Waterloo station to drop off Agnes.

'Yes, let's. You and Bernard must come and stay with me. I'd love to to have you and to show you the Island – it's really lovely.'

They embraced. Madge Hillier was one of the few people Agnes did not mind embracing her. She thanked her too, but silently, for not referring at all in any way to the disastrous happenings at Penny Stratton before Agnes had left. Many people would have found it impossible not to speak of them. Madge was the exception and Agnes was grateful.

She waved to the departing taxi and made her way to the platform which showed the indicator reading 'Isle of Wight'. She was glad she was returning; the Island was a lovely place to live, marred only by the mystery that she felt she must solve – and perhaps, too, by loneliness.

On the train she let her mind wander back to Bruce as he had been – a little boy lost, wandering up her drive, his torn dungarees, the bleeding knee – there was only one person he meant anything to in the Turner household and that person was a paid girl without even child-care qualifications. Certainly the little boy, now called Mark, looked a happier child. And in such a short time his new family had apparently gained his love and confidence.

Agnes was, in a way, reluctant to face Stella. She resolved to say nothing to her about knowing that her identification of Bruce had been a lie.

The day after arriving home, returning on her way back from shopping at one of the local grocers, she met Linda. 'Stella is away in London, Miss Carmichael, and I am looking after the house. Mr Turner has gone fishing on the mainland with his doctor friend and Rick has gone to spend a few days with his people before he goes to America. He's the lucky one.' All this news – so much had happened in the days that Agnes had been away!

'When did she go to London?' Agnes was surprised, although she had not seen Stella for some time and her last communication had been the rather abrupt refusal to come out to tea with her. She felt that Stella might have been so excited about a trip to London that she had not thought to let Agnes know she was going. It was a strange coincidence, too, that Stella should be there at the same time as herself.

'I'm still useful now that she's gone away. It's not Nanny now that poor little Bruce is dead. It's a job, though, so I'm hanging on at the moment.'

Agnes risked one query. 'I didn't know Stella was going to London. Still, I suppose the change will do her good after all that has happened.'

Linda sniffed and resentment coloured her next remark. 'I could do with a change as well, Miss Carmichael, but I can't afford it.'

Agnes was quick with her sympathy. 'Yes, I do know how much it must have upset you and how much you loved little Bruce. His loss must have been a great grief to you.' She said this, feeling the truth of it. This girl had shown Bruce practically the only affection he had received from that household.

Linda was obviously touched by the remark. 'Have you been away, Miss Carmichael?' she asked with a little more warmth and interest. 'Did you have a nice time?'

'Yes, I did, Linda. I met an old friend and we did some shopping together.' She was careful not to make the visit sound too pleasurable in case Linda became even more resentful than she appeared; also, she didn't want her to repeat or even think 'It's all right for some.' She continued, 'What made Stella decide to go to London so suddenly?'

'I don't know. She had a telephone call some time ago – well, several. She's got a boyfriend, I think. Anyway, he telephoned, if it was him, soon after Bruce was buried. I heard her talking, all excited, but she didn't tell me and I don't think she told anyone else who it was. She just said on the telephone . . .' She looked down at her shoes and then up at Agnes. 'I wasn't really listening, Miss Carmichael, I just happened to hear.'

Agnes interrupted her with a fairly gently worded reproof. 'I don't think you should repeat what you heard, Linda, even if it was heard by accident.'

Linda bridled a little. 'All right then, Miss Carmichael. I must go.' She flounced off up the road, obviously put out by the last remark and probably longing to tell Agnes what the conversation between Stella and the boyfriend, if it was one, had been about!

Agnes carried her shopping indoors and proceeded to put it away. So – Stella had gone to London after a telephone call and had not yet returned! A boyfriend? Maybe it was a product of Linda's imagination, but Agnes could not be sure. Did Stella know who had adopted Bruce? Was she in on the whole deal?

Agnes paused and as she looked into the garden a picture of Stella seemed to appear before her – of Stella's candid eyes. No, she couldn't be, she was sure of that – or at least she was almost sure.

She wondered if Stella would confide in her when she returned – but then, why should she? The young can be very secretive, and Stella certainly was a girl who could hide her feelings.

Agnes's thoughts turned to Bill. She was pleased he had managed a little holiday with his doctor friend – his life didn't seem to be very happy. She felt a longing that surprised her; to put her arms round him – see him relax, smile. The feeling was strong. Was it maternal or sensual? No, the feeling was not maternal, she wanted him – but would he ever want her?

14

During the time Agnes was in London Dr Bryn Jones and Bill Turner had met several times and walked along the beach together. Nevertheless Bill had been quite surprised when he answered the door bell and found him standing on the doorstep. The doctor said, 'Hope you don't mind my calling, Bill, but I've a proposition to put to you.'

'No, glad to see you. Come in.'

Linda had heard the door bell and was in the hall. 'Will you rustle up some coffee for us, please, Linda?' Bill led the way into the main room, passing his own study, the door of which was open.

'Is that where all the work is done and the ideas come flooding in?' Bryn asked.

'Well, where the work is done, yes – but ideas don't always really flow.'

They sat down.

'Mind if I smoke?' Bryn asked.

'Not at all. There's an ashtray beside you.'

'Do as I say; don't do as I do,' Bryn said, laughing as he lit up. He sat back comfortably in the armchair. 'Pleasant room,' he said.

Linda brought in a tray of coffee and biscuits and put it down on the small table between the two men. 'All right?' she said. Bill thanked her and she disappeared.

'I wondered if you'd be interested. I'm going fishing, a fishing weekend actually, just coarse fishing. Cheap weekend, too, really. The bloke who was going with me has dislocated his shoulder and I wondered if you'd like to take his place. I don't want to go on my tod.'

Bill was delighted with the prospect – a few days away from the house...

'Yes, that's really civil of you, Bryn. I could do with a break. The problem is, though, I've no fishing gear – used to have, but got rid of it.'

Bryn answered him. 'Don't bother about that. I've got an extra rod you can borrow and a spare net. We can hire waders if we need them.'

The matter was soon settled. Bryn drank his coffee and the time and place were arranged. It was decided that they would go in Bryn's car. Bill said goodbye and watched his friend departing. As he did so Rick came down the stairs.

'Reckon I'll be off the day after tomorrow. That OK, Bill?' he asked. Bill wondered how Rick had managed the fare and to pay his debts – but it wasn't his business. 'Fine, yes. I won't be here, though, so will you leave the key with Linda? Let us hear how you get on.'

'Yep, right. You away then?' Rick asked.

'Yes, going fishing with my friend Bryn.' Bill felt a feeling of exhilaration as he said it.

'Good-oh,' Rick answered, not sounding particularly interested. 'Have fun. Bring back a whale or two.'

Bill went into his study feeling a bit more like work. He'd try and finish another chapter of the current book before he left. *Death on the Pier*, rather a macabre title, he thought, after what had happened, but it had been decided on between him and the publishers and he felt it had better stay. Poor little Bruce – sad... sad. He could suddenly see the child, brown eyes looking up at him. Ah well...

Stella was in London. She had departed rather suddenly; been gone three days now. Rick would soon be gone as well. Agnes Carmichael, too, was away.

Linda came in for the coffee tray. 'Linda, I'll be away for a bit, a few days, and I'm not sure when Stella will be back. Rick goes the day after tomorrow, he says. Do you mind holding the fort while we are away?'

'No, Mr Turner, I don't mind. I haven't got another job, anyway.'

'Good. No, I didn't mean that exactly. It's good for us, I mean, to have you to stay on here, but I'm sorry you haven't got a job.'

Linda smiled at him. It was obvious that he was her favourite person in the rather uncaring house. Bill hoped that Rick would give her a good tip before he left. Thank goodness he had paid the back rent that he owed. Bill wondered, again briefly but not too deeply, how he had suddenly managed to get in the money – young ones seemed to do this kind of thing. It was quite a bit, apparently, enough to get him to America anyway. Well, maybe he would make his fortune there, even get a hit with his 'Heat Up The Past'. He sighed; probably Rick would be coming back to England with the customary white Rolls Royce while he was still hacking out the next crime novel for £2,000 and hoping that plenty of people would borrow his books from the library to increase his income from the Public Lending Right.

Death on the Pier ... He typed away, but only for half an hour or so, then the thought of Bryn Jones and the fishing trip interrupted his thoughts. Nice fellow, great few days it should be, too. He'd come back revived, refreshed. He forced himself back to the book and soon the typewriter was clicking away in the now empty house. Linda had put her head round the door to say she had left him a cold lunch and had gone out to do some shopping at Tesco's, and Rick had mooched off somewhere.

When Bryn called for him the following day Stella had still not come home. She had telephoned saying that she was staying in London if he didn't mind and was all right, enjoying herself. Bill had thought she sounded a bit nervous, a bit tense, and as it had been about eleven o'clock at night he hoped she was behaving herself, not drinking or getting into the drug scene. He didn't know the school friend she had told him she was staying with – couldn't recall her at all.

Agnes Carmichael had not returned home either. All the windows were shut and there was a notice, a circular, sticking out of her letterbox, a sure invitation to would-be burglars letting them know that the house was empty. Bill had gone round and pushed the circular through; it had fallen with a dull thud on the carpet inside the house.

Bill rather missed Agnes, her trim figure, her level and unflirtatious gaze. He suddenly remembered her perfume, lovely, light and understated. He missed her. Strange that he should remember her perfume so vividly. Was he falling for her? He grunted with contempt at his own thoughts. What had he to offer a woman like Agnes Carmichael? A hack writer like him, who wasn't doing so well anyway. He dismissed the thought from his mind, but he couldn't quite dismiss the perfume.

Often nowadays, though, his mind went back – perhaps it was age – to his wife, the car crash, the birth of her daughter (not his) whom she had never seen. He wondered, had she lived, would she have remembered, with love perhaps, the young boy whose passion had produced the fair-haired, rather discontented young mother he had named Stella? In his memory he could still conjure up that thin, immature student she had pointed out to him, the streak of white hair across his head. Why had she been almost anxious to point out her impregnator? It had not been malicious, that was not Estelle. He thought now that she had perhaps wanted to show him that it was not a question of love or even lust for the boy. In pointing him out perhaps she had tried to tell him that she didn't love anyone but himself. But he could not bear to look at the youth except that once – he hated him. Had he hated Estelle? Yes, perhaps at that moment he had, but now, looking back, he could see that the longing for a child was almost every normal woman's wish, her fulfilment.

Poor Estelle, she had had all the usual investigations regarding her infertility. He had had no tests, he had been so sure it wasn't his deficiency. He'd refused examination for years, then when he had been proved the one at fault . . . She had found someone, a callow boy, to do what he couldn't do, give her a child. He knew she had never seen or got in touch with the youth again – no need to. How many times had she asked him to forgive her? Even on that night, the night of the crash, she was still begging him to try and love the child, saying it was theirs – the boy was nothing to her.

Well, he'd done his best to make it up to her. He had sworn at Estelle's graveside that he would never let Stella know that she was not his daughter. He had sworn that over the poor mutilated dead body in its coffin in the ground and he had kept his promise and, no matter what, he always would.

It was raining slightly when Bryn Jones called for him – a light, fine rain. Bryn assured him that it was perfect for fishing. They set off, both smiling, like two schoolboys let out of school, Bill thought.

After the ferry crossing they set out for Sussex and the river.

15

Agnes would never have guessed that she would have missed so much the comings and goings from the house next door. Her neighbour the other way, Mrs Timpson, she saw occasionally and made some polite remark or greeting, but it meant little to her whether she was in or out. The other side, though, gave life to the scene and she had to admit she missed them.

Stella was away, Bill Turner had not yet returned from his fishing trip and Rick had departed for America. He had come to bid Agnes a rather stilted goodbye. He had not mentioned Bruce or his previous conversation with her, or Hebe. He had even declined Agnes's invitation to come in and sit down, but had remained standing on the doorstep.

'I hope you do well in America, Rick. I expect you will keep in touch with the Turners?'

He had looked quite sceptical and said, 'Yes, maybe I will,' and he had said goodbye, shaking her hand rather limply, and that was that. Agnes had closed the door on him with little regret; charm he had not, she thought. But she did wonder if he would make any kind of dent, any impression, on the New York music scene; or would he be, as the pop song said, 'Parking cars and pumping gas,' instead of attaining some kind of celebrity success? Would he just be hawking his songs around to indifferent listeners who would wave him away? Well, at least he was trying and maybe he'd make it. Who could tell in the shifting sands of the music world – today anything could happen.

Two days later a telephone call took Agnes completely by surprise. It was Stella. She sounded breathless and excited, yet there was an overtone of slight anxiety. 'Agnes, I've telephoned the house twice and got no reply, where's Daddy? He's normally in and working during the afternoon.'

Agnes explained that Bill was away and Rick had departed to the States; that Linda was there in charge, but had probably been out shopping.

'Oh thank goodness everything is OK, Agnes, I was a bit worried. I've got something to tell Dad, but as he's not there I must tell you. I was going to tell Dad first, but as he's away I can't.' Her voice tailed off and a man's voice spoke, but Agnes could not catch what he said. Stella went on, 'Agnes, I'm so happy, so happy. I'm married!'

Agnes was speechless for the moment, but Stella went on. 'It's little Bruce's father, Agnes. At last he found out where I was and he ... Well, we've been writing for some time and now ...'

'I'm so glad for you, Stella.' Agnes felt there was nothing else she could say, the deed was done.

'His name is Miles. I'm Mrs Miles Hunt now – isn't it wonderful?'

'Yes indeed.'

'Look, Agnes, we're booked on the ferry this morning so may I bring Miles to see you? We'll be there about twelve o'clock. We're booked in at the Gloucester, just in case Daddy is mad with me, is furious about my ...' She stopped.

'Why should he be mad at you, Stella?'

'Well, Miles is a little older than me, Agnes, and Daddy may say ...' She paused.

'I see.' Agnes visualized a white-haired sugar daddy, but surely the man in Switzerland had not been so much older!

'Well, we'll see you about twelve o'clock, is that all right?'

'Yes, all right, I'll be here.'

'Great.' The telephone clanged down.

Agnes put her receiver down more quietly and caught herself murmuring, 'Marry in haste and repent at leisure,' then suddenly felt rather old as she argued against her own thoughts. It was hardly in haste: she had known and slept with him three years ago and borne his child – though of course he hadn't known that. And what of Bruce, had she told him the same lie as she had told everyone else, that it had been him, her dead son, on that slab in the morgue? Well, if she hadn't ... What a muddle! Only she knew, and presumably the man Hebe, that Stella's new husband was the father of a little boy alive and well and living somewhere in Scotland. What power did Hebe possess? She hoped it was not a manipulative power. She was intrigued and curious to meet the new Mr and Mrs Hunt. She was also aware of a feeling of envy, jealousy. How wonderful if it were her just setting out on a marriage to a man she loved. She knew love now – 'to hold a man in your arms is wonderful'. She knew how much she had missed – just a taste of love and that was all; but that small taste had made her long for more.

She went to the hall mirror and gazed at herself. Yes, to be loveless and alone was not good, but she was fifty. Still, she buoyed herself up by thinking it was not so long ago that she'd had a lover. He had desired her and she wished that he was beside her now and not dead.

Miles and Stella arrived promptly at twelve, probably because of the car ferry's arrival – Stella was usually late. The car that drew into Agnes's drive was a pale fawn Mercedes, its number plate showing that it was a new car – this year's model. It shone in the sunlight.

Miles got out first. To welcome the pair Agnes had come to her front door and opened it wide. Miles looked up and raised his hand in greeting before he came round the car to open the door for his new wife. He was a handsome man, tall, slim, athletic-looking. Agnes judged him to be perhaps in his late thirties or maybe very early forties. He had one distinguishing feature that Agnes noted as he came up the drive. His hair, thick, slightly wavy and brown, had a white streak about an inch wide, which began at his forehead and was brushed back across his head. It brought back a sudden memory to Agnes. In the orphanage where she had spent many of her young years there had been a little boy – his hair had been slightly more fair than this man's, but the white streak had been much the same. The little boy had been teased over it. Even as she moved forward to greet her guests Agnes remembered the little boy's name: it had been Adam.

The two, Stella and Miles, walked up to Agnes, Stella looking shy but radiant. The man held out his hand to Agnes and his handshake was warm and firm. Stella embraced her. 'Oh Agnes, I'm so happy I can't tell you. Are you surprised about it all? Whatever is Daddy going to say?' The words poured out of her.

Miles laughed indulgently. 'Give Miss Carmichael time to speak, darling,' he said.

In her sitting-room Agnes fetched drinks and listened to Stella, who seemed unable to stop. 'Agnes, Miles knows about poor little Bruce and has forgiven me.'

Agnes was not sure how to take that remark – 'forgiven me' what, she wondered.

Miles took Stella's hand. 'I know it wasn't her fault, Miss Carmichael. Little boys can wander a long way, I know that.'

Agnes registered in her mind, so she had lied about the morgue!

'I did not even know she had my child or I would have . . . I don't know what I could have done. I couldn't trace her, although I wanted to so much; I couldn't forget her.'

'I didn't let him or answer his letters because I had told Miles so many lies about my age and being on the pill.'

It seemed to Agnes that all these explanations should have been given to Bill Turner, not to her, but there was little she could do about that. Thus she listened with, in some cases, failing sympathy; wondering how they would react if she were to blurt out the truth – tell them that what Miles was being so forgiving about was not true, that the child he mourned was still alive and that Stella was telling lies even now.

The familiar feeling of power came over Agnes. Stella might be young, desirable, beautiful and, it appeared by the look of it, have married a rich man who loved her, but she, Agnes Carmichael, could destroy everything if she wished. All their complacency and future happiness could be destroyed with one sentence – 'But Bruce is still alive, Stella, and who was it in the coffin?' She liked the feeling, as she had always liked the feeling, of knowing something that others didn't know. There was only one other person who knew and that man she felt she must confront – Hebe Grant!

Stella got up suddenly, kissed Miles. 'I'll go in and leave a note telling Daddy that we're back and staying at the Gloucester.' They heard her running down the drive.

'She must have been through a dreadful time, Miss Carmichael. If only I'd been with her when she found she was pregnant.'

'Well, that could hardly have happened, Miles. After all, you didn't know that she was under age and that she was not taking any precautions.' Agnes tried to keep the slight tinge of criticism from her voice.

'Oh, I don't care about all that, Miss Carmichael. Now she's my wife and I adore her. What she did was wrong, but it was mostly my fault.'

'She's very beautiful.' Agnes had to say that, and indeed the change in Stella was dramatic – her haircut, her shoes, her clothes, were expensive. She looked more mature. Gone was the sloppy-jumpered, torn-jeans girl of such a short time ago.

They sat in silence for a moment. Miles shook his head when Agnes offered him another drink, then Stella came back into the room. She immediately sat down as close to Miles as she could and he put his arm round her.

Agnes looked at her again, and again she felt cheated. Was it the physical contact with her husband that made her feel like that? Yes, probably. Stella had lied – lie had followed lie and yet there she was, grasping her happiness with both hands. She was so young, so beautiful and, if one could judge, ideally happy with her new husband. Was the last lie upsetting her? Was she worried about it? Did she still wonder where her young son, the deaf child, was – living or dead? Agnes, looking at her, thought not. No one could be hiding worries and look as radiant as that!

So preoccupied was Agnes with her own thoughts that she only suddenly became aware of what Stella was saying. 'Do come, Agnes, please.'

Agnes realized that she was being asked to join them for dinner at the Gloucester that evening. She hesitated, not knowing whether to go or not, then she accepted. She wanted to know more, she wanted to see more of them, but she was not sure why. She knew so much that these two happy people did not. They were so blissfully happy and that was pleasant – pleasant at least for her to know that she could make that happiness disappear. Yes, it would be pleasant to go to dinner with them – more than pleasant, exciting.

They left. Miles backed the opulent car expertly out of the drive and on to the busy road, Stella smiling and waving. Where did Miles's money come from, Agnes wondered? Well, she would probably find out that evening over dinner. He looked like a man who worked in the City – maybe he was a lawyer, a banker, something that brought in quite a lot of money, she was sure.

She thought about Bill Turner. His fishing trip was taking rather longer than she had expected. According to Linda he was supposed to return on Tuesday. But he hadn't. He couldn't be anything but pleased at Stella's marriage, surely? Yes, there was a fairly large age difference, but even so... Agnes decided to have no lunch, dinner tonight would be enough. She was always careful to do what she could to keep her figure. She went upstairs to decide what she would wear.

Agnes noticed at the hotel that evening that her feelings were rather mixed. Perhaps she slightly sympathized with Stella's determination to be silent about Bruce. After all, what good would it do to tell Miles now? This thought was countered now and again by what she did consider to be unwise, to start a marriage with an outright untruth. Still, many women and men lied about their loves before they met Mr or Mrs Right and kept quiet about previous lovers, even pregnancies.

If she herself married, would she tell about her lover or not? If it would put the marriage in any kind of danger and she wanted the marriage, she would certainly not confess any past mistakes. She thought of Bill Turner – he had never told. The past once it had happened became the past and was best forgotten and, if necessary, buried in silence.

Miles and Stella greeted her in the foyer and they went straight through to the dining-room. A low bunch of red roses decorated the centre of the table and a bottle of champagne was chilling in an ice bucket beside the table. They sat down.

'We could have fetched you, Miss Carmichael,' Miles said.

'Agnes, please.' Stella interrupted before Agnes could reply. 'Agnes has a lovely car, Miles, a Porsche.'

'Oh, a lovely car indeed.' Miles poured the drinks. The bottle leaving the ice bucket made a cold tinkling sound that brought back memories to Agnes. She sipped the drink with enjoyment.

The service was good. As the small plates on which pâté had been served were removed, two people came to the table next to theirs, a pretty, dark-haired girl in an incredibly small amount of dress, low-cut, short and bright scarlet. Her hair, sleek and well-cut, fitted her head as closely as a cap. Stella, facing the table, obviously knew the man who was with the girl; he was quite outstanding. He was in a grey, well-tailored suit, his hair brushed back into a short pony tail. In his left ear glittered a thick gold ear-ring. His face was unusually pale, his mouth thin-lipped and straight. There was a certain arrogance in the way he summoned the waiter and glanced round the dining-room. Then he noticed Stella. He immediately left his table and came over to her.

'Stella, how are you?' His voice was slightly husky.

Stella flushed and looked slightly uncomfortable. Her glance travelled to Miles, then: 'Hello, Hebe. I haven't seen you for a long time.'

'Rick has departed for America, I hear.' He looked at Miles.

Stella nodded. 'Yes, I believe he has gone. This is my husband, Miles.'

Hebe looked surprised. 'Your husband? Rick didn't tell me you were engaged.'

'No.' Stella was almost abrupt. 'This is Miss Carmichael. Agnes, may I present Hebe Grant, a friend of Rick's.'

'And yours, Stella,' Hebe said smoothly. He smiled and acknowledged Agnes, then looked again at Miles.

'Congratulations.' Then, in the American style, he said, 'Miles, Stella, Miss Carmichael,' turned and went back to his own table.

'That was a friend of Rick's,' Stella said.

Miles poured more champagne. 'Oh yes, darling?' He sounded uninterested. Agnes, however, was quite the opposite, she was fascinated. He was the one person who knew what she knew!

She looked across to Hebe's table. There was something... perhaps something a little sinister about the man – or was it because Rick had told her that Hebe had killed little Bruce, even though she now knew this accusation was untrue. She couldn't help thinking there was something about Hebe Grant that was curiously menacing. Was it his rather narrow-eyed look, his slightly ironic smile, his hair, the ear-ring? His hands, too, she had noticed – they were white. She didn't know why, but the very look of Hebe Grant made her shiver slightly. Still, she was glad that she had met him, seen him, and she knew that shortly, somehow, somewhere, she had got to talk to him. That she would find a way she was quite certain.

After a delicious meal Stella, Miles and Agnes walked out to the car-park. They strolled along together to the Royal Yacht Squadron, the necklace of lights tumbling across the water on the mainland and the distant cars appearing to move like glow-worms. They stood for some time watching, looking across the Solent. The night was warm. Miles had his arm round his new wife's shoulders. Stella looked up and smiled and kissed his cheek. Agnes again felt the urge to destroy it, the happiness that she had never had. The water lapped softly against the stone of the wall below, the headlights behind them occasionally lighting up the slumbering stone lions on the parapet.

'It's a lovely place, the Isle of Wight, Agnes,' Miles said.

Agnes agreed. 'Thank you for a very pleasant evening, both of you.'

Stella kissed her. 'Do you think Dad will be back tomorrow, Agnes?' she asked.

'Probably, but I'm not sure – you will have to telephone.'

'Well...' Stella looked at her rather pleadingly. 'You don't know what time he'll be back?'

Agnes shook her head. 'No, I'm sorry, Stella, I've really no idea.'

Miles accompanied Agnes to her car and as she drew away from the parade she watched as, hand in hand, they crossed the road towards the hotel.

16

Bryn Jones drew up at Bill's driveway. 'Thanks, Bryn – door to door, eh?'

Bryn smiled and turned off the ignition. 'Boot's locked. I'll open it for you.'

The two men went to the back of the car. 'Double yellow lines,' Bryn remarked as he unlocked the boot, took out Bill's suitcase and handed it to him. He then banged the boot shut, this time not bothering to lock it. They walked back to the front of the car.

'Anything else?' Bryn Jones asked.

'Yes, my mac on the back seat.' Bill opened the passenger door, leant over, got out the garment and closed the door. 'Great time, Bryn. I really enjoyed it. I feel completely refreshed.'

'Me too. We must do it again.'

Bill nodded. 'Like to. That hotel was mega, as my daughter would say.'

Bryn laughed. 'Mega it was. Nice not to have to change in the evening.' He got into the car. 'Better go, don't want to end the trip with a fine. See you.' He drove off.

Bill felt sorry to see him go. The long weekend, longer than he had anticipated, he felt had really done him good. He felt rejuvenated. It had been wonderful. He dumped his suitcase down on his doorstep, then his mac on top of it. He started to dig in his pockets for the front door key. Not there. Even as he failed to find it he remembered where he had left it – on his tallboy in his bedroom. He'd known he wouldn't need the front door key, nor his car keys. He rang the bell. No answer. He tried again. Still no one. Where was everybody? he wondered. Stella, was she still in London? Rick might have already left. But Linda, she should be here. He rang once more and waited. Then at that moment, as he stood back to look up at the windows, Agnes drew into her driveway in her car.

'Locked out, Bill?' she called. She smiled at him.

'Where is everyone? Do you know, Agnes?'

She nodded. 'Come round and I'll make some tea.' She drove into her garage. Bill walked back round his drive, leaving his suitcase, and joined her as she unlocked her front door. As she passed him he noticed again her well-remembered perfume.

'Go in and sit down. Linda has probably gone down to the beach.' Agnes motioned towards the sitting-room. 'I'll make us some tea – won't be a minute.'

Bill went into Agnes's sitting-room. He did not sit down, but walked around. The room was so attractive, the curtains, the carpet, the furniture, so different from his. He went over to a side table and picked up a small silver frame and looked at the white cat in the picture. Agnes came in with a tray, cups and saucers, but as yet no teapot.

'Special cat?' he asked.

'Yes, very special. One day I'll tell you the story.' Agnes went out again to make the tea. She came back and sat down by the tray, put down the teapot. The front door closed with a slight bang. Bill looked up. 'It's Mrs Mack, my help, departing.' She looked at her watch. 'She usually leaves about now.'

'You're pretty well organized, Agnes – your garden, the house. We're always in a mess somehow.' He sighed, smiled and sipped his tea.

He went on talking. It was wonderful, he thought, he had someone to tell. He told Agnes about Bryn Jones, the beauty of the river and the country around, the comfort of the hotel. He just drank tea and talked; then he suddenly realized it might be boring her. Agnes looked as if she wanted to say something.

Agnes smiled and looked at him warmly. 'Don't apologize, I liked hearing all about your trip. I don't like fishing, though, I hate hurting animals.'

Bill, looking at her, thought, She would. She is a sweet, kind attractive woman and very, very easy to get fond of – no, more than that, to fall in love with.

Agnes suddenly got up. 'I'd forgotten to get the biscuits,' she said.

'Oh, don't bother for me,' he said.

'I want one. I didn't have any lunch.' She left the room to go back to the kitchen, conscious that his gaze was following her. In the kitchen Agnes opened the tin of biscuits and fetched a plate to put them on – she did it very slowly. She decided she must tell Bill about Stella. She did not feel happy about breaking the news to him, but she'd have to. It would have been better if he'd been able to get into his own house, tried to telephone Stella in London, or anything. Indeed, Stella and Miles might have telephoned him later in the evening and suggested they came over. As it was, they didn't even know he was home. She must telephone and tell them.

She went back into the sitting-room and decided she had waited long enough. Bill gave her the opening she needed straight away. 'Stella's not back yet, is she, Agnes? She was staying with a girlfriend up there. Maybe she is enjoying herself and staying longer than I thought she would. I'm quite glad.'

Agnes took the opportunity to tell him of Stella's marriage to Miles and the fact that they were staying at the Gloucester Hotel. Bill was astonished, curious – but Agnes did not detect from his manner that he was particularly hurt by Stella's secrecy. She mentioned that Miles was a little older than his daughter.

'Why didn't you tell me before, Agnes? Well, I hardly gave you time, did I?' He smiled. 'Chatting on the way I have been.'

'I hoped Stella would come or telephone today. She said she would, because I said you might arrive home and that if you did I'd tell you where she was – but of course it hasn't worked out like that!' She got up and as she passed Bill he took her hand and pressed it.

'Thanks, Agnes,' he said, retaining her hand.

'What for, Bill?'

'For being sensitive to my feelings about Stella's marriage.'

Agnes withdrew her hand, but slowly, and went towards the phone. As she did so, through the bow window she saw the pale fawn Mercedes drawing up into her drive. 'Oh dear,' she heard herself speak aloud. Agnes had wanted the three to meet in the privacy of their own home, but it wasn't to be. She went back into the sitting-room. 'Stella and Miles have just arrived. I'll go and let them in.'

Bill looked very relaxed. 'Oh well . . . I wish I had had time to smarten myself up a little. Still, they must take me as they find me, Agnes – holiday clothes and all.'

Agnes opened the front door. 'Your father is back, Stella.' She let them in. They were both dressed in navy and white, with sailing shoes. Perhaps they had been sailing; perhaps Miles even had a yacht. Agnes, of course, didn't know. She thought he looked very handsome and Stella very pretty. She pointed to the sitting-room. 'Come in and have some tea with us, I've just made it,' she said.

They entered the sitting-room, Bill stood up – then it all happened!

Bill dropped his cup and saucer. They crashed to the table, the saucer splitting into two pieces, the cup spilling the tea over the tray.

Stella and Miles stood there. Stella said, 'Dad.'

Bill sat down heavily, his face as white as a sheet. Stella went over and sat down beside him. Her face was full of concern. 'What is it, Dad, aren't you well?'

Bill did not take his eyes off Miles. At last he spoke. 'I'm all right, silly of me. I – I felt suddenly giddy.'

Miles came over and held out his hand. 'Forgive me, sir,' he said. 'It's my fault, not Stella's. When I heard all about our child I persuaded her –'

'No, it's all my fault . . . well, both our faults, Daddy. Please forgive us.'

Bill seemed to try to pull himself together. 'No, no, it's nothing to do with that. I'm sorry, Agnes, I've broken . . .'

Agnes had already picked up the tray to take it to the kitchen. 'Don't worry, Bill. I'll make some more tea,' she said, utterly unable to understand the drama of the scene. She had noticed Bill's refusal to take Miles's hand. Perhaps it was just confusion; perhaps Bill really had felt giddy.

In the kitchen Agnes cleaned the tray and put extra cups and saucers on it. The kettle was nearly boiling and she made more tea, but she took her time. She wanted to give the trio in her sitting-room an opportunity to talk, at least to say something to each other that maybe couldn't be said whilst she was there.

She went back into the sitting-room, carrying the tray. Complete silence greeted her. Miles was still standing. Stella was crying, her arm round her father's shoulders. Bill's colour had returned, but it seemed he still couldn't take his eyes from Miles. Did he think he was that much too old for Stella and, even so, would it upset him as much as it apparently had? She put the tray down, Miles moving politely forward to take it from her, a little too late.

'Do sit down, Miles,' she said. 'Do you feel better, Bill?' Bill nodded, but he still looked more pale than usual and seemed for the moment unable to speak.

The tension did not lessen and Miles suggested to Bill that he might like to have dinner with them that evening. Bill shook his head. 'Thank you, Miles, but I'm a little tired, I only got back just over an hour ago. If you don't mind . . . not tonight?'

Miles was obviously too polite to press him further, but Stella said, 'Oh Daddy, please.'

114

Miles took her hand. 'Tomorrow perhaps, Mr Turner.'

Bill seemed to take that suggestion a little better. 'Yes, yes, I'll come tomorrow, I promise you I will.'

Miles pressed Stella's hand more firmly. 'There, darling, we'll see your father tomorrow.' He turned again to Bill. 'About seven o'clock, the Gloucester Hotel. It's on the parade at –'

Bill interrupted almost rudely, 'Yes, yes, I know where it is.' He got up. 'I must go.' He turned to Agnes, 'I expect Linda is back now. I forgot my key.' He made this remark to Stella, hardly looking at her, then turned away again.

She foraged in her handbag, her eyes still full of tears. 'I've got a front door key, Daddy.' Bill took it and left the room.

Agnes followed him to the door. 'Is something the matter, Bill?' She asked. She opened the door, turned and looked at him.

'You don't understand, Agnes. How could you?' He left and Agnes watched him walk down her drive and disappear. He was right, she could not understand.

A tearful Stella and her new husband left soon after. Miles looked upset. Agnes watched them drive away. She took the tray of tea things through to the kitchen; she was glad to have something to do. Why was Bill so shattered by Stella's marriage? Miles seemed nice enough – surely it could not be just his age?

Agnes wondered if Bill would come back that evening to explain to her. She hoped he would, but he didn't and it grew dark. Agnes went out into the garden at the back of the house. The house next door showed two lights. Linda's bedroom window was stippled with colour; Agnes knew she had a television set in there. Bill's smaller study window also showed a light. She could imagine him sitting there, not doing anything. She was sure he wouldn't be writing and she longed to comfort him. She almost felt like going round to her neighbour's tonight, now, but after hesitating decided against it. If he wanted to tell her why he had been so upset, he would come and do so. Perhaps tomorrow morning.

She locked her front door and went into the sitting-room to look at her television, but the programmes seemed to have little meaning for her – her thoughts were with Bill Turner.

As she sat there the room darkened and the television flickered on. A play that Agnes particularly wanted to see failed to capture her interest. She switched off the set and again went out into the garden. The study light next door was still on, the curtains drawn.

Agnes stood watching the light, wondering at her own feelings. She would have given a lot at that moment to be with Bill, to put her arms round him and try to get him to tell her what was wrong.

She wandered round the moonlit garden. Was she in love with him? This feeling was nothing like she had had before, nothing like what she had felt for . . . No, this was different, warmer, more – dared she even think it? – maternal. Anyway, whatever it was, she felt it!

She looked at the rectangle of light again, put out her fingertips and lightly touched a red rose looking dark in the pale light, then she went back indoors and locked the kitchen door behind her. Her hot drink was cold now, but it didn't matter. She no longer wanted to sleep; she would rather lie awake and let her thoughts take her where they could. She remembered Bill's hand clasping hers just for a second earlier in the day and she remembered, too, letting her own hand stay in his for those seconds.

But something had happened since then; some shock had happened to him. The marriage? Surely not, it couldn't be just that. Tomorrow she must go and see him. Perhaps he would confide in her. Perhaps he wouldn't care to, but it would be sad if he couldn't tell her what was troubling him. If he could confide in her it would mean . . . and here her dreams took her . . . There might be a bond between them that would go on to become something bigger, something lovelier. As she lay sleepless she was beginning to realize more and more what she wanted most – to be near him.

The moonlight disappeared from the window and the hazy blue colour of dawn grew pink before Agnes dropped asleep.

She woke with a half-pleasant, half-worried sense of anticipation.

By a quarter to ten she was up, dressed and breakfasted on toast and orange juice, had instructed her cleaner what to do that morning and was standing, her heart beating a little faster than usual, at Bill Turner's front door.

Bill Turner himself opened the door. He was dressed, shaved and looked moderately composed. Before Agnes had time to speak he said, 'Oh Agnes, I'm so glad you have come. You are the only one I can tell.' He took her hand and drew her in.

'I was worried about you, I hardly slept.'

'Sleep! I didn't go to bed.'

'What is it, Bill? Why did Stella's marriage have such a fearful effect on you?'

Bill opened the study door. 'Let's go in here. Linda won't come in here, she never does.' He closed the door firmly behind them.

The room they entered was untidy. Screwed-up papers almost filled the waste-paper basket and some were lying round the basket itself – thrown, Agnes thought, in rage and frustration when the novel was not going well. There was a layer of dust on the word processor; a stack of books, new-looking, were balanced precariously on the corner of the desk; a dirty glass stood on top of them. The curtains were drawn back untidily. The room smelled of smoke and the window was shut. A very pretty vase sat incongruously among the litter of manuscripts. It contained pencils and pens and a pair of kitchen scissors. A box of paper clips had spilled out and were scattered over everything.

Bill crossed the room, took a thick file marked 'Letters' and some magazines off a chair near the window, carried the file over to his side of the desk and placed it beside his own chair. He did this with quick nervousness. Then, as if remembering himself, he said, 'Coffee, can I get you some coffee?'

Agnes shook her head. 'I've only just had breakfast.'

They both sat down. Bill looked at her for some seconds before he spoke, then: 'Agnes, I wonder if I should tell you what I want to. You're the only one I can tell, but it will involve you in something . . .' He put his hand to his forehead and paused, rubbing his head as if it ached.

Agnes leaned forward and very gently touched his cheek. 'Bill, whatever it is, whatever it involves me in, I want to help you.'

He grasped her hand and pressed his lips to it. 'I'd better be brief. I'd better tell you straight away. Miles is Stella's father, Agnes.'

For a moment Agnes did not take in what he had said.

Bill proceeded with the story. Estelle, his own inability to father a child, the young student, the car crash, Estelle's death – everything came tumbling out. 'What can I do, Agnes? All these years I've let her think she's my daughter. I didn't know the man in Switzerland was my wife's lover.'

'But the name Turner, wouldn't Miles have . . . ?'

Bill shook his head. 'I didn't know the young man's name. I saw him only once – could never forget him. But Estelle never told me his name, why should she? She taught French history at the school under her maiden name Estelle Dubois. Then I killed her in the car.'

'No, no, that's not true – you went into a tree, that's what they said.' Agnes put her hand over her mouth as Bill looked at her in amazement.

Then her long-kept secret had to be told.

'So you knew when we met that Stella was not my child?' Agnes nodded. 'And you never told anyone, not even any of the other nurses?'

Agnes shook her head. 'You told me in confidence, Bill. It wasn't my secret to tell.'

'Oh Agnes, this at least is a happy coincidence. But how can I handle it all? It's beyond me. I can't tell Stella she's not my daughter – and I can't tell her about Miles, can I? Yet I must. Oh God!'

There was a soft knock at the door. 'Yes?' Bill's voice was hoarse.

Linda poked her head in, her eyes curious. 'Would you like some coffee?' She asked Bill Turner, but her eyes were fixed on Agnes. They said plainly, 'What's going on?'

Agnes answered for Bill, who was sitting with his chin resting on his hand, his eyes closed. 'Yes, Linda, it would be nice. Some coffee, thank you.'

Linda disappeared and Bill spoke as if he had suddenly remembered. 'Agnes, I've got to go and have dinner with them tonight. I can't do it. I cannot do it – face Miles, face Stella. I'm a coward, I know, but I can't do it unless you will come with me. Please, is it too much to ask of you?'

Agnes took his hand. 'No, nothing is too much to ask of me, Bill. Of course I'll come with you.'

Bill put his hand over hers. The door was pushed open and Linda brought in the coffee, this time without knocking. Agnes noticed with what rapidity the coffee had been made and brought in and it made her smile a little. The smile reached Bill and he smiled back. He looked a little more relaxed, a little less tortured, and Agnes was thankful for that.

17

'Darling, you'll just have to act younger.' Stella and Miles were breakfasting on the same morning as Agnes was calling on Bill Turner. Stella laughed as she said this and put her arms around her husband's neck, pressed his head down and kissed his lips – a long, long kiss – and they parted reluctantly.

'You taste of oranges,' Stella said. 'Last night you said I tasted of champagne.'

Miles smiled at her. 'True, darling, but I love you tasting of both.'

Her smile faded then and a worried frown returned. 'It's Daddy leaving like that, without explaining.'

Miles was more conciliatory about her father's behaviour. 'Fathers are like that. He thinks I'm too old for you and not good enough. I think he'll come round. Perhaps there are others, too, who think like that.' He stroked Stella's hair. 'You're so beautiful, darling. Of course he cares for you and your future.'

'You're sweet, Miles.' Stella returned his caress. 'Look,' she pointed to some yachts just starting away. It was a beautiful scene – the white sails, coloured spinnakers. 'I love it here.'

'What are you going to do today, darling? Sail with me or see some more of the Island?'

The telephone rang in their bedroom. Miles got up and answered it. He spoke for a moment or two and then rejoined Stella. 'It's for you, your father. He sounds cheerful and he's coming this evening.'

Stella ran to the telephone. 'Daddy!'

Miles sat down at the table. He was glad Bill Turner had telephoned. The last thing he wanted was to be the cause of alienation between his wife and his father-in-law. He heard Stella put back the receiver. 'Miles, what do you think? Daddy's coming to dinner tonight – and he wants to bring Agnes!' Her eyes sparkled. 'Miles, do you think they're an item?'

'An item?' Miles put his arm round her.

'I mean . . .' Stella made a little face at him.

Miles laughed. 'I know what an item is, darling.'

'Wouldn't it be lovely if . . .'

'Yes, it would, if your father were as happy as I am. Agnes seems a nice person, but I shouldn't jump to conclusions too quickly, sweet.'

'She is. And he'll be lonely now. She'd be ideal for him.'

Miles laughed again. 'Now stop being a matchmaker, my love.'

Stella put her head on his shoulder. 'Will you love me always, Miles? Even if I don't – don't always . . .'

'Don't always what, sweetheart?' Miles's voice was tender.

'Don't always . . .' Stella was suddenly crying, not noisily, just tears running from her eyes.

'Whatever you do, darling, or whatever you've done, it doesn't matter. I will always, always love you.' He held her away from him so that he could look into her tear-filled eyes.

'No matter what?' she asked.

'No matter what,' Miles answered, kissing her wet cheek.

Stella turned away. She leant over the balcony railings, her long hair stirring in the light breeze. She felt so happy, so safe with Miles, but in the background of her mind there was always Bruce. She would never know his fate, never be able to thrust entirely from her mind that terrible lie, a lie she had now repeated to her husband. She couldn't alter it now – to her father, to Linda, to Miles, to Agnes, Bruce was dead and cremated, but that little note at the funeral haunted her. Someone knew, someone knew that she had identified the wrong child, had lied. The police were still looking for a little boy, but they didn't realize it was Bruce and if they ever found him... She shuddered.

'Are you cold, darling?' Miles's voice was full of concern.

Stella was startled. 'Cold? No, Miles, it's warm – it was just a grey goose.'

Tomorrow, as her mood grew a little lighter, perhaps everything would be all right. If they found Bruce's body they wouldn't know it was her son – except, of course, if the mother told them it was not hers, not her son they had found. Oh God, what a muddle she had made just to be free. But it wouldn't happen. Both little boys were dead and Bruce's body would never be found. That she hoped and prayed – after all, both deaths were through no fault of hers.

She had Miles now and if only Dad could be happy, too. He had borne so many burdens; the burden of her pregnancy, her expulsion from the convent, her refusal to tell who was Bruce's father and the expense of it all – Linda. She had put on him constantly.

'Oh, I wish Daddy could marry and find happiness with someone like Agnes and write a bestseller or have one of his books made into a film.'

Miles gave her a hug. 'We're so happy and I'm so happy, you want the same for everyone. That's what happiness does, my love.'

'I hope we don't meet that Hebe man again tonight,' Stella said suddenly.

'Who? Oh, the ear-ring man. Why?'

Stella went to the dressing-table and started to comb her hair.

She shrugged. 'I don't know, Miles, he's so menacing isn't he? Wicked-looking.'

Miles shrugged his shoulders too. 'Not really, darling. Perhaps it's that pony tail.' He laughed.

Stella put down her brush, went over and ran her hand lightly on Miles's hair. 'I'm glad you haven't got a pony tail, Miles, and I love that white streak across your head.'

'It didn't do much good at school, I used to get ragged for it,' Miles answered.

They went out on to the balcony again, reluctant to leave their privacy.

The dinner that evening went off well. Stella was determined to thrust her worry behind her. Miles was charming to Bill and to Agnes. His prosperity was demonstrated to Bill by the well-chosen delicious meal and the quality of the wine. All, Agnes felt, should have contributed to a happy occasion, but as she watched Bill she could sense the reserve, the silences. She watched, too, the effort Miles was expending on the relationship, trying to make Bill accept and like him.

She felt a tremendous pity for Bill, hiding and perhaps trying to accept something that must be almost repugnant to him – his wife's lover was now the husband of her child. She felt a surge of love and concern going out to him. It was such an unusual feeling for her that she hardly knew how to conceal it. She reached out and touched his hand, she wanted to comfort him, to love him, to try to make up for a life spent in real poverty, struggling with what was, after all, the product of his wife's adultery and the offspring of that adultery. No wonder he sometimes looked tired and worn, she thought.

After the meal was over and they had taken coffee in the lounge of the hotel, they left. Stella and Miles strolled along with them to their car. The moonlight on the sea was like a picture, a silver path leading towards them, sparkling and rippling in the calm water. At last Miles and Stella moved off and made their way back, hand in hand, to the hotel, as Agnes had watched them do before.

'Phew! How did I get through that?' Bill, his hands on the steering wheel, rested his head against them for a moment, then looked up and turned to Agnes. 'What am I to do, Agnes? Without you I couldn't even have coped this evening.' His expression suddenly changed. 'I'll never be able to face up to life without you, Agnes.'

She shook her head. 'You don't have to cope without me,' she said softly. Their lips met, his arms went round her. After the kiss he almost abruptly drew away.

'What am I doing? What have I got to offer you, Agnes? A struggling, poverty-stricken novelist, no prospects, a run-down house.'

'I love you, Bill,' Agnes answered him; her own words, her own feelings surprised her. She had never felt like this before. If anyone or anything hurt him it would hurt her as much. She remembered the man she had never married and her lover; neither of them had made her feel like this. Was this really love – forsaking all others?

'Oh my darling Agnes, you don't know.' He started the car; the engine sounded rough to Agnes compared with the gentle purr of the Porsche. Perhaps that worried him, her money, his poverty. It needn't, she had enough for both of them. But would his pride ever accept it?

They drove home almost in silence, each engaged in their own thoughts.

18

When she got up the next morning Agnes remembered with some dismay that she had asked her next-door neighbour, Mrs Timpson, to coffee at ten thirty. She looked at the clock. No biscuits and not enough time to go to the shops and get any. She would knock up some scones. Agnes was learning to cook such things now that she was alone with lots of time to spare – sometimes too much time to spare, she thought.

Mrs Timpson arrived on the dot of ten thirty. 'You *have* got it looking nice in here,' she said as she entered Agnes's sitting-room. 'It's a little smaller than mine, I fancy, but so beautifully appointed.' Agnes felt that the word 'appointed' savoured more of a kitchen or a bathroom than this room, but she smiled and accompanied Mrs Timpson across the room to stand for a moment at the french windows. Outside, Agnes's gardener, who came for two hours twice a week, was mowing the lawn; the fresh smell of the grass was pleasant.

'They are so expensive, aren't they?'

Agnes paused as she went to leave the room to fetch the percolating coffee. 'Who?' Agnes was feeling somewhat distracted and could not for the moment get her mind to focus on Mrs Timpson's remark.

'Gardeners. Quite expensive. £7 an hour, I've heard.'

Agnes stopped at the door. 'Oh yes, that is so.'

'I wait for Denis, my son, to come and advise though now he's divorced of course he has no garden of his own so hardly wants...'

'Of course. I can quite imagine.' Agnes escaped into the kitchen.

Her mind was continually drifting to her other next-door neighbour. She was aware of an overwhelming wish to be with him. She took the coffee back. Mrs Timpson had seated herself on the settee. She too, as Bill Turner had done, picked up the little silver-framed photograph of Fluffy, the blind white cat. Indeed, it was the only photograph in the room. 'You like cats?' Mrs Timpson asked, handing the picture back to Agnes after she had put the coffee down.

'Yes, I'm a lover of animals – dogs, cats, sheep, goats, any animal, snakes even.' Agnes added the last rather out of mischief.

'Ugh, snakes. I dislike animals, they're so dirty, even birds. I'm always cleaning their droppings off the tiles of the terrace.'

'Yes, I expect you are,' Agnes said and smiled.

Mrs Timpson left at about twelve thirty, having sipped daintily at a glass of sherry. Agnes was pleased to see her go, though she had tried to make her visitor welcome and had added the sherry to the morning's entertainment of her visitor, feeling a trace guilty about her rather abstracted manner. However, over the sherry she had listened with feigned interest to Mrs Timpson's gossip about people in the road. One woman had apparently walked out on her husband and two children and the judge had awarded her custody of the two children. 'The poor father is desolated – she's left the Island with a new boyfriend and the children.' Mrs Timpson sounded scandalized.

After listening to more of such talk Agnes saw her to the door.

Hewson, Agnes's gardener, had worked his way round to her front garden and was clipping a few straggling twigs from the hedge. 'Just finished, miss,' he said, thrusting the secateurs into his gardening apron pocket. He made his way across the garden and through the side gate to put the secateurs back, put away the mower and lock the shed.

'Thank you, Mr Hewson. See you on Tuesday,' Agnes called to him.

'God willing,' he called back.

He always said that. Agnes smiled slightly and was about to turn back into the house when something stopped her. Linda came out of the house next door carrying two small suitcases, her handbag slung over her shoulder. As she saw Linda, Agnes also noticed to the right a 'Taxi' sign, just visible through the rather dilapidated hedge bordering the bottom road end of the next-door garden. Bill followed with a large suitcase. He was out of view for a few seconds then reappeared in the drive, waving. The taxi drew away.

Agnes, for a reason she could not fully understand, did not want to see him, was frightened of seeing him. She backed through her front door, closed it and stood in her hall. Why had she done that? Why had she hidden from him? Yet she had been thinking of him all the morning and most of the night. She stood quite still until she heard the next door shut.

She stayed there, wondering at herself and her feelings. Linda was now gone, for good perhaps or maybe for a holiday – but hardly, three suitcases . . . and the one carried by Bill looked heavy. If she had left for good, gone to another job, Bill would be alone except for the cleaning woman who, as far as Agnes could remember, only came once a week. So Bill . . . The thought of him alone in that big house – bigger than her own – the weed-covered garden, the untidy kitchen. She'd never been upstairs in the house, except to bandage Bruce's knee in the bathroom. Why did she feel this need to hide? Was she afraid to get involved?

Last night she had loved the feel of his embrace. Agnes hated being unable to analyse and put into correct departments her own feelings. Her last, and only, lover she had wanted; she had wanted to go to bed with him. But when he had died so tragically, what had she felt? A sense of relief as if she had been released from something? She could hardly remember her own feelings. Things were blotted out in her mind, she decided – subsequent events had erased them. Was everyone like that, she wondered?

With a familiar gesture she shook herself. When she did this it always reminded her of a dog getting rid of water on its coat. The thought amused her. She straightened her shoulders, trying to thrust out of her mind the picture of Bill standing at the gate, not noticing her. Standing there, she imagined him going back into the house, shutting the door with that little bang she had heard– then what?

She looked at her watch, lunchtime. Had Linda left something prepared for him? Probably not. She went into her kitchen to prepare her own lunch. But the thought of Bill, maybe in his kitchen looking helplessly around, still haunted her. Or perhaps he was in his study gazing at his typewriter, there amongst all those screwed-up pieces of paper in and around the waste-paper basket. The picture was so clear. Or perhaps he was standing, looking with despair out at the wreck that was his garden – the brambles entwining the hedges, the roses (some dead but not deheaded), the weed-infested lawn. What was he feeling?

Agnes felt impatient with herself, picked out a knife from the drawer and started to slice cold chicken for her own lunch. The new potatoes she had put on were beginning to bubble in their water on the stove. She was dreaming it all, dramatizing. In all probability she was quite, quite wrong; the picture she was creating was not apt at all. Bill was sitting down at his dining-room or kitchen table demolishing a helping of casserole that Linda had left him . . . But no, it was no use. She turned off the stove, picked up her front door key from the hall table, locked the front door behind her, walked round and rang the door bell of her next-door neighbour's house.

Bill opened the door and his face lit up when he saw who it was. 'Agnes, come in.' She walked in and she glanced into the study as she went by. There were no screwed-up pieces of paper around the waste-paper basket. No work had been done that morning, it indicated.

'I saw Linda go. Has she gone for good, Bill?'

'Yep. Found a job looking after two children. Great for her – you know how she loves kids. I'm glad! I was worried about sacking her.'

'What about you, though?'

He made a little grimace. 'I'll manage, somehow.'

For the first time Agnes noticed how blue his eyes were. 'Well, not today, Bill. Come and help me eat spaghetti bolognese, I've made far too much,' she lied.

Back in her own house with Bill, Agnes cooked the spaghetti and the meat, added tomatoes. Bill was in her sitting-room, smoking and drinking a gin and tonic. She joined him as the meal cooked.

'Agnes . . .' She wondered what he was going to say. He looked serious, his eyes fixed on her face.

'Yes, Bill?'

'Your perfume, what is it? It haunts me whether you are with me or away from me.'

'It's called Joy,' she said, and felt herself almost shy.

He took her hand and tried to make her sit down beside him on the settee. 'I've got something else to tell you,' he said.

'The spaghetti will overcook,' she said.

He released her hand. 'Afterwards?' he said.

She paused a moment. 'Afterwards,' she replied.

When they had finished the meal Agnes was about to clear the table. 'I'll make coffee,' she said.

'No, you won't.' Bill's voice was firm, his eyes full of triumph. 'I've got something to tell you. Now stop playing housewife for one minute and sit down, woman.'

Agnes sat down again. Across the table he grasped her hand.

'What is it, Bill? You sound so pleased with yourself.'

He paused for a second or two. 'I've sold one of my books to a film company. I had a letter from my agent this morning.' He watched her face.

'How wonderful, Bill! How absolutely wonderful! I'm so thrilled for you.'

'A thrill for both of us, darling, I hope. It means you won't be marrying a pauper. If, that is, you will agree to marry me – will you? I couldn't ask you before this – though God knows I wanted to.'

Agnes squeezed his hand. 'As if that were true and as if it mattered anyway,' she said. 'Of course I'll marry you – but not just because you may be richer now. I love you, Bill.'

Bill took a letter from his breast pocket and handed it to her. Agnes unfolded it and, as she read it, she could not recall ever before feeling so much joy for another human being.

They went on talking, talking about everything. It seemed that his success had opened the floodgates for Bill and he could now discuss his life more openly with her; to some extent, she also felt freer with him. It was quite a time before they felt there was only one way to celebrate and that was to make love.

Agnes knew now why she had felt that tinge of fear and had felt the need to hide from him. She had known that commitment was near her – once again. But this time, when Bill had proposed marriage so suddenly, all her fear had gone. All she wanted now was to be his wife.

*

Agnes lay beside Bill, the little bedside clock ticking beside her. It was her clock and her bed. She wasn't quite sure why she thought that, but it was so. Her single bed hardly accommodated the two bodies side by side. Agnes looked down at her breasts; well shaped, small, they were still slightly pink from his kisses. She smiled to herself. Her first lover had had no moustache!

First lover! She had only had one before this, Peter alias Philip. His lovemaking had been so different, so passionate, so demanding; she had sacrificed her virginity to him. But this man . . . She raised herself on one elbow and looked down at him. He was sleeping with his back to her. She lightly touched his hair: silver, shining, silky. In spite of his fifty-eight admitted years he was muscular but not fat. She watched the pulse beating in his throat – slow, calm. He turned slightly and she glimpsed his face for a moment, then he turned back again and buried his face in the pillow – her pillow. The clock said 7.35; they had been in bed together for two and a half hours and had made love twice.

After lunch they had talked – talked about his wife Estelle and his life since, without her; about his books, the bringing up of Stella, the problem of the baby, the fact that she had been pregnant so young. He spoke not in a complaining way but as if stating facts.

Agnes got out of bed and went into the bathroom. She put on her shower hat and the warm water ran over her body. Then, wrapped in a large, fluffy white towel, she went back into the bedroom.

Bill was awake. He lay with his hands behind his head. 'I didn't feel you get up or I would have stopped you,' he said.

Agnet shook her head. 'I want to be taken out to dinner.' She leant over and kissed his mouth and as he was about to clasp her she drew back, her eyes laughing. She felt young, satisfied, slightly smug.

'Right.' He swung his legs out of the bed. 'May I shower in your shower?'

'Of course.'

'Come with me?'

Agnes shook her head. 'I'm going to dress up,' she said.

'Oh Lord, that means I've got to change into my "going to see my publishers" suit.'

'That's right, darling. I want to be seen with you; I don't mind what you wear.'

She sat at her dressing-table making up her face. The sound of the shower cascading on the glass in her bathroom pleased her – someone there, she was not alone.

'You're man mad,' she said to herself, then corrected the remark. 'No, just at the moment one man mad – and I think this is for keeps.'

The shower stopped. Bill came out, shrugged on his shirt, stepped into his trousers, slipped his bare feet into his shoes. He went over and ran his hand across her shoulders.

'Won't be long, my love,' he said and ran downstairs and out of the front door. Agnes went on getting ready.

19

Hebe Grant was feeling wretched, out of sorts and at odds with the world. The cause: money, or lack of it. He needed some support from Bango, his associate in London, so named because he had been banged up so many times for drug offences (unproved), assaulting policemen (proved), burglary with violence (proved), another drug charge (unproved). He always had a good brief who got him a short sentence or a fine. Bango had helped Hebe many times but now, in answer to Hebe's guarded phone call, he'd been as cagey as hell.

'Money up front, Hebe – no credit,' he had said. 'New rules, mate. Can't afford to take chances any more.'

'Come on, Bango – just a small delivery to keep me going, for Pete's sake. You always help me. Have I ever let you down?'

'No, I'm not saying you have, Hebe, never, but things are not the same nowadays up here. Supposing you get busted down there? Where would I be?'

'I won't get busted, Bango, for God's sake,' Hebe had protested.

'Well, you did up here and I nearly dropped a grand.'

Hebe lost his temper – a silly thing to do with Bango, but he just couldn't help it. 'Look, I've got other irons in the fire, Bango, big money involved. I know what I'm doing down here.'

Bango reacted to Hebe's rather angry voice. 'OK then, man, pay me and I'll deliver.' He banged the telephone down.

Hebe cursed. The money from Bruce's kidnapping had been spent – new clothes, new car, embellishing the disco a bit. The kids liked to come, but you'd got to give them something, some enticement. If they found he was not supplying, if they couldn't score there, they would soon take off to where they could get the Big E, or white dust – or anything that would give them a big jolt or a high or whatever it was they wanted. They'd got used to Hebe's place; they weren't just teenage glue sniffers or solvent jerks, they were more into the serious stuff and brought their money with them.

'Hebe, are you in?' There was a banging on the glass of his door. Bloody Evie, he was sick of her, too. She expected him to be a universal supplier, not only of drugs but money too, for clothes and ... He wanted rid ... But she knew a lot about him. She'd even looked after Bruce for a night. He must have been mad to let her, but at the time there had been no one else he could trust – not that he trusted her all that much!

He opened the door and the dark, pretty girl burst in. 'What gives, why is the door bolted? I couldn't get in with my key.'

Hebe answered her. 'Shut the bloody door, I'm cutting.' Evie looked at the glass slab, thick and green, on the table, a razor blade beside it. On the glass were little lines of white powder, and plastic bags were piled on the table round the glass slab.

'Not much there,' she said.

'What do you want?' he asked.

Evie looked greedily at the little lines of powder. He noticed her look. 'Take your eyes off that. It's all I've got for the rave tonight and no money to buy more.'

The girl looked incredulous. 'Where's it gone, the kid's money?'

Hebe didn't answer. He sat down at the table, picked up the razor blade and went on dividing the powder.

Evie went on grumbling, walking about the small untidy room. 'If you hadn't bought that damn car and those suits, and that ear-ring – eighteen carat, so what, no one would know if it was brass – you'd still have the money.' Hebe didn't answer. 'And you needn't have given Rick that £10,000.' She pouted. 'He didn't do anything worth that.'

Hebe had lied about the amount he had paid Rick, so again he let her rant on, not answering. 'What about the baby? What's that girl's name, Katy? Have you got a buyer for that kid? What is it – a girl?'

Hebe started putting the powder into the little plastic bags. Each time he used the razor blade to pick up the powder it made a little screech as it travelled on the glass. 'Don't do that.' Evie covered her ears. 'It sets my teeth on edge.'

Hebe stopped. 'Kate's thinking twice. Bloody girl thinks she can't part with the baby now. Women!'

Evie moaned. 'Oh no, silly cow. She'll be sorry when it's a bit older when she can't get a sitter to come to the house and wants to go out.'

'Too late for me then, I want it now. The dame's fifty at least. Don't like the look of her much – mouth like a rat trap and a rough-looking partner.'

'Porno number?' Evie asked.

'Dunno, can't tell. Don't think so. They can't all be like Bruce's buyer.' He shrugged and went back to his task.

Evie went to the window and looked down on the small box-strewn yard. 'I wouldn't give up a kid, not these days, if it were mine.'

Hebe laughed. 'Just see you in the loving mother role, Evie,' he said.

Evie blushed. She had recently had an abortion and she didn't want to think about it. Anyway, she hadn't sold the kid. 'When will you know about Katy, Hebe?' She went and put her arm round Hebe's shoulder. She was going to kiss him, but Hebe shoved her off. 'Not in the mood, Evie.'

Evie let go immediately. 'When will you hear?' she asked again.

'Hear what?' Hebe got up and stretched his back. Evie noticed he had on new soft suede shoes.

'New shoes, too. How about the baby, Katy's baby? Has she really decided to keep it?'

'I reckon so. I don't know – haven't seen her for a couple of days.'

'Well, why not do what you did with Bruce – just nick it?'

'Get real, Evie, no one on the inside to help. Besides, too risky. I need money right now – just to tide me over, to get more shit.'

'How's that Stella, Bruce's mother?' Evie asked. She was combing her hair, sleek and black, in front of the mirror over the fireplace.

'Funny you ask that.' Hebe picked up his car keys. 'Yeah, she's married; we met her the other night, you know. I was just thinking about her.'

Evie's brows drew together in a frown. 'You don't fancy her, do you, Hebe?'

He shook his head. 'No, but I fancy her new husband's bank balance.'

'What do you mean, Hebe?' She watched him put the tiny plastic bags of powder into his jacket pocket.

Evie came closer to him again. Hebe moved away. 'Never mind what I mean.' His voice was cold. 'I'm going out,' he said, twirling the keys round his finger. The door of the flat closed behind him.

Evie, left behind, opened one or two drawers and cupboards, looking for a fix, but she did it without much hope. Hebe never left anything worth pinching about. She gave up and soon the door slammed behind her, too.

She looked around for Hebe, but he had gone – his car as well. That was just like him, wouldn't ask her if she wanted a lift – oh no, just split. Why did she bother with him? Sometimes he was different and other girls wanted him. He could be nice. She ran for a bus and just managed to swing on board as it was taking off. Where had he gone? she wondered.

Hebe drove a short distance, stopped at a phone booth, got out and slammed the car door. In the booth he thumbed through a directory, found the number of the Gloucester Hotel and dialled.

20

Next morning Bill had stayed for breakfast. Agnes cooked him bacon and egg, the smell was delicious. Something new to the house, that breakfast smell. He left about ten thirty – to work, he said. He looked so much happier. He talked again about Stella and her incestuous marriage, but he'd come to no conclusion about what was to be done. Agnes gave no advice about it; she felt it was a decision he must come to by himself.

The night and the morning had been wonderful. There seemed to be a chemistry, a rapport, that made for comfort and relaxation between them. Something quite different from any of the other men Agnes had contemplated spending her life with.

He whistled as he walked down the path, his walk slightly jaunty, and Agnes knew she loved him. The feeling frightened her slightly, just in case it was evanescent and disappeared like sunlight behind a cloud.

Back in the house Mrs Mack had arrived and was washing up

the breakfast things. She worked for Mrs Timpson also and Agnes felt that Queen's Road would soon be regaled with her arrangements. She smiled widely as she realized this. She did not care a scrap who knew!

During the morning Agnes got her car out and drove to the local supermarket – smoked salmon, a crisp lettuce, some tomatoes, fillet steak, mushrooms. She wanted to prepare a super dinner for that evening to repay Bill for last night – for his tenderness. She realized that Bill was not well off and she had appreciated very much the lovely meal with which he had indulged her.

She had not been back in her own house for more than five minutes when the telephone rang. She had an answering machine which she had automatically switched on when she got back, but there had been no messages. Agnes sometimes wondered why she bothered with it as calls to her were so infrequent. This time the call was from Stella, a very frightened and upset Stella who could hardly speak at all. Agnes heard the click of a pay phone and realized that Stella was not calling from their hotel suite but from a call box.

'What is it, Stella? Try and calm yourself. I can't understand what you're trying to tell me.'

At last Stella did regain a little of her composure. 'I must see you Agnes – this morning. Please!'

'Very well. I've just come in, so if you come over now –'

'No, no, I can't come to your house. Daddy might see me and wonder why I don't go in and see him. I couldn't.'

Agnes grew a little impatient; she had not yet put away her purchases. 'Well, what do you want me to do, Stella?.'

Stella was weeping again, but managed to stop long enough to beg Agnes to meet her at a small café in Newport in about half an hour.

'Stella, I've only just come in,' she said. But this made no difference.

'Please, please, Agnes. I can't tell you what it is on the telephone.'

'All right, I'll meet you.'

Stella named the place where they were to meet and Agnes put the phone down, slightly cross. But she was curious. Was this just a lovers' tiff? By the sound of Stella she thought not; she was conscious that lies washed about those two. Had something been said – had someone . . . ? Her irritation gave way before her curiosity. She put the steaks on top of the refrigerator and covered them, then put away the rest of the purchases she had made for tonight, picked up her handbag, checked the back door. The White Mouse, that was the name of the café where she was to meet the tearful Stella.

She started the car and drove out of her gate to Newport and the White Mouse. She would soon learn what the tears were all about!

As she drove through Wootton, passed the lake, and eventually paused at the traffic lights, her thoughts were on Bill. She could not help wondering whether, if the film offer had not arrived – and with it the promise of money and maybe success – Bill would have asked her to marry him with such suddenness. She thought not – she felt that his pride and her money might well have kept them apart. What a dreadful thought!

The traffic lights turned to green. She drove on. Well, what a strange proposal it had been. 'Sit down, woman,' she remembered – she would always remember that order. It was so lovely to obey someone you love; and how unusual for her to want to obey anyone! She smiled to herself. Her secret smiles were becoming more frequent.

Agnes had to park quite a long way from the café and she had some distance to walk. Even so, when she arrived at the White Mouse there was no sign of Stella.

Agnes sat down at a table. The place was almost empty. It was, she supposed, a little too early for lunch to be starting and a little late for coffee. A waitress approached her table, but Agnes did not order anything, just told the girl she was waiting for someone. It seemed to her that maybe Stella might not turn up at all. She was feeling irritated that, after sounding so upset and weepy on the telephone, Stella was not here waiting for her.

However, after about ten minutes Stella appeared, full of apologies and tearful excuses about not being able to find a parking place and the heavy traffic. She sat down and immediately the waitress approached them again.

Agnes looked up at her and glanced towards Stella, who was not looking at her, then ordered two mineral waters. Stella took little notice of the order. She looked wretched. She had on no make-up, not even lipstick, and her hair looked less shining and well brushed.

'Stella, what's the matter? Have you quarrelled with Miles?'

She looked up quickly. 'No, no, nothing like that. He's in

London today, he's a financial adviser – I told you, didn't I? He tells people how to invest their money. He's really good. In his firm he . . . ' She clasped her hands together. 'No, no, Agnes, it's not that. Miles will be back this evening.'

'Well?' Agnes prodded her.

The waitress brought the mineral waters. Agnes picked up her glass and drank half the liquid. She was thirsty. This morning's breakfast . . . Bacon, she thought, with a sudden surge of pleasure, seeing Bill again in her mind's eye, seated at the kitchen table demolishing his breakfast.

Stella did not appear to have noticed the glass that was put in front of her. 'It was last night, someone telephoned me. Miles was in the shower, it was lucky I answered it.' She picked up the glass in front of her, sipped the sparkling water and put it down again. Then she put up her hand and pushed the dangling tress of hair behind her ear, to Agnes a very familiar gesture. Then she looked up again.

'It was Hebe Grant. You remember, Agnes – we met him, he came over to our table that night.' Agnes nodded. 'He was a friend of mine a bit, not much.'

'So . . . Stella, why did he ring you?' Agnes did not feel particularly interested.

Then the whole story came tumbling out amid bursts of tears and 'I didn't mean to.' The only small fact that Agnes did not know was the story of the wreath with its terrifying message. Agnes sat unmoved, her eyes fixed on her companion's face. Her thoughts were slightly amusing to her. She had difficulty in curbing a smile. Agnes loved knowledge, secret knowledge.

Hebe thought he was the only one who knew of Stella's deception – but *she* knew, she, Agnes Carmichael, knew it all. Stella's big lie. She knew too how Hebe had kidnapped and sold the child, even where the little boy was. Well, almost – if she needed to she could track him down, knowing that Lady Preston had adopted him. Of course she knew about Rick, too, but her thoughts were more with Hebe Grant. He wouldn't stop at one child, nor would he be particularly caring about who got the child. Bruce had no doubt been lucky, but the next one might fall into the hands of a pornographer, child abuser, any form of horror.

She dragged her thoughts back to Stella's revelations of the note on the wreath. 'But still you went on with your marriage to Miles, knowing that someone knew about your lie, Stella?' she asked.

'Yes, Agnes. I really love Miles and I feel safe with him, and after all I thought he would take me away somewhere. Oh, I don't know. I've done wrong and it's all caught up with me now. Hebe says he will tell everyone it wasn't Bruce at all and I identified the wrong child unless...'

Agnes waited for the inevitable.

'...unless I give him £1,000.' She started to weep again and Agnes could willingly have shaken her when she added, 'I'm going to ask Daddy if he can raise the money. He might be able to borrow it from his publisher. I can't ask Miles. He'll wonder what I want such a large sum for.'

Agnes's one thought was for Bill, nothing else, no one else. She realized how much he mattered to her. 'You will not worry your father with this, Stella. I'll give you the money myself.'

Agnes was rather surprised at her own instant response, then realized she was protecting Bill. The feeling she had for him was certainly new to her. Maybe the old memory lingered, seeing him lying helpless in the hospital bed, his rejection at that time of the baby who had been cut out of his brain-dead wife. He hadn't wanted the child at all. She remembered well what he had said about it then – even so, he had, it appeared to her, done his best for the child... and what trouble she had brought on him! Another baby to feed and clothe and pay for, no admitted father – and now further troubles, further anxieties for him. Incest, Stella marrying her own father. She hardly heard the girl's thanks and protestations of repayment.

'I'll pay it back, Agnes, I'll pay it back somehow,' Stella said.

Agnes stopped her almost abruptly. 'How does he expect you to get it to him? I presume he made some arrangements – and I also presume he wants money, not a cheque?'

Stella nodded, digging out a handkerchief, screwed-up and wet, and starting to dry her eyes.

'I'll let you have the money tomorrow. You can come over and see Bill and drop in on me.' Agnes had found herself purposely using the word 'Bill', not 'your father', to Stella.

She rose to leave, looking down at the girl's upturned grateful face. 'You do realize that if I judge Hebe Grant right, and probably I do, he'll come back for more?'

Stella nodded. 'Yes, I have thought of that, but at least this will satisfy him for the moment, Agnes. I just don't know how to thank you.'

Agnes left the café – she realized, rather abruptly. She would cash a cheque at her bank this afternoon and have the money ready for the stupid girl tomorrow, but meanwhile a plan was forming in her mind, vague, but it was forming. Just supposing she told Bill the whole story, Rick's part in the affair, Hebe Grant, his so-called daughter's deception at the mortuary, her lies to Miles about the child's supposed death, her own knowledge that Bruce was alive and well and happy. Would all this bring them closer or force them apart? Agnes favoured the former. Surely such shared knowledge . . . But the fact that Stella had lied to him, and the fact that all this knowledge came from her – would it drive them apart? After all it had been, Agnes believed, a criminal offence that Stella had committed. No. She was wrong. It must remain untold.

As she drove home, her usual well-tried practice of keeping knowledge to herself won – she would keep her own counsel. She always had. She would give Stella the money and wait. What did worry her, however, was that if this Hebe creature wanted more and Stella could not supply it, he might tell Bill everything.

As Agnes put the car away a decision had been reached, for the moment anyway. She had called at the bank on her way back and cashed a cheque; the money was ready. But if ever Hebe harassed Bill she would have to take other measures; what measures, Agnes at the moment had no idea. But something would work out for her, it always did.

Bill had heard nothing further from his agent about the film project. He telephoned him. 'Oh, they always take ages. Don't worry. We shall hear from them.' Bill suggested that George, his agent, telephone or write to jog their memory a bit. But his agent didn't like this idea at all. 'No, old man – don't show them we are anxious, for God's sake. Just let it rest until we hear. We shall, don't you worry.'

But Bill did worry. The excitement and his feeling that he was about to land a contract which would bring him in fairly big money had made him feel that poverty, or at least extreme poverty, was behind him.

Had he been too impulsive in asking Agnes to marry him? He certainly hoped not. To lose her now would be more than he could bear and her answer to his proposal had been just as fervent.

Bill had to comfort himself that his agent's assurance was probably right – the contract would be dealt with in their own time, and his bank balance would eventually be healthier. All these thoughts were going through his head as he made his way to meet Bryn for their usual beach walk.

The dog frolicked around them on the grass beside the sea wall. The tide was well in and the waves broke against the wall, but not high enough to send spray over Bill and Bryn as they strolled along in the rather uncertain sunshine. Bill liked these walks with Bryn. He would liked to tell him about Agnes and ask him what he thought about rich people marrying poor people, stuff like that. But he was repressed in his feelings. Money. She was too well off and he was too poor. Damn money and everything to do with it, he thought. At least he was relieved of Stella, but that too was on his mind. Genetically what would happen? Was Bruce's deafness anything to do with the fact that the sperm that had created him was that of his mother's father? Dear God, what a question! He shied away from it and talked about something else. After rambling on he was aware that Bryn Jones was looking at him with a questioning look.

'What's up, old man?' he asked.

Bill started and stopped the story he was recounting. 'Why?' he asked.

'Well, you told me that yarn yesterday and it's not like you to repeat yourself.' He laughed his genial, friendly laugh. Bill knew why he had slipped up on that piece of his story – on his mind was one question he did not want to ask his doctor friend, but then he forced himself.

'Bryn,' he said suddenly, 'in my next book I'm thinking of having a case of incest – the man rapes his daughter and she has a child. Would it be likely to be affected – you know, deformed or deficient in anything, even deaf?' Then he hastily added, 'Or blind?' He waited anxiously for the answer.

Bryn didn't seem to think the question very important, but before replying he picked up the piece of stick the dog had dropped and threw it a short way along the grass. 'No, I think not, Bill. After a lot of inbreeding, yes, perhaps, but no . . . And deafness or blindness – I've never heard of that as a sympton of inbreeding, old boy.'

'Good.'

'Well, that makes the plot well and truly all right, does it?'

Bill nodded anxiously. Bryn laughed. 'You authors! I bet you get yourselves in some tangles, eh?'

'We certainly do, Bryn.'

They paused and Bryn snapped on the dog's lead before they made their way across the road to their usual pub. Once there, they sat with their usual half-pints of bitter in front of them; both men had got the habit of two half-pints instead of one pint. There were many things that they agreed about. But Bill could not leave the subject alone, he had to ask some more questions. 'How about those tales of Glasgow, Bryn – you remember when the brothers made their sisters pregnant?'

Bryn took a pull at his beer, thanked the barman who had just put down a bowl of water for the dog, who drank thirstily, then accepted a crisp from Bill. 'Well, I can't tell you really, Bill. I suppose these family couplings produce their share of mentally or physically handicapped offspring, but I don't really know much about incest.'

Bill dropped the subject and let his mind return to Agnes. Sex had been good with her. He allowed himself a bit of self-congratulation, too – he had been good, and he thought she had enjoyed it. She wasn't the kind of woman to feign an orgasm, he was sure of that. He tried to suppress a complacent smile, but Bryn noticed it.

'I've solved the incest bit for you, have I, Bill? I shall expect a bottle of sherry for that.' He laughed. 'You look pleased with yourself now.'

Bill came back to earth. 'Yep, thanks, Bryn.' He picked up the glasses, which were now empty. 'I'll get the other half,' he said and made his way to the bar.

On the walk home after he'd left Bryn, Bill's mood changed a little again. It was all very well, but what would it ever be but a mirage? Would his book get made into a film? A film would be great, though. Could he cope with Stella's marriage? Agnes could, of that he was sure, but could he? After all, it was his fault that his wife had taken a lover.

By the time he arrived home he was low once more. Would he ever attain peace of mind again in his life? Would he always feel deeply guilty about Stella, Bruce even? He had never loved the child. Money. How glibly people said it didn't bring happiness. It would to him now – he'd be able to offer a good life to Agnes, to match her Porsche with a similar car of his own. Oh well...
He walked up his weedy drive trying not to look at the state of his front garden. For some reason Rick flashed across his mind. He wondered how he was making out in the US. Was it grinding him down, was he working as a soda jerk somewhere, or parking cars? Oh well. He slammed his door behind him and went into the study. At least Agnes had had enough faith in him to accept him.

21

Agnes had not slept very well; the meeting with Stella worried her. However, the source of her concern was not the telephone call from the blackmailer. It was Bill, and how he would be affected if Stella poured out her problems to him, which she might well do – Agnes was sure – if Hebe asked for more money after a short while. Blackmailers were never satisfied with one payment and, Agnes knew, went on and on demanding more and still more.

A plan was forming in her mind and was one of the reasons she had been unable to sleep. Surely she knew enough about this man Hebe to be able to frighten him. But how? Telephone? No – a letter, or maybe just a note perhaps, enclosed with the money. The money was ready. She had asked for an assortment of notes – £50, £20, £10 – although when she was asking for the assortment she had not then thought of enclosing anything else. Another idea had seeped into her mind during the night. She would put the money in a manilla envelope and the note, when she had composed it, in the middle, seal the envelope and tell Stella to hand it to him. He might, of course, open the packet just to check that it really was money, particularly if Stella gave it to him in a fairly private place. Stella had not yet told her where the meeting was to be.

Now the note – how to write it, compose it. Agnes had no typewriter now, but as she went into the kitchen to make herself a cup of coffee there on the kitchen chair was yesterday's *Daily Express*. Agnes's paper came late, the *Telegraph*, but her daily sometimes brought the *Express* with her to read while she was having her coffee break. She must have forgotten to put it back, as she usually did, into her capacious handbag.

Agnes made her coffee, took it through to the sitting-room with the newspaper and the kitchen scissors. In her desk she knew she had some sheets of typing paper and some glue. Her idea was crystallizing – her ideas usually did. The things she needed just came to her; when she wanted something, there always seemed to be the required implements ready to hand. It always happened and today seemed to be no exception, everything was there.

Agnes drank her coffee with enjoyment, then opened the *Express*, took up her scissors and began to turn over the pages to find the letters she needed. She did not realize that as she did so she was smiling.

The task was fiddly and took some time. Agnes took the sheet of typing paper – it was from a packet she had purchased long ago when she was engaged in a rather similar task, which she had also enjoyed, although on that occasion she had typed her message. This one, she felt, would look more dramatic. The result when she had finished was like the anonymous messages made this way that she had seen on television – indeed, it looked as dramatic as she had hoped.

When she was sure it had dried completely she folded the note carefully, making it narrower than the notes, and slipped it into the envelope in the middle of the money. The envelope was large enough to take the money flat and unfolded. She sealed it carefully. Only one risk, she thought, and that was that Hebe would take out all the notes to count them, but somehow she felt he wouldn't. Stella was too frightened to give him less than he had asked.

Agnes thought that he would have telephoned Stella by now, telling her the place to meet him to give him the money. Agnes hoped the meeting would be in a fairly public place so that careful examination of the contents of the envelope would not be easy and only a cursory glance would take place. Anyway, that was a risk that she, or actually Stella, would have to take. Stella would not of course know that there was anything but money in the envelope so she would hand it over innocently enough. Agnes could not foresee how the plan would work out.

Would Hebe be frightened that someone had seen him and the child? Maybe he would think it was Stella herself. The note warned him that no more money would be passed to him no matter how well off Stella's husband appeared to be. Somehow she didn't think he would put the note down to Stella. Anyway, she would have to wait and see. Meanwhile, one thing she was determined about: she would not give Stella any more money to pay this man.

Stella called in at about eleven o'clock looking white and strained; she took the sealed envelope with more thanks. 'Miles thinks I've come over just to see Daddy so I'd better call in,' she said.

'Of course, but not a word of this to Bill or I shall certainly regret helping you – you understand that, Stella?' Agnes's voice was firm and her expression serious.

'Oh no, I won't tell him. How could I, Agnes? He thinks it was Bruce in the mortuary. How could I mention anything to him that would make him . . . ?'

Agnes suddenly felt the urge to say to the girl, 'Well, anyway, it's really nothing to do with him. You're not really his daughter and Bruce is not his grandchild – you are all, all, nothing to him!' She resisted the urge, of course, and watched Stella walk down the driveway and out to the new car that Miles had just bought her.

Agnes wondered if Bill would call her that day, then decided to telephone him. 'Stella's just been in, only a half-minute visit but nice to see her,' Bill said. Agnes could hear the sound of a Hoover in the background. At least, she thought, there's someone to clean the house and perhaps tidy up and wash the kitchen floor which, when she had been in the house, had never been too clean. On impulse she added, 'Stella came here too, just for a minute. She's pleased with her new car.'

'Yes.' He sounded abstracted. 'I was talking to Bryn about, you know . . . the fact that Bruce . . . I told him it was part of the plot of my new book.'

Agnes stopped him. 'Do come in and have a scratch lunch with me, Bill. I'd love to hear what he said.'

'I'd like to, sweetheart. May I?'

'Yes, I'd really love you to, it's lonely without you.'

'Sweet. I'll be around in about half an hour.'

'Yes, bless you. Don't worry about Stella, Bill.'

There was a sigh on the other end of the telephone before he answered, 'I'll try not to, Agnes.'

Agnes flew round her kitchen. The anonymous note, the thousand pounds, Stella, Hebe, all were pushed right to the back of her mind. Only one thing mattered, Bill was coming to lunch. Thank God for the microwave.

Hebe saw Stella before she saw him. She was quite a good-looking piece, moved well. He noticed her in appreciation, the sway of her hips as she approached him. She had got out of her new red Mazda. Union Street was not an easy place to park but she had managed it. His own car was parked across the road. Hand over and a quick getaway was all he wanted. Hebe looked admiringly as she came up to him in the Arcade. Stella handed him the envelope; it felt thick. He flicked back the sealed flap with his thumbnail and looked inside. Satisfied, he slipped the envelope into the pocket of his thin navy anorak.

'How did you know – I mean, about Bruce?' Stella whispered the question, her eyes wide and curious.

'My business, girlie, my business.' He felt secure. She was scared of him and he liked women to be scared of him. He turned away. 'Cheers for now, gorgeous. You may hear from me again.' He walked quickly away, ran down the four steps from the Arcade to the pavement, crossed the road and got into his car. He looked back. Stella was still standing on the top step leading into the Arcade in partial shadow but there was enough light to allow her smooth fair hair to shine.

'Could fancy her,' Hebe said aloud then did up his seat belt, signalled and drew out into the busy street. The car in front of him braked, slowed, stopped to allow a man in a maroon BMW to back into a parking place. Hebe waited with more patience than was normal to him. He patted the slight bulge in his anorak pocket. Nice to have money. Now he had a boat to meet and a dangerous packet to collect. It was Big E for sale at tonight's rave. He hoped to turn the money Stella had just handed to him into four times that amount. The kids were good payers. 'No money, no honey,' that's what he said to them. 'No money, no honey.' They'd get the money – steal it, even graft for it sometimes. 'Please, Hebe, I can't pay tonight but I'll have it tomorrow.' That cut no ice with him, no ice at all. He could do anything with the kids who were on junk, anything. Make 'em fetch and carry, bend over, though he wasn't much for that, preferred regular sex. That was easy to get too. He put up a hand and caressed his ear-ring.

He was longing to get back to London, this place was rustic. Still, he'd leave it a bit longer. The fuzz wouldn't let him alone if they got wind he was back – not yet.

He parked the car on the front and walked; he needed the exercise. He was proud of his body, didn't want to put on flab. He made for the entrance of the hovercraft. The breeze was pleasant. Two giggly girls passed him. One was very pretty; she looked at him and he looked back at her, their eyes locked for a couple of seconds, just long enough for him to see a flush of admiration and note that her eyes were greeny grey. If he hadn't got a boat to meet he might have picked her up. He looked at his watch, ten minutes, he could do it easily – he wasn't that far away. Feeling confident and powerful he strode on.

The catamaran was coming in when he got there. He watched

carefully as the passengers got off. His contact was well known to him. The Old Man, that's what he was called. He wasn't old at all but his hair was snow white though he was only thirty-five. He was a furtive bloke. Hebe supposed it was carrying drugs that made him look around him carefully. The cat was empty, all the passengers had disembarked. He was not there; what about tonight? He'd got to have the stuff. He'd have to meet the next boat, and the next. He went into the waiting-room. It was empty. He took out the envelope and looked at the notes, riffled through them, and then saw a folded piece of paper. He took it out and read it. Suddenly he felt slightly sick and he also felt a sweat break out on his upper lip. The note said, KIDNAPPING IS A CRIMINAL OFFENCE PUNISHABLE WITH LIFE IMPRISONMENT.

Who knew? Who knew? Had Rick shopped him? No, never. It couldn't be Stella, she wouldn't dare, he knew too much about her. There was only one person – her father, Bill Turner. He had given her the money and put this in the envelope. He looked around him, there was nobody there. He smoothed out the letter and examined it again. Letters cut from a newspaper, stuck on. Yes, yes, stuck on typing paper and who used that but an author, bloody Bill Turner. He'd get him for this. The nerve of it, putting the note in with the money. Clever, too clever.

The Old Man was on the next cat. He came off, furtive as Hebe had remembered. He didn't greet Hebe at all; as Hebe turned he walked behind him to his car. Hebe unlocked the door and slid into the driver's seat; the Old Man walked round the car and got in. He was carrying a light mackintosh draped over his arm. He dived into a pocket of the mac and took out a small black packet, which he put in the glove compartment. Hebe knew his companion well enough not to examine the packet. He glanced sideways. 'One thousand,' he said. Hebe nodded and handed him the envelope, the anonymous letter having been thrust into the pocket of his jeans. It seemed to be burning a hole there. The Old Man did not attempt to count the money but slipped the envelope into his breast pocket. 'Ta,' he said, reached for the door handle and got out of the car. 'See you,' he said, raising a hand and touching the glass of the window, one thumb in the air, then he was gone.

Hebe drove back to his flat. The exchange with the Old Man had calmed him but the letter in his pocket was still there and he could picture it in his mind's eye. He stopped at the traffic lights; he could even see it on the back of the car in front of him, picture the cut-out letters. The IS was a little crooked, slanted a little. The

CRIMINAL was small, a word cut from the paper in its entirety, not made up in bits. His hatred for Bill Turner began to seethe. What a crafty way to try and tackle him... him... Hebe. To give his daughter the money with that note enclosed. What did he intend? To blackmail back? But how much had he seen? Had he actually been peering down from an upstairs window whilst they loaded the child into his car? Had he seen Rick? Yes, of course he must have, and not mentioned it to him, just let him go off to the States. He didn't want the kid so he had just let them take him. How low can you get!

The red car in front started off when the lights changed. By God, he must be a ruthless son of a bitch. To let the kid go like that, not raising the alarm. He'd deal with him – he'd deal with bloody Bill Turner. How, he didn't know, not yet, but he'd fix him and fix him good!

22

Bill was a little late coming in for what Agnes had called on the telephone 'a scratch lunch'. She was rather glad, although she was longing to see him – the very thought that he would soon be coming through her welcoming front door thrilled her. She was glad too that her habit of making meals and freezing them had not died away or deteriorated now she was alone and had hardly any guests.

In Penny Stratton, the ill-fated village that she had lived in before she came here, people did drop in but usually for a drink or a cup of coffee – sometimes lunch but not very often. Nevertheless, she had always been ready and the making of meals for two or three had persisted.

She had decided to give Bill corned beef hash – men loved that, at least a couple of her men friends had in the past. That and an apple pie and cream. She had almost finished her preparations and was cutting slices of Cheddar cheese to go with the apple pie; some people, she knew, liked that – a piece of information she had gained lately from a magazine and heard, too, from North Country nurses.

'Agnes, may I come in?' Bill stood for a second at the door.

She walked into the hall to greet him, a little uncertain, a little diffident; shades of the old insecure Agnes would often overtake her even now. But there was nothing uncertain or diffident about Bill. He kicked the door shut behind him and immediately took her in his arms. He smelled of tobacco, she loved the smell. His kiss was passionate and Agnes returned it as passionately.

'Oh my darling, I love you.' He still held her tightly and Agnes put her hands over his shoulders and caressed the short bristly hair at the back of his neck. At last they drew apart.

Agnes was breathless. 'What is happening to us, Bill? Whatever it is, it's wonderful.'

'We've fallen in love, a situation which my dear, so-called daughter would find almost impossible to believe and probably laugh at.' He paused, then a look of pain crossed his face. 'It's strange, isn't it, to think that her own father has fallen in love with her. Little does she know!'

Agnes shook her head. There was a bitterness in Bill's voice she did not want to hear; she wanted him to be totally happy. 'Now, darling, they don't know. They're happy. Don't worry, or anyway try not to worry about them.'

'You've helped me, Agnes, you don't know how much.' He paused and again Agnes was struck by the sudden change of his expression as he looked at her.

'Come through to the sitting-room, darling, and I'll get us a drink,' she said. He went through and sat down on the settee and was about to speak. She thought he was about to talk more about Stella and she stopped him. 'No, don't say anything else. Just let me get us a drink, there's a dear.' She came back quickly with the two glasses.

Bill was still seated on the settee; he looked so comfortable and right, she thought. She sat down beside him. There was a little frown between his eyebrows. 'Is anything the matter, Bill?' she asked. She felt so sensitive to his every mood.

He sipped his drink, then put the glass down. 'It was probably nothing but I had rather a strange phone call – a wrong number, I expect!'

'How was it strange, Bill?'

Bill stroked his hair back, first one side and then the other, just above his ears, a gesture that Agnes was growing to love as well as recognize. His hair was thick and slightly wavy but he, as did most men, tried to make it smooth, take out the wave.

'Well, it was some man, he said something about a note. Why had I put it in some money or something. I couldn't get the gist. He had obviously got the wrong number and thought he was talking to someone else. He sounded a tough sort of bloke. I tried to interrupt him but he wouldn't listen to me.'

During this speech Agnes had felt herself freeze. Oh God, why hadn't she thought of this when she had given the money to Stella, when she had so gleefully made up her note? Of course that awful Hebe man might well think it was . . . Probably he felt sure it was Stella's father who had given her the thousand pounds and included the note . . . Hebe would think that Bill had seen the kidnapping!

'What is it, darling? You've gone quite pale.' Bill put his hand on hers. 'It was nothing,' he went on, 'just a telephone caller who had got the number wrong, nothing to worry about at all. I wish I hadn't told you.'

For a second or two Agnes could hardly speak, hardly answer him. The consequences of what she had done whirled round in her head. The type of man Hebe was might retaliate in response to what he assumed to be Bill's threat, might really think that Bill had seen the child being abducted. How else could he think Bill knew? Hebe was a drug-pusher, a child-abductor, maybe a child-abuser. That kind of man would stop at nothing. She had unwittingly placed the man she was to marry in terrible danger.

'Bill . . . ' She placed her hand over his, then her heart failed her. If she said anything, what good would it do? At the moment he thought the call was just a crank call or a wrong number, nothing of importance. She couldn't tell him anything. She gave Bill's hand a little squeeze then got up.

'I must see to lunch, darling,' she said and tried to smile down at him. Her mouth felt dry. She realized more acutely than she had done before how much she was in love with this man . . . and by that note and that money what might she have done to him! The feeling she had for Bill was like nothing she had experienced before. The thought that she might have put him into such a situation almost panicked her. This must have shown in her manner for Bill said again, 'Don't worry, Agnes, about that call – it was nothing.'

Agnes left him and made her way into the kitchen and stood for a moment looking out into the back garden. She couldn't see the garden; she could see nothing but the terrible picture of Hebe harming Bill, blackmailing him . . . and Bill had no money. Or perhaps threatening him with a knife or with a revolver or anything . . . She must pull herself together. She went and opened the oven; the lunch was ready and she had to be ready to serve it and act as normally as she was able.

*

The lunch served, Agnes watched with pleasure, in spite of her anxiety, Bill's enjoyment of the corned beef hash and afterwards the apple pie and cheese. Hardly a healthy lunch, she admitted, but it was such a joy to see his almost boyish appreciation of the apple pie liberally accompanied by cream.

When he had finished he leaned forward and grinned at her affectionately. 'If that is one of your scratch meals, sweetheart, I daren't think what one of your carefully thought up meals would be like!'

Agnes smiled. 'We'll find that out soon, darling,' she said. She had managed, in spite of her worry about the telephone call, to eat her own lunch but they were rather small helpings. She was about to leave the table and go and perc the coffee when she remembered. 'Oh Bill, you were going to tell me about your talk to your doctor friend about Bruce.'

Bill shook his head. 'Yes, I meant to tell you, Agnes, but that telephone call rather put it out of my head.'

'Well, don't let's talk over the dirty dishes.' Agnes started to clear the table and Bill helped her carry the few plates and cutlery out to the kitchen.

The coffee was already percolating on a low heat. Bill looked round the immaculate kitchen. He made a face. 'A bit different from my kitchen,' he said a trace glumly.

'Well, this is a woman's kitchen. You do very well in yours. I'm sure Stella did her best; after all, teenagers are hardly as tidy as older people.'

'Well, between me and Rick and Stella, and with a little help from the cleaning lady, it didn't stand much chance; we were all at fault.'

As Agnes loaded up the coffee tray he stood behind her, put his arms round her and kissed the back of her neck. She felt a shiver of delight run through her body and turned in his arms till their mouths met. His tongue parted her lips and she opened her mouth, then pulled back. 'Coffee and tell,' she said and her voice was soft and loving. He nodded.

'Let me take the tray.' He released her.

They went into the sitting-room and out through the french windows to sit on the white chairs under the umbrella. The day was quite warm for autumn. A slight pleasant breeze ruffled Agnes's hair. She poured the coffee and handed a cup to Bill, and prepared to listen to what he had learned from his doctor friend.

'Well, he thought Bruce's deafness was unlikely to be due to the fact that Miles was –'

Agnes broke in. 'I'm glad. I didn't think it was hereditary, Bill, but of course you didn't tell him –'

This time it was Bill's turn to interrupt her. 'No, darling, I just said it was part of a plot in my latest book, but . . . ' He stopped.

'Yes, Bill?' He looked so serious and seemed almost reluctant to speak, then he appeared to pluck up courage for the next sentence.

'This morning when Bryn called to bring me a book he had promised me he met Stella for the first time. As you know she was in a great rush, but she was very sweet and polite with him and after she left he said, "Well, she's a very pretty girl, Bill, and she's like you. There's a strong family resemblance." It really surprised me, Agnes, but I'm trying not to read too much into his remark – after all, it's something that anyone might say.'

Agnes was silent for a moment. 'A strong family resemblance' didn't mean much, she thought, and she personally had not noticed such a resemblance. 'Could she be your child, Bill? I mean, did you . . . ?' She found the question embarrassing, or was it perhaps that she shied away from wanting to think of Bill having sex with anyone else – even his wife?

Bill understood her unfinished remark. 'Oh yes, Agnes, we went on trying. Estelle wanted a child so much that I suppose I always hoped that maybe . . . Wouldn't it be wonderful, Agnes, if I was her father and Miles was not?' He seemed to suddenly realize that Agnes was looking away from him. 'Oh, I'm sorry, darling – it's boring for you listening to my troubles and problems.'

Agnes turned quickly back to him. 'Your troubles and problems are mine too, Bill,' she said. She had been thinking of Hebe and the note, Stella's lie about her child's corpse. They were problems that she was not sharing with him; she was carrying them for him entirely alone. Really, the relationship between Miles and Stella was just one problem, one of many, but it was the only one Bill knew about.

He went on. 'I asked him about a blood test – purely for the plot of my new book, of course – but he said that would be no use as proof of fatherhood. If Stella, or the child in my book rather, had a blood test and compared it with a test from Miles, then all it would show would be that he was not her father, which of course is what I would love to prove – but however can we?'

Agnes nodded slowly. 'I know blood tests show only negative parentage, but you could hardly ask for one!'

Bill sighed. 'Well, there's no chance of us learning even that. I'll have to live with it, I suppose, Agnes, try to forget that there may be such a relationship – but Bryn's remark did make me hope a little.'

'Of course it did, darling, I can understand that.'

Bill took her hand. 'You understand so much and are so sympathetic, Agnes.' Agnes half resisted as he got up from his chair and said, 'Shall we go upstairs?'

'Only on one condition, Bill dear.' Agnes remained seated, Bill holding both her hands.

'What condition is that?'

'That you marry me before you wait for the film company to decide – it may take ages.'

'Do you really mean that?'

Agnes got up. 'I do mean it, Bill. I don't want to lose you now I've found you.'

They kissed again and he leant back to get a better view of her face, smiling. 'You're not marrying me for my money then, just my literary genius.'

Agnes laughed. 'What else, Bill?' she said. Their arms entwined, they went back inside.

After Bill had gone back to his house to do some work, as he always put it, Agnes went into her garden. She felt quiet, safe and satisfied. No more loneliness, no more. Her love for Bill was a gentle thing and his love for her surrounded her like warm air. She felt like constantly smiling. Even the thought of Stella and Miles, of Stella's trouble, did not ruffle her complacency. Only one thing did – she was still upset about the telephone call! She wondered whether Hebe would try again – try what again? A telephone call to extract more money? She didn't know what Hebe was capable of; she couldn't read his mind and decide what he would do. One thing did make her a little more anxious – would he call on Bill? Bill wouldn't even recognize him or understand what the unknown man was accusing him of. What note? What money?

Agnes could almost picture the scene. The white-faced Hebe – yes, he did look capable of anything. She must watch over and protect Bill. She felt again his arms around her. She knew his feeling of guilt about Stella and Miles would never leave him and, no matter what people said, if Stella became pregnant he would worry and worry about the child – would it be normal? That remark of his doctor friend, Bryn, about the family resemblance had raised his hopes a little. If only there was some way she could take that care away from him and make Hebe's threats disappear should they rise again! She hoped that fate would help her as it so often had.

As the day grew dark and she prepared for bed her happiness for herself and Bill remained intact and comforting. She realized, of course, they must tell Stella and Miles about their marriage. She settled into bed; she was suddenly certain that all would be well. What gave birth to such a certainty she had no idea. Something would happen, she knew it! She had had this feeling before and it had always proved correct; she had been able to cope with the situation herself. Where it came from, this certainty, she didn't know. So confident was she in it that she fell asleep almost at once.

23

Hebe, meanwhile, in his rather grotty flat, was feeling no such confidence. The call he had made to Bill and the answer he received had thrown him, though only slightly; he did not believe Stella would have approached Miles for £1,000 without giving him some good reason, but a father surely was a different matter. Probably she could tell him anything, get anything out of him. But Bill Turner had sounded genuinely puzzled on the phone, as if he really didn't know what Hebe was talking about. He'd have to approach him again – after all, it must be him. Bill Turner might know about the kidnapping, he might have seen it, but only Hebe knew about his daughter's wrong identification. Did one bit of knowledge cancel out the other? What a bloody muddle.

Anyway, he thought, he would wait a couple of days and then call on him, face him with the complete denial of the abduction or perhaps beat the old bastard up. Not his style really, but he knew one or two druggies who might oblige and do the job for him – then he would have to pop up to the Big Smoke, too. But was it a good idea? He threw his cigarette end across the room; it smouldered on the carpet. He crossed the room and ground the butt into the floor. It was a right bugger. He knew about Stella and her bit of criminal activity and Bill Turner apparently knew about his and Rick's job. Hebe shrugged his shoulders and ignored the thin spiral of smoke still coming up from his cigarette end. He must get in first, really frighten him. Anyway, if Bill knew about Stella's lie he would pay to have it kept quiet, no matter what. And if he knew, and had seen him and Rick kidnapping Bruce, as it said in the note, why the hell hadn't he reported it, called the police then and there? Why keep it to himself?

He felt he'd like to give up the whole set-up. He had some money still, but the latest thousand wasn't much, not enough.

He planned to go back to London, but he'd want about £100,000 – that would get him a little down-beat flat somewhere, but not much else. Yes, he'd give it a couple of days then go and see Turner. Maybe he'd ring Stella again, but after he'd seen her father, find out what reason she had given to get £1,000 out of him. He saw the spiralling smoke coming from the patchy carpet, picked up a glass which had contained beer and still had a little in the bottom and poured it over the stub. Psst, it went out. A black patch formed on the carpet. Well, it wasn't his bloody flat. He felt he must get out; he grabbed his jacket, banged the door behind him and made for the Horse and Groom, a pub he had fancied recently. After all there was a rave night; he couldn't really leave anyone else in charge, he'd have to see to it himself. Blast it. And for what? Peanuts. Wasn't really worth the trouble and bother – selling kids was much more profitable, but even then you'd got to find the kids or the mothers.

The rave night and his club were pretty quiet until about a quarter past eleven when a large crowd came in, obviously mainlanders. There were about twenty youths and four or five girls. They looked round at the room, the lights, the soft drink bar; Hebe had no licence. Some sneered, some sniggered.

'Let's get booze, eh?' one said. 'This is boresville plus.' There was a short consultation, money changed hands, then four youths pushed off into the night again. The two that Hebe hired to serve behind the bar looked at him. Hebe shrugged. A girl came up close to him and looked up into his face.

'Any bags going?' she said, looking at him with a trace of admiration, which Hebe was quick to notice.

'Bags?' he asked, feigning innocence.

'Oh come on, there's always something in this joint.' She

touched his lapel with a bright blue painted nail. 'Big E perhaps, crack, even hash?' Hebe's eyes narrowed. 'No money, no honey, baby dear.' He smiled at her.

'Nice suit'. The painted nail traced down his lapel. More kids were coming in now, to Hebe's relief. He'd spent quite a lot on dope for tonight. He'd have to make a decent profit, that was important. He hoped they were loaded.

The girl's mascaraed eyes were unwavering. 'I've money for honey,' she said, pursing her lips and making a kissing sound. She followed him to the bar. He went behind it, pretended to get the stuff from behind the tins; obviously it wasn't there but he made out it was – he always kept it in his pocket, it was safer there. Hebe trusted no one. The girl sat on a bar stool, her hands under her chin, elbows propped on the bar counter. Hebe pushed his hand towards her. Under it was a tiny plastic bag; inside, one white tablet. He tipped his hand sideways. She lowered her eyes, saw the packet then raised them again. 'E?' Hebe nodded. 'How much?' she asked, putting forefinger and thumb in her cleavage.

'£10,' he answered softly. Then at her obvious easy acceptance of the price he wished he'd said £20. She slid two notes under her hand, imitating Hebe's movement. Their hands touched. Hebe put his hand on hers for a second and took the money.

The girl's heavily lipsticked lips smiled, revealing white even teeth. 'Ta.' She palmed the packet. 'Is there drink anywhere?'

Hebe felt he liked this woman. He moved up to the end of the bar and she followed him on the other side. The strobe lights were flashing round the big space, the floor was full of gyrating kids. The group playing was getting into its stride, the noise increasing. Hebe had been promised a singer with the group, but so far none had turned up.

'Gin and tonic?' He looked at the girl again. Her hair was ear length, bushy, straight; a fringe came nearly down to her eyes.

'Oh God – no beer?' she said. Hebe poured a G and T from his private hiding place under the bar.

'Nope.' Hebe handed her the glass. She sipped, wrinkling her nose.

'Must get on.' Hebe went back to the middle of the bar where a pale-faced youth stood, hand resting on the shiny counter top, fingers tapping impatiently. Hebe knew the signs, he knew the boy. Sometimes the kid had money, sometimes he hadn't. He was into crack but Hebe didn't push that particular drug. He had once but found that cracksters were apt to run amok and smash the chairs and tables, so the pale-faced youth would have to make do with heroin or nothing. He pushed the money over the counter much as the girl had; his hand was covered with letters made with a biro spelling Hate, his nails were dirty. He accepted the tiny bag of white powder but made no comment. Hebe thought he was pretty strung out. He made for the lavatory, taking a packet from his pocket as he went. Hebe guessed he was going to shoot up. Well, let him, it was no business of his how he took the stuff, snorting or shooting.

Hebe treated all druggies with contempt. They were hooked and anyone who could be hooked on anything was a fool – it made them vulnerable to others, they got in other people's power.

More money and more Ecstasy went over the counter; more heroin and a few uppers for the kids who hadn't really got into the hard stuff yet. The four Mainlanders had returned from the pub carrying a few six-packs of lager. They joined up with the others and the dark girl with the blue nails joined them too. Out of the corner of his eye Hebe had seen her splitting the plastic bag, popping the pill into her mouth and gulping it down. She then slid off the stool and joined the fifteen or so tough-looking guys who had just come in. Their T-shirts were all different. One had 'Murders OK' printed in large black letters on the white material. Another had 'Suicide is Self-Expression', another 'Deny me Nothing'. After that Hebe lost interest in reading the things. You could have anything put on a T-shirt in the High Street, even in Ryde. So these shirts were no big deal really.

Another girl had come in after them, big-breasted. Hebe did read her printed message, 'Touch These and You're Dead'. Hebe sighed, he was bored. The raves were always the same, the same type of crowd, predictable. They were all trying to be different, to dress differently, but they didn't, they all ended up alike – T-shirts, washed-out jeans, faded. That's why he liked his well-tailored suit, his neat hair-style, his split gold ear-ring. He fancied the dark-haired girl, though – but she was obviously with a burly-looking bloke with a very short haircut almost like the old American crew-cut, who was wearing a black seamless jumper, a gold necklace round his thick neck and a matching bracelet. Both looked like real gold to Hebe. Whether the dark girl had told him Hebe had given her a gin and tonic he didn't know, but the burly one looked at him now and again belligerently, a look full of malice – not a man to mess with.

As the evening wore on Hebe began to feel lower, more

depressed, sick of the dancing kids, the noise, even selling the drugs, though he'd made a nice bit of money – not enough, but a nice bit. He automatically went on pushing, pushing, pushing, assessing each buyer with a practised eye, and looking round all the time for the cops. The noise, the dancing, dragged on. The Island kids weren't really ravers, not like London or Brum or even Edinburgh. He'd tried them all. Selling illegitimate babies was the best – tricky but not so damned boring. Oh boy, that brought his thoughts back to the note. He had got to see to that; go and see that bloody writer, Stella's father, Bill – what was it? Turner.

A scrawny young girl touched his arm. 'I'll pay next week, Hebe.' Her eyes were pleading; she was pretty but spaced out. Hebe recognized the symptoms. As usual, 'No money, no honey, pussy,' he said and felt a frisson of enjoyment at the anxiety on her face.

'I'm hurting, Hebe, really hurting. I need a fix, please.'

He walked away, crossing the room, looking this way and that, keeping his eye on everything. The girl made no attempt to follow him.

The rave was disintegrating. Two o'clock, he tried to get them all out by that time, he didn't want the pigs around moaning about noise. Two kids were snogging on the steps leading to the loo and were oblivious to everything. He went up to them. 'Time to split, lovers,' he said.

They broke apart and hand in hand made for the door. Gradually the hall cleared. The barman wiped the counter for the last time, picked up a box clattering with empty drink cans to take outside. The dark girl and the boys drifted out.

'Night.' The barman picked up the money Hebe had put on the counter – his night's pay – and went, slamming the door noisily behind him. The other soon followed.

Hebe lit a cigarette, went and locked the door, checked the loos for druggies, poured himself a gin and tonic and sat down to count the money. The drink was heavy on gin and short on tonic, he felt like that. His mood of depression persisted in spite of the drink. The lights were switched off; only a single light over the bar remained. He paid the group and they departed. He wouldn't give them the full amount because the singer hadn't turned up and they hadn't been all that good, but there wasn't much to choose from in this goddamned place. He downed the gin, wiped his mouth with the back of his hand and switched off the remaining light. He was right out of drugs, would have to get some more the day after tomorrow. He put his hand in his pocket, one tiny packet remained. Well, the takings weren't bad – middling, he supposed. Oh well.

He crossed the dark space. Now that it was empty his footsteps echoed. He opened the door, closed it behind him, turned and locked the padlock, and then the resolution flashed into his mind. He wouldn't wait any more, he'd go and see Bill Turner tomorrow, in the morning and have it out with him. He checked the padlock then walked to his car.

As he got in he fingered the last remaining packet in his pocket. He might even use it himself just before he visited Stella's bloody father. He hadn't the habit, rarely took anything, but tomorrow he might try a fix. For his size and build he knew he wasn't in all that good shape for a punch-up. He closed the door behind him. Besides, the heroin might pep him up a bit, make him more aggressive – more like that burly-looking bloke who'd been with the dark girl.

He started the engine, leaned back a moment; he still felt tired and dispirited. For some reason the dark-haired girl with her pouting mouth and blue nails kept coming back into his mind. He wouldn't mind giving her one, but that bloke she was with seemed to own her, wouldn't take kindly to any competition even if they ever came back; probably wouldn't, though.

He opened the glove compartment. Some cigarettes fell out and an empty matchbox, some sweet wrappers. He felt at the back of the little compartment and his hand closed over a large fat object, leather-covered. A flick knife, might come in useful tomorrow. He pocketed it, slapped the little door back and drove home.

24

'What is it, darling? You're looking so pensive and sad.' Miles sat down beside Stella and put an arm round her waist. She almost jumped at the sound of his voice. She was sitting on the hotel balcony outside their room, her eyes fixed on the yachts: their yellow and white striped sails made a lovely picture. She was not taking in the scene at all. At that moment the beauty and the colour of the sea and the yachts meant nothing to her. Her thoughts were dominated by the thought of Bruce and the lie that had ensured he was presumed dead. The search was still going on for the other little boy, the one she had identified as her son, but no trace of a child had been found.

From the account she had read in the papers he had been a poor unwanted little chap with a mother who was a drug addict and an alcoholic father who had left the mother when the child was a baby. She could not remember all of it except that he had spent most of his time being fostered or in a home. Where was Bruce's body? She always thought of it as 'Bruce's body' for she was certain he was dead. Looking for the other child, mistakenly, as they had been for so long, why had they not found Bruce? That thought always frightened her. She didn't know how long it took for a body to become unrecognizable and she hated herself for praying that Bruce would never be found or, if they did find him, they would never know who it was.

It was at that moment in her thoughts that Miles's voice had broken in and she answered him. 'Nothing, darling. I was just watching the yachts – they look so pretty.' She smiled at him, trying to make her smile bright and natural.

'You're beautiful.' He kissed her and she was about to return his kiss when the telephone summoned Miles back into their room. Stella listened, fearful. All telephone calls now made her anxious: thoughts of Hebe; thoughts of Bruce.

'Oh really, Bill? That's wonderful! Congratulations. I'll call Stella. I'm so pleased for you.' He put the phone down and came out on to the balcony, his smile wide. 'Your father wants to break some wonderful news to you, darling.'

Stella left the balcony and crossed the room, thinking that he'd sold a book to a film or TV company. She picked up the receiver. 'Yes, Dad?' she said. 'Dad! What wonderful news! Agnes and you are going to be married! How great!' Stella put her hand over the receiver and looked towards Miles who was standing watching her. 'Did he tell you?' she asked. Miles nodded.

Stella took her hand from the receiver and spoke to her father again. 'We are so pleased, we must have a celebration straight away. Are you engaged? Are you going to give her a ring? Have you thought when you're going to be married? Have you fixed a date for the wedding?'

Miles came forward towards her. 'Give them a chance! I expect they've only just –'

'Daddy, I'm so pleased. I'm so very fond of Agnes – can I ring her and say . . .' She listened to her father's voice for a second or two, then: 'Right, I will, it's wonderful news. We'll come over and see you both – when? This morning – champagne? Yes, of course.' She put the receiver back on its rack. 'Daddy wants us to go over at about twelve o'clock. He's got champagne. And what do you think? A film company may be taking one of his books!'

'Good, we'll take a bottle too. What time is it now?' He glanced at his watch. 'Ten thirty.' There was a knock on their door. 'Oh, that will be room service. You looked so comfortable on the balcony I thought I'd join you and I've ordered some coffee for us.' The coffee was wheeled in, the waiter tipped, and Stella and Miles resumed their seats on the balcony.

'Miles, I'm so pleased for Dad. Agnes will be just right for him. Poor Daddy, he hasn't had much luck in life, what with me and . . .'

Miles poured the coffee, but paused to stroke her shoulder fondly.

'I'm so glad Daddy has had a film offer at last. I hope he makes a pile of money. Agnes is quite rich, don't you think, darling?'

Miles nodded but was reassuring. 'Somehow I don't think that will matter – whether either one is richer or poorer than the other. I don't think it will make any difference to Agnes or to Bill, darling.'

At half past eleven Miles and Stella set off for Ryde. In the back of the car lay a bottle of champagne carefully wrapped up. Miles stopped by a florist in Cowes and Stella chose a bunch of twelve yellow roses for Agnes. She was smiling with happiness; her other anxieties had faded into the background of her mind. She cradled the roses in her arm as she got back into the car. 'Oh isn't it wonderful! If only they're as happy as we are.'

Miles turned and kissed her lips and the scent of the yellow roses wafted around them like a fragrant cloud.

When they arrived at Bill's house Agnes was already there. Stella rushed over and kissed her on both cheeks, giving her a big hug. 'Oh Agnes, I'm so thrilled.'

Her delight was so genuine and unforced that it pleased Agnes. Miles, slightly more formal, shook Bill's hand. 'Congratulations, Bill, great news.' He then went over to Agnes and took her hand, but Stella burst out in her impulsive way, 'Oh Miles, gives Agnes a kiss too. Don't be stuffy, darling, she's one of the family now.' She turned to her father. 'And a film, too, Daddy!'

Agnes offered her cheek to Miles with a smile.

The champagne was poured. Miles stepped through to the

kitchen and popped his bottle into the refrigerator – noting with some dismay that it was almost empty. It contained just a sad-looking lettuce, a tub of margarine and a rather ancient pack of bacon. Thank goodness Bill would have someone to look after him, he thought. He was so happy with Stella that he wanted everyone else to have the same.

They drank the champagne and ate the crisps and little squares of cheese and biscuits that Agnes had brought round with her. Soon the second bottle was opened. The first excitement had subsided a little and everyone had grown more quiet.

'When are you going to be married, Daddy?' Stella asked the question again.

Bill looked at Agnes. 'Any ideas, dearest?' he asked.

Agnes took his hand and looked at Stella. 'As soon as possible, Stella. I don't want him to get away.' She laughed; she surprised herself. Never before had she felt so contented, so secure and so sure that what she was doing was absolutely right – never had she felt so in love.

Their conversation was interrupted by a ring on the door bell. The bell in Bill's house never worked properly, it always gave a sort of croaky sound.

'I'll go.' Stella sprang up and crossed the hall to the front door. 'Hebe!' Agnes heard Stella's startled exclamation. Her heart sank. What did he want? Was he going to face Bill with a note he knew nothing about? Thank God Miles and she and Stella were with Bill.

'I want to see your father.'

They heard footsteps crossing the hall, then Hebe stood in the doorway of the sitting-room.

'Who are you and what do you want?' Bill's voice was brusque.

Hebe looked at each person in turn and recognized Agnes and Miles. He did not speak to or even acknowledge any of them. He immediately confronted Bill. 'Are you Stella's father?'

Bill did not answer him but turned to Stella. 'Do you know this man?'

Miles answered for his wife. 'Yes, we met him, at least I met him, for the first time one evening at the hotel. He was dining there.'

Hebe broke in. 'I'd like a private word with you, Turner.'

Agnes looked at Stella, whose face had drained of colour. 'Oh Daddy – no!' she said. 'Don't have anything to do with him. It's nothing to do with you.'

'Very well, let it not be in private then.' Hebe's voice was menacing. He put his hand into the pocket of his jacket, took out a piece of paper and handed it to Bill.

Agnes recognized what it was by its shape and size – the anonymous note she had made up to go into the envelope with the money. He had found it as she hoped he would, but she realized that she had not thought her action through. It was Bill he suspected of including the note. She almost stepped forward to confess her part in the affair but Hebe did not give her time to speak.

'Look at this.' He pushed the paper further towards Bill. 'Read it.'

'What is it?' Bill took the note from Hebe's hand and was about to reach into his breast pocket for his reading glasses when the contents of the note, as he opened it, reached his eye and he realized he had no need of spectacles to read the large printed letters. 'What does it mean?'

'You sent this to me in the money. Your daughter delivered it and I don't think she knew you'd put it there.'

Bill's irritation obviously grew. 'What the hell do you mean – note, money? I've never sent you any money or any note.'

'You're accusing me, practically saying you saw me kidnap your grandson.'

Agnes looked at Hebe more closely. The pupils of his eyes gave him away. He was doped and, she thought, dangerous.

Stella went and grasped Hebe's arm. Hebe shook her off. Bill controlled his voice and manner. 'Look, young man, I have sent you no money, no note. When Bruce was lost he was not kidnapped – he wandered away and was found drowned under the pier. You know that – it was in the papers.'

Hebe was silent for a moment.

Bill went on, 'I simply don't know what you are talking about, so will you please leave my house – or shall I call the police to evict you?'

Miles moved over and stood beside Bill. When Hebe did not attempt to leave he said quietly, 'I suggest you do as Mr Turner says.'

Again Hebe did not move. His narrowed eyes were fixed on Bill Turner almost as if there was no one else in the room.

Stella said, 'Hebe.' She might as well have not spoken by the notice taken of her almost pleading tone. He remained perfectly still.

Agnes moved a little closer and in doing so she got a better and closer look at Hebe's face. It was as white as she remembered it when she had met him at the Gloucester Hotel. His lips, too, were almost colourless and at the moment pressed tightly together. It was his eyes, however, that alarmed her. They were bright and the pupils contracted to a pin-point in size. That and his aggressive manner made her guess he was high. Either he had taken something before confronting Bill or he was an habitual drug-taker. Either way she felt there was a danger that he could act violently and with malice.

His hands, white as his face, hung harmlessly enough, the fingers slightly clenched. He remained quite still and silent for a few moments, then turned his head a little as his gaze drifted over the four people in front of him; the narrow, bright eyes lingered on Stella, Agnes and Miles almost without interest, then returned to Bill.

'Kidnapping is a criminal offence. What does that mean? Is that a trick to accuse me of something? Why did you send it?' Hebe's voice was low and hoarse. Whether it was a threat or not Agnes was not sure, but Hebe raised a clenched fist. Miles stepped between Bill and his aggressor. Bill tried to push Miles aside, his temper roused.

'I've already told you I know nothing about the money or the note you are talking about. I don't know you. Will you leave, please.'

Miles interrupted. 'Shall I ring the police, Bill?' he asked.

'Yes, please, do, Miles.'

Miles took two or three steps towards the telephone.

'You will regret it if you do, Turner.' Hebe's voice was clearer, louder.

Agnes's and Stella's eyes met. Agnes could see the fear in the girl's eyes.

'Miles – please don't get the police in.' Stella said.

'Why, darling?' Miles looked puzzled.

Before she had time to give her reason Bill almost shouted, 'Unless this man leaves immediately, ring them.' He took hold of Hebe's upper arm, trying to push him towards the door. Hebe's fist unclenched and flew to his jacket pocket. He withdrew a flick knife. Click – the blade, sharp shining and evil, pointed at Bill. Miles rushed to his aid, pushed him away from the blade – but too late to avoid its thrust, and he, not Bill, was stabbed. Stella screamed. Miles was almost surprised at the spurt of blood that followed as Hebe withdrew the knife. He dropped it and it clattered, hitting the low table on which stood the empty champagne glasses, and then fell to the floor, its blade smeared with blood.

Miles stood for a moment, his face growing as white as Hebe's, whiter, then he slumped to the floor.

Hebe took in the scene as Miles fell down. He had not intended this and fear took the place of aggression. He turned, left the room, ran across the hall and was gone, his running steps crunching on the gravel path.

Agnes for a second felt paralysed. Then it was as if something snapped into place and she became a nurse – Sister Carmichael.

'Ring for an ambulance – say it's urgent.' She knelt down by the prostrate man. Bill stood beside her. 'Have you a handkerchief, Bill?' He handed her one; she folded it into a small pack and put it over the bleeding point as far as she could see it. 'Help me with his jacket and shirt.' Stella, she could see, was in no state to cope with blood. Once the jacket and shirt were removed, the pumping artery was revealed. Agnes pushed on it with the handkerchief. 'Fold up the shirt, Bill – as small as you can.' Bill did this, folding the bloodstained part inside. He handed it to Agnes, who put the larger pack on the already blood-soaked handkerchief. How she wished all this had taken place in her own well-ordered home where she knew where everything was, where first-aid material was to hand.

'Have you a bandage of any sort, Bill?' she asked, still pressing firmly on the injured area.

'Yes. Stella, there's a crepe bandage in the bathroom cupboard. Fetch it, dear.' Stella ran upstairs and Bill looked at Agnes. 'Will he be all right?' Miles looked hardly conscious; the carpet around his arm was heavily bloodstained.

'Yes, yes. I hope so, but he's losing blood.'

Stella came down and handed Agnes the bandage, which looked none too clean. However, with that and the shirt Agnes contrived a makeshift tourniquet. Miles was still bleeding but not so copiously.

The ambulance arrived and Agnes thankfully surrendered her charge to the capable hands of the paramedics. Miles's blood pressure was taken, a tourniquet – this time not a makeshift one – was applied and a drip needle put into Miles's other arm. Only then did they lift him on to the waiting stretcher and load him into the ambulance.

Stella followed, after glancing at Agnes. 'Thank you,' she said. The ambulance doors closed and Agnes watched it go down the street and away to the hospital.

She entered the house. Bill was washing blood off his hands in the kitchen sink. Agnes did the same, taking a clean tea towel from an open drawer and handing it to Bill. As he took it she noticed his hand was shaking and she took it in hers.

'Poor girl and poor Miles,' she said. 'But the ambulance men were good. I think he'll be all right, Bill. Though they'll have to transfuse him, I think.'

Bill looked distracted. 'Why did Stella seem to be so upset at the mention of the police being called, Agnes?' They moved out of the house to Bill's car.

'Probably the very thought of the police after all the questions she had to put up with about Bruce made her feel she just couldn't bear to go through it all again.'

In the car Bill looked at her. 'Yes, of course, I didn't think of that. But surely now . . . and with such an attack on Miles . . .?'

Again Agnes was cautious. 'Look, darling, let's take it a bit at a time. After all, if Miles doesn't want to bring charges . . . Stella may persuade him not to . . . I don't know. Let's leave it to them, shall we?'

'Yes, but what's it all about, carrying on about anonymous letters? I got the feeling that Stella knew something we didn't, Agnes. I hope I'm wrong.'

Agnes was silent, not replying to what she knew to be the truth. If questions were asked, what about Stella's involvement? A lie that Bill knew nothing about – Hebe might blurt that out if he was questioned by the police. She felt in her heart that it would be better not to bring charges but to leave it. Still she said nothing.

Even in these circumstances Agnes loved being driven by Bill; the feeling that they were engaged and that one day soon they would be married – that she belonged to him and he to her. She loved to look at his profile as he drove along to the hospital. Now and again he turned and looked at her and smiled. As they stopped at some traffic lights he pressed her hand. 'You're wonderful, Agnes. Without you I feel Miles . . . would probably . . . have died. I've never seen anyone bleed like that, you were so calm and composed.'

They parked the car opposite the gates of the hospital. A long line of consultants' cars were parked in front of it, each in an allotted square marked by white lines. At the end of the parking area there were two large doors both held open by iron hooks. CASUALTY ENTRANCE was on a lighted sign over the door. The whole façade of the old hospital looked to Agnes to be slightly old-fashioned. Another ambulance was parked at the entrance and as they walked by it an elderly woman was being wheeled out of it. Bill and Agnes stood back to let her trolley go by. She had white fuzzy hair and as her eyes met theirs she nodded and smiled.

'Fractured femur,' Agnes said, almost automatically, then made a little grimace and felt herself blushing, wishing she had said nothing.

'How do you know that, Agnes?' Bill said, obviously impressed.

Agnes shook her head. 'Oh it's nothing, Bill. I was just showing off.'

Bill would not let it go at that. 'Tell me, darling,' he said. 'I want to know.'

'Well, it's just that one of her feet was lying sideways as it does sometimes when the hip is broken – that's all, I was just showing off.'

Bill still looked at her admiringly. Then his anxieties turned again to Miles.

In the waiting-room they sat down. A woman with a little boy sat opposite. The child was silent, his small hand wrapped in a tea towel, but his red eyes and cheeks showed that tears were not far away. 'He's cut his hand,' the woman volunteered. 'This hospital is closing and it's a shame. I would have had to take him all the way to Newport on the bus. It's not right, but these people don't think about things like that, do they?' The little boy began to sniff. 'Now don't go on, Trevor. They'll soon make it better,' she said.

The door opened and a nurse put her head round. 'Trevor Brown,' she said. 'Will you come through?' The woman smiled at Agnes. 'Better ring the bell, dear, or you'll sit there all day.' The door closed behind them.

'What did she mean?'

They noticed a bell labelled in rather small letters PLEASE RING FOR ATTENTION. Bill pressed it. Nothing happened and he came and sat down again. About five minutes passed and another nurse appeared. 'Have you registered?'

Agnes spoke. 'We're not patients. We came behind the ambulance that brought Miles Hunt in, with what I think might be a severed brachial artery.'

The nurse's demeanour changed at Agnes's knowledgeable remark. 'Oh right, I'll fetch Sister.' She too disappeared, this time leaving the door slightly ajar. Almost immediately an older woman in a blue dress, her short white hair covered by a cap, came in. She crossed the room towards them with a pleasant smile.

'Are you relatives of Mr Hunt?' she asked.

'Yes,' said Bill firmly. 'He is my son-in-law. How is he?'

The sister sat down beside Bill. 'He is being attended to by Mr Geoffrey Jevons, a consultant surgeon. He is in the Casualty theatre. The surgeon is suturing the artery and he is being transfused.'

'Will he be –?'

The sister cut in. 'Certainly he'll be all right. He received attention promptly. If he had not, it might be a different story. He has lost a great deal of blood.'

Bill looked at Agnes. 'That attention was due to . . .' He indicated Agnes.

'I was a Casualty sister,' Agnes explained almost apologetically. She felt now that amongst all the new technology this department bristled with she would be totally lost.

The sister acknowledged her remark. 'Lucky for the patient you were there,' she said. 'Mr Hunt will be admitted to the private floor when Mr Jevons has finished with him, then you may probably go and see him.'

She was about to leave them when Stella emerged through the door. She looked white and ill, but a little more composed.

'Do you feel better now, Mrs Hunt?' Sister asked.

'Yes, I'm better. It was just . . .' She turned to Agnes and Bill. 'They said they were a little short of blood so I offered some of mine and when they pricked my thumb to take a sample . . .' She looked at the sister, who nodded at her.

'So that we could ascertain your blood group, Mrs Hunt,' she corrected.

Stella continued, '. . . I passed out – stupid.'

'Never mind, it's done. We will let you go up to the ward, but first perhaps the consultant will have a word with you. Just wait a minute, will you.' She left them and shut the white door into Casualty firmly behind her.

About fifteen minutes passed, with nothing more dramatic than a young doctor dashing through, banging the Casualty door behind him, white coat flying, stethoscope hanging from his neck. He looked furious; he did not even glance at them but rushed through, kicked open the plastic doors and disappeared from sight.

'What was all that about?' Bill asked.

'Thoroughly tired out and irritable,' Agnes suggested.

'Well, I hope he's not going to be looking after Miles, Daddy,' Stella said.

A green-coated woman appeared carrying a tray on which were three steaming cups of tea and a small saucer containing packets of sugar. 'Sister thought you'd like some tea.' She drew up a small table, took off some magazines and put the tray down. She too disappeared.

Another ten minutes passed. Once more the door opened but this time a doctor, an older man, appeared accompanied by Sister. 'This is Mr Jevons, the surgeon who has been attending Mr Hunt.' The surgeon shook hands with Bill and then turned to Sister.

'Would you be kind enough to let us have your office for a few minutes, Sister?' The woman nodded. 'Will you come this way, please.'

They all trooped through the Casualty door, past some curtained cubicles, across the treatment room and into Sister's office. She left them to it.

The consultant went round the desk and sat down, motioning towards the three chairs on the opposite side of the desk, which had obviously been arranged to seat patients' relatives.

Stella sat next to Agnes, taking her hand as she did so, Bill next to Stella.

The consultant began at once. 'Your husband has been transferred to the private floor at his request and will do very nicely now, I think.' He put the tips of his fingers together and looked benignly at the three of them. 'He will need a few pints of blood to replace what he lost, which was a considerable amount.' He again paused and looked at them. 'Mrs Hunt very courageously offered her blood – we are a little short. So we grouped Mrs Hunt.' He turned to Stella. 'Your group is O, by the way and your husband is AB, comparatively rare. However, I don't think he will need as much as we feared as he was promptly treated.' Then his expression became more grave. 'One wonders how he sustained such a wound?' He looked enquiringly at the three people in front of him.

'Accidentally, Mr Jevons, accidentally.' Bill spoke firmly and Agnes felt the pressure of Stella's hand on hers.

Poor Bill, Agnes thought, he was concealing the very name of Hebe and was clearly not going to mention the anonymous note and the money.

'Well, so be it.' Mr Jevons obviously did not believe them.

Agnes felt that the consultant, who looked on the edge of retirement, would not press the matter – nor did he. The interview was concluded and they left the office. Agnes, possibly more than any of them, was conscious of the consultant's speculative eyes following them.

They reached the private floor by lift and Bill and Agnes were taken to a small comfortable waiting-room while Stella went in to see her husband.

The moment the door was shut Bill turned to Agnes. 'AB – O – blood groups? What does all that mean, Agnes?'

Agnes was silent for a moment. She too was thinking of the consultant's words. She had been meticulous about swotting up for her nursing exams, but of course that was a long time ago. Still, she was almost sure that a person who was group O, as Stella was, could not be the child of an AB. Stella would have had to be A or B, was that right? Much as she would have liked to reassure Bill, she dared not.

'Darling, why don't you ask your friend Dr Jones – he will know. I don't believe . . .' She hesitated. 'I believe I remember that the child of an AB must be either A or B, but it's so complicated I can't be sure.'

Bill's eyes lit up. 'Do you mean, as far as you can remember, that Stella might be my daughter because of being group O?'

Agnes nodded but before anything else could be said Stella came out of Miles's room. 'He spoke to me, he seems . . . well he seems a little better.' She sat down with a bump on the easy chair across the room. A nurse appeared.

'You two can go in just for a word with the patient, but only for a minute.'

Agnes and Bill followed the nurse along the short corridor and into the room marked 6. The room was quite airy, with a large window whose pretty flowered curtains matched the upholstered chair by the side of the bed. Neither Agnes nor Bill sat down; they stood by Miles's bed for a few minutes. He looked white, and his left arm and shoulder were heavily bandaged – Agnes presumed to keep the wounded arm still. The other arm was lying on the folded-back sheet, a needle fixed in place by two strips of plaster, the blood bag up on the stand, the drip below it; as the blood dripped, life flowed back into the white-faced patient.

'Only just to say get well quickly,' Bill said. 'We mustn't stop.'

'Many thanks to you, Agnes. I was a bit out of my senses but I was able just . . . to realize what you were doing.'

Agnes gently patted the hand below the bandage. Hebe was not even mentioned; it was as if he had not existed.

They left the room.

Stella was waiting outside. 'I'm staying here, Daddy.'

'Of course, my darling.' Bill clasped her in his arms with unusual warmth. Stella returned his hug. Leaving Stella, they went out of the room and entered the lift.

'How wonderful if you're right, Agnes.'

She believed she was, but could not be a hundred per cent sure – and that was Agnes. She would never repeat such an important fact without being sure, but she hoped and hoped that Bryn Jones might verify what she had said and that Stella really was Bill's daughter. What a difference that fact would make to him!

25

When Hebe left the Turners' house after stabbing Miles he felt sick and afraid. The drug he had taken had lasted until he had seen the blood. He had never seen anything like it before, like a fountain. He pulled his jacket closer to hide the little dots of red that the sprayed blood had made on his shirt. He opened his pocket for the knife. Blast it – it wasn't there. He must have dropped it and left it there. Was it still stuck in . . . what was his name? Miles's arm. He couldn't remember taking it out. He felt confused as he drove home. The drug which had at first helped him, stimulated him, now muddled him. He wished to God he hadn't taken it. He wasn't violent, it was that drug. He was no druggie, he wasn't really used to it . . . Those people who said they could stop whenever they liked, he was one of those. He hardly ever took anything, but now – just one, just one dose and look what it had done!

At his flat he parked the car and locked it. Inside he stripped off his shirt and put it in the bathroom hand-basin, added some washing powder from a box on the ledge of the bath and turned on the hot water tap. He liked that shirt, he didn't want to lose it, throw it away; that's what they did when they'd done something like this, but no, he wasn't going to.

He put on a clean shirt, took his jacket from the back of the chair and put it on carefully, pulling the lapels straight and smoothing them down. He didn't want to injure the suit that had cost him a bomb. No tie, he didn't feel like a tie. Hebe combed his hair, ran his hand across its smoothness and began to feel better. That knife though ... stupid. Still, maybe he could ask Stella for it. He grinned into the mirror; he'd ask her when he asked for more money. He believed her father – no one could act as good as that.

But if it wasn't him – who was it? Miles – did he know what Stella had done? Hebe sat down and lit a cigarette. Think, think ... If she hadn't asked Miles for the money and she hadn't asked her father, who was left? That bloody woman Agnes something – what was her name? Of course! She looked rich; he had smelled her perfume too and knew it was expensive. Of course, she might have seen him; she lived next door. She might even have seen Rick and him – might well have – putting the kid in the car.

Hebe felt muddled again and put his head in his hands. He thought again drugs were not for him, they scrambled his brain. Supposing it was Agnes? She obviously wanted to protect Stella, but what for? Did she know about the kid in the morgue? Unlikely, surely, but had she given Stella the money? And if she had ... He rubbed his forehead. And the note – had she put that in? Had Stella known it was there? Perhaps not; perhaps yes. Well, there was nothing he could do at the moment but wait for the bloody police to come and arrest him, accuse him. 'Grievous bodily harm and kidnapping.' He could almost hear them saying it. But if they didn't come – well, then he'd know they didn't want to charge him because ... what? Because they'd something to hide. After all, if that Agnes woman had seen Rick and him why hadn't she called the police then? In fact, why was everybody keeping quiet if they'd seen anything? God, he couldn't work it out.

He was right. A week later, nothing had happened. No police had arrived and the next rave party was due in two nights. He'd got to get going again; he'd got to meet with the Old Man to collect some E. He had the loot to pay for it and it certainly looked as if they weren't going to arrest him. No police – surely, if they'd been coming to question him, they'd have done so by now.

Friday. He must meet the Old Man at the end of the pier tomorrow night. It was a good place that, down by the boat, the little passenger tourist boat. The Old Man liked that trip up the Solent, mixing with the grockles, having a sandwich and a beer with them, looking innocent – perhaps relishing the fact that he was carrying a pack of Joy and looking like a grockle. Well, everyone is different and in a way all the same. He was not happy, not here in this god-forsaken island. He longed for London and wondered how soon he dared risk going back there yet.

He'd been clever, crafty, he thought. He'd rung the hospital a couple of times to see how Miles was progressing. 'Comfortable' was all they would say, but that showed at least he hadn't died. Then the last time the switchboard hadn't even put him through to the ward, they'd just said, 'Mr Hunt left the hospital yesterday. Who is calling?' He'd put the phone down, not answering the question. So that was all right. No accusations, no bleeding to death. Now what? He still knew Stella's secret. Should he hit again now for more money? She might decide to confess to Miles what she had done, then it would be no good. No. Hebe decided she wouldn't do that. He'd lie low for a bit, but he wouldn't forget her or that Agnes woman. They might accuse him of kidnapping the bloody kid but... Anyway, if it came to a battle of wits he'd probably win and he had an advantage – or had he? Was the lie that Stella had told still a secret? He wasn't sure. Anyway, let it be, he'd other irons in the fire that would bring in far more than their measly thousand.

The weekly rave was definitely catching on. Kids came from the other side of the Island – Freshwater, Ventnor, and from the mainland too. They slept on the beach or on the bowling green – stoned, some of them. Some brought their own shit with them – he knew that, but didn't bar it. They mostly wanted Big E. Easy for him to get. The Old Man brought smack too, and a bit of acid, but acid seemed to be out at the moment. E was what the kids wanted, what they were after – at his rave, anyway. Half-wits, messing up their health with drugs, their ears with Heavy Metal, ruining themselves one way and another. He'd seen heavily pregnant girls, too, dancing like mad, and they looked as if they'd been drinking, never mind drugging. He'd sold them E. Some hope for the kids, born addicts. Oh well, it wasn't his responsibility. After all, if he didn't supply what they wanted somebody else would!

He thought again of that downward thrust of the knife; that wasn't in his character, not violent. Crafty... astute... clever... all those things, yes, but violent, no. That blood, the way it had gushed out... Jesus! He'd never have done it unless he had taken that dope. A little packet like that, so small, so harmless-looking. No wonder the kids went ape, no wonder.

Hebe had stopped jumping now when the telephone or his door bell rang. After all, if they were going to charge him they would have by now, the fuzz would have been around. Hebe sighed. He felt flat; perhaps that was the dope too, high and then low. Oh come on, it wouldn't be, it was a week ago. He made a sudden decision; he must leave after the next rave, go back to London, risk it, stay at his sister's till he'd got a flat somewhere. Take the bloody risk, it was worth it. He felt better after he'd made the decision; he'd melt away, leave them all guessing – London, London. Back to the crowds, the red buses, the tube, the smells – that was where he belonged, not here!

26

After Miles left the hospital he returned to the hotel. Apart from having his left arm in a sling he had practically recovered from the blood loss. Stella felt that his, as she called it, 'accident' had drawn them closer together. Her plea that they should not charge Hebe, but just leave the whole thing alone until he was better, proved understandable to Miles. Now it was too late to do anything about it.

'I can understand, darling, why you don't want to answer questions or to have anything more to do with the police after what you went through.' However, Miles couldn't quite hide his curiosity as to why Hebe had come to Bill's house at all and why he had accused Bill of sending a note saying something about kidnapping Bruce. And the money – what money was he referring to? It was all a mystery he'd rather forget.

However, Stella was so upset by the whole thing he felt it was better left, not talked about. After all, it was Bill that this strange man, Hebe, had been intending to stab, and this in a way justified Stella's remark that it was an accident. It was all very baffling, though...

They had hesitated, on his discharge from hospital, as to whether they should go back to London or stay on a while at the hotel. The manager of the Gloucester was very upset by the fact that he had, as he put it, 'been attacked by some hoodlum in Ryde'. He said he must have come from the mainland – he would not admit to the boy being an Islander. They had been more than kind, offering to bring Miles his meals in bed if he didn't feel strong enough to get up, or to serve the couple dinner in their room if they didn't feel like coming to the dining-room. It had been an incentive for them to stay on in the Island, although Miles was not altogether sure that Stella would not have preferred to go back to London. However, when Miles said he would like a little more rest and convalescence at the hotel, she immediately agreed.

'You know Hebe, don't you, darling? Why do you think he accused Bill of sending that note?' His curiosity had impelled him to ask her that.

Stella had shaken her head. 'I don't know Hebe well, dearest. He was Rick's friend not mine. I never liked him.' She seemed so uncomfortable at the mere mention of Hebe's name that Miles stopped referring to the matter.

He too had a sense of guilt that in Switzerland he had perhaps not enquired too deeply into her age. Indeed one of the other skiers had accused him of baby-snatching. He had just laughed: he had thought she was lovely and had found her so very compliant and passionate he had never suspected she was so young. Although he had tried to contact her in London many times he had perhaps not persisted enough. Guilt is a great inhibitor; Miles felt that he had done Stella harm and that now he must indulge her by doing what she wanted rather than what he thought was wise. After all, they might never see Hebe again. And about that Miles was quite right.

Their time at the Gloucester passed pleasantly. Miles went back to the hospital to see Mr Jevons for a final blood test and check-up, and was allowed out of his sling. The incident, it appeared, was closed.

27

The thought of making more money and fast dominated Hebe's mind. Grab and get away, he thought. He was losing his marbles and stabbing bloody Miles had been a stupid mistake, but as the days went by and still no charges were brought he realized he might be safe. Just why they were doing nothing about it, he was not sure. Probably Stella had had enough of the police, especially in her doting husband's opinion. Police questions? He couldn't bear to have his wife tormented again. Stella probably took the 'I can't bear any more questions, darling' line with her husband.

Because of her misinformation it seemed to Hebe that, even if he didn't hold the trump card, he might not be without a decent hand of diamonds. He was stronger, he felt, and it would do more harm to Stella to reveal her secret than she could do to him, even aided by her friend Agnes. They'd have to prove he had anything to do with the kidnapping; and had they really seen him? No, he felt confident enough to have another go.

This time he decided to concentrate on Agnes rather than the, in his opinion, feeble-minded Stella. How, that was the problem. A telephone call? A meeting? A note?

Eventually he decided on the telephone. With this method of communication he could await Agnes's reply in silence at the other end of the phone while she made up her mind what she would say. But he must be brief and to the point, and give her absolutely no time to cut him off or argue; just make her think whether to do as he said or not and, if possible, make her realize she'd got to pay to keep him quiet!

The first time he rang there was no reply; the second time he got Agnes's answering machine which, before the bleeper had even bleeped, made him put the receiver down like a hot coal; his voice recorded on that was the last thing he wanted! But the third time he was successful and Agnes answered the phone herself.

He was all ready – in fact he had made a note of what he intended to say to her. Luckily he had remembered her name, Carmichael. He had not wanted to address her by her Christian name. Formal and businesslike was the tone he wanted.

'Miss Carmichael,' he began, his voice slow and controlled, 'I believe I may know something of which you are not aware – not the rumours of a child being kidnapped but something else, something very harmful to your young friend Stella. I would like another £1,000 for the information. I have a feeling that the first thousand came from you and no doubt the note too.' He then decided to await her reply. It had been quite a long speech and there had been no sound from Agnes Carmichael, no sign of an interruption or an ejaculation, nothing. He gave her full marks for control, but when the silence after his sentence was prolonged he began to wonder if she was still listening.

She was, and her reply surprised him more than a little.

The first time the telephone rang Agnes had heard it. She was in next door with Bill. The letter about his book being accepted by a film company had been followed by another suggesting that he came up to London to meet his agent and a Mr Bernstein from the film company. He was busy typing his reply.

On hearing the phone Agnes went round to her own house and switched on the answering machine then went back to Bill, who had finished the letter and was signing it. He stuck down the envelope, put on the stamp and addressed it. Then he got up immediately to post it. 'I won't be a minute, darling, but I want to get this off.'

Agnes heard her phone go again and decided it might be something urgent so she returned home.

Bill was eating with her every day now. She loved feeding him and longed for her marriage. She checked her phone, but whoever had rung her had not availed themselves of her answering facility. The receiver had been put down before the bleep. She started to prepare lunch and then the telephone rang again. Three times, she thought, maybe the same person, maybe not. Agnes did not get all that many telephone calls.

It was the man Hebe and Agnes listened. 'Miss Carmichael, I believe I may know something of which you are not aware . . .' Agnes listened, almost holding her breath, then waited a little longer and in those seconds she decided on her reply.

'That sounds reasonable, Mr Grant. I certainly would like to talk to you. As to the money – well, we shall see what you know that I don't!'

'Right. Well, where shall we meet, Miss Carmichael?'

Something flew into Agnes's mind like a large black bird, just as her ideas always did, out of nowhere and into her mind. She knew something was going to happen. She would leave it to fate. She felt in some way that this man Hebe was digging his own grave.

'Where do you suggest, Mr Grant?' she said.

Another pause. At last Hebe answered in a slightly arrogant manner, 'I have to meet a boat tonight, unfortunately late, eleven o'clock.'

'Boat?' Agnes queried.

'Yes, a boat,' he answered but he volunteered no more.

A tiny tremor of fear quickened Agnes's pulse. Eleven o'clock, the end of the pier . . . She thought of the darkness and the water. Why did the fear bring a faint tremor, perhaps of pleasure? She reached behind the telephone and her hand closed over Hebe's knife.

'I'm sorry, I'm going to London and that's the only time I –' Hebe's words were not apologetic, just factual.

Agnes broke in quickly. 'That will be all right. I'll be there.'

'With the money?' Hebe's voice was rougher now. 'I mean what I say, Miss Carmichael. I want that thousand.'

'I'm sure you do, Mr Grant. Eleven o'clock at the end of the pier.' She put the telephone down, still fingering the knife. It felt comfortable in her hand; the blade was drawn inside it. She threw it from one hand to the other as she stood by the telephone, thinking. Bill, Bill, Bill, he was everything to her, everything. Nothing more must hurt him, nothing, through Stella, through Miles, through Bruce, but most of all through Hebe Grant. Hebe was in it for the money – and money, as Agnes knew, could make anybody do anything; but there was something else that was even stronger and that was her love for Bill Turner. That, she felt, could overturn a mountain or stop a wagging tongue.

She was glad Hebe had suggested a meeting tonight. She did not want too much time to think. Think about what? All she could think of at the moment was that she should wear something warm and dark. The end of the pier could be very chilly in the autumn. She was still handling the knife and she almost (was it subconsciously?) knew she was going to take it with her. To return it to him? To dispose of it? Genuinely at that moment she did not know.

It was still early afternoon. Suddenly she did not feel able to continue her lunch preparations without a drink. A brandy. Not a terribly usual drink for her, not these days, only when there was tension. Often a time of tension would make her shoulders ache, then the brandy warmed her. Why was she so tense now? Her shoulders were not aching yet but she knew they would. It was that black bird that had flown into her mind. It had folded its wings for the moment but at any time soon it might spread them again and take off.

Bill would soon be back from posting his letter and ready for lunch. She must hide her mood from him. That would be difficult, almost impossible, but she must do it. She sipped her brandy, finished it, felt better for it and went back into the kitchen to continue her preparations.

She thought as she worked that Hebe Grant had seemed slightly thrown off balance by her quick agreement to meet him. She had not, however, answered his request for money in any way.

The council had been divided about having a display of fireworks at the end of the pier, but those in favour had ultimately prevailed. After all, the old-fashioned paddle steamer no longer brought passengers to the pier head. The hovercraft did, but that took up very little room and did not come in late at night. There was the small passenger boat that ran up and down the Beaulieu River and around visiting ships, but that tied up nowhere near the site suggested for the fireworks.

'Fireworks over the sea! How romantic!' A woman councillor had thrown the remark into the discussion

'Silly old fool,' a councillor had whispered to his next-door neighbour, but the one with the eye to the money did not agree with him.

'I think Mrs Snowden is right. Fireworks reflected in the sea – charming and romantic, the reflections and all that. People will love it.'

'And safer in a way,' another councillor had remarked. 'You can't set fire to the bloody sea.'

Anyway, fireworks at the end of the pier, a £1 charge at the entrance to the pier, a ride down and a ride back when it was all over. It had all been arranged two months before the actual carnival. Nearer to the event the time and place were confirmed and the arrangements for the carnival and fireworks were printed in *What's On in the Island*. When the day approached posters appeared around the town and the main street was decorated with flags, electric lights and flower baskets.

A man had been hired to stand at the turnstile at the entrance to the pier to take the money. The carnival crowds queued, they'd watched the carnival and now for the fireworks. More footsteps sounded on the wooden slats leading down to the sea than had been heard for some time. The tide was in and lapped around the stanchions. Much laughter, catcalls, wolf whistles disturbed the night air. Everyone seemed to be chattering and in high spirits. Children were clutching helium-filled silver, gold, pink and blue balloons. Candy floss sold like hot cakes and a hot hamburger stall scented the night air.

Two people only were not in carnival mood. Hebe Grant arrived at about ten forty. Agnes kept to the letter of the law and walked down the slats, now almost deserted, at eleven o'clock.

There was no charge for them; the man at the turnstile had gone. She could see at the far end the sky lighting up with cascades of colour, stars bursting and disappearing as small explosions echoed through the might. As she moved closer she could hear the 'oohs' and 'ahs' of the assembled watchers.

When Agnes arrived at the end of the pier the slatted wood floors changed and the ground was concrete; she noticed the change in the sound of her own footsteps. The crowd still had their faces turned upwards. Agnes mingled with them momentarily in spite of the fact that her reason for being there was not to see the fireworks; the beauty of their bursting bunches of red, green and white stars like huge flowers in the sky, falling, falling, reflected in the rippling sea, was eye-catching. After a moment or two she made her way to the dark side of the pier where there were no people and it was hardly lit even by the fireworks. The sea looked black there and the steps leading down to that black sea looked like ebony.

Agnes drew back. A steamer was moored at the bottom of the dark steps. It was just casting off. Its lights were not brilliant; a row of small cabin windows threw yellow shafts of light on to the landing stage, while its deck lights pointed ahead, lighting up the water.

There Hebe stood, an equally dark figure, watching the boat depart. He raised a hand as if to signal goodbye to someone on board. In his hand he held a small black packet. His usually sleeked-down hair stirred slightly in the breeze. He dropped his arm and put the packet in his jacket pocket, still watching the boat, its engines throbbing like a heart as it drew further and further away. Still he watched, a tall black figure. He turned and looked up . . . At the top of the steps was a figure as dark as his own.

He called out softly, 'Miss Carmichael?'

'Yes, it is Miss Carmichael,' she answered, slowly descending the steps towards him.

'I'll come up,' he said and repeated the remark again as the figure did not stop coming down towards him. 'I'll come up.' This time there was no answer, only a sharp click. The descending figure was nearly level with him now.

'Mr Hebe Grant?' The voice was ice cold.

'Yes. Have you got the money, Miss Carmichael?' He could see a little better now. She had on a black headscarf tied under her chin and a black mackintosh that gleamed with a satiny shine in the little light there was. Funny to wear that, he thought, on such a warm rainless night. Still . . . He looked down at something that glistened in her hand. 'Good God, you're not –' He had no time to say more.

There was a sharp searing pain in his chest as the knife plunged in. He made a faint grunting sound as he fell backwards, the knife still in his chest. As he hit the water the crowd let out a shout: the final set piece had burst into light, a Catherine wheel at each end of a sign that read GOODNIGHT, the wheels whirring and scattering fiery darts around.

Agnes mounted the steps, taking off the dark mac and headscarf as she walked across and joined the crowd. A child called out, 'Is that all, Mum?'

'Good, wasn't it?' A fat woman turned to Agnes with a wide toothy smile.

'Very good indeed, very impressive,' Agnes replied pleasantly.

'Thank goodness we get a ride back. It's a long walk down that pier, I reckon.' Agnes agreed and followed the woman as she made her way to the train that was rapidly filling with holiday-makers, tired now and hot.

'I could do with a beer,' a man said. 'Pint of lager would go down a treat.'

'Not half, so could I,' someone answered him.

It was all so normal, so ordinary. They were the sort of people Agnes had been used to as patients. People who broke their hips, got burned with too much sunbathing, were stung by wasps, collapsed on the promenade, got sick with eating too much. Children were there too and she knew them – they would come into Casualty with cut feet because someone had left glass on the beach, or with fish hooks in their hands. They had been part of her life at one time. Now it was all different. Now she had, or soon would have, a husband, a stepdaughter and a son-in-law. She was part of a family, and what she had just done had been to ensure its safety and happiness.

She had to stand on the train and she swayed to and fro to the movement of it. Then she was conscious of a wonderful feeling of something achieved, something done, something cleared up, put right.

When at last she reached her own house she felt quite tired and breathless after the walk up the long hill from the sea. Bill's light was still on in his bedroom; she had left the light on in her own and drawn the curtains before she had set off to the pier. She let herself in through the front door very quietly. She hoped Bill had not telephoned her to say goodnight. He would, of course, have got no reply. If he had she would tell some little white lie – say she had fallen asleep with the light on, or was having a bath, or had not heard the telephone.

Agnes doggedly went through her normal routine; cleaned her face of make-up with her usual cleansing cream, brushed her hair, cleaned her teeth, had a quick shower and then to bed. Only then did she give a thought as to what she had done. A knife in his chest – her aim, she knew, had been anatomically correct. The packet in his pocket – she was certain he had received drugs from whoever he had met on that boat. The knife and the packet in his pocket – what more did she want! The black bird that had flown into her mind had been a messenger. He had now flown for ever away from her mind.

She switched off the light. It had been strange how the GOOD NIGHT sign and the whirling Catherine wheels had covered the splash as Hebe hit the water. Things helped her. They always did.

She snuggled down in bed wishing Bill were with her, but soon he would be with her for ever. She sighed luxuriously. How wonderful, and how lucky she was. Her eyes closed and she drifted off to sleep, a dreamless sleep.

In the house next door Bill was in a complacent mood. Since leaving Agnes at about four o'clock he had sat at his word processor working. The film offer seemed to make using the hated machine more pleasant. When at last he looked at his watch and read ten past twelve he could hardly believe it – the working time had flown by.

He went outside and looked up at Agnes's bedroom window. The light was on, the garage door firmly closed. He wished he was there beside her but it was too late to telephone. As he went to go back indoors the light in Agnes's bedroom was switched off. Maybe she had been kept awake by the sound of the exploding fireworks. He knew they were happening this evening, but so immersed had he been in his new book that he'd hardly heard them at all and had certainly not been disturbed by them.

He locked the back and front doors, went upstairs, had a shower and climbed into bed. He too was asleep in minutes.

Mrs Timpson also was just retiring. She had been annoyed by the exploding fireworks. She considered them dangerous and an extravagance the council could well cut back on. The money could be better spent ... to help the shortage of school books, the lack of places for the mentally disturbed, the shortage of policemen on the beat, the disgracefully long waiting lists at the hospital. All these things, Mrs Timpson felt, justified the abolition of fireworks. Every 5th November she made her feelings known by writing to the editor of the local paper. He never responded, though she had put in her letters how she had heard of children and adults with eye injuries, burns ... 'Oh, what is the use!' she said aloud and snapped off her bedside light. She certainly did not share any of the complacent feelings of her two next-door neighbours and she did not manage to fall asleep for some hours in spite of a sleeping tablet.

Her thoughts wandered round. Miss Carmichael, she felt, was a strange one. Oh, on the surface she was correct, rich and well dressed, but there was something in her manner ... Was it a mysteriousness or was it just reserve? No, that wasn't it, it was something else. 'I just wouldn't like to cross her,' she said aloud. And Mr Turner, that was a strange household – the child disappearing like that, and that awful boy, Rick, he'd gone now, but where? She had often wondered if he was Mr Turner's boyfriend. Well, everyone knows how it is these days.

Stella, she was a queer girl too – pretty, but she was young. At the thought of Stella Mrs Timpson remembered she had not used her moisturizing cream; she had not put it on her face and neck. She sighed, switched on the light and got out of bed. At the dressing-table she put on another small light. This, she felt, was a mistake; it showed up the wrinkles round her eyes and mouth, and her crepey eyelids. She had the cream but she often forgot to use it as it was expensive ... it was the thought of Stella with her fresh young skin that had made her remember her cream. She unscrewed the lid of the jar and began to rub a generous helping on to her neck and chin.

How old was Agnes Carmichael? she wondered. Her face was quite smooth. She seldom smiled – perhaps keeping so impassive made wrinkles less likely. Still, she'd never managed to catch a husband – at least, she didn't wear a wedding ring, not that that meant anything these days!

She rose and switched off the dressing-table light, got into bed and picked up the latest Jackie Collins novel. She'd read a bit to see if that made her sleepy. It didn't and suddenly she was again disturbed by footsteps walking up the gravel path. Her path or the next-door one? She couldn't decide. She went to the window and peered out, moving the curtain only a tiny slit. She saw Miss Carmichael just opening her front door. She watched her go in and close it behind her. The bedroom light was on so . . . She dropped the curtain back into place and smoothed down the crease.

So that was the way it was! She'd obviously been in her next-door neighbour's house, in with Mr Turner. There'd been no sound of a car and she would hardly have been walking the streets at this hour. Well, she supposed it was sex – it always was these days. 'Fancy Miss Carmichael . . .' She again spoke aloud and then got back into bed. 'Some people . . . they think of nothing else.' She sniffed. She opened the Jackie Collins again and settled down to read, but try as she would she could not get the thought of Agnes Carmichael and Mr Turner out of her mind. They were together . . . what did they call it now? . . . a couple! No one had any morals these days, but . . . She put her hand up and smoothed the light cream under her eyes and she was conscious, she was honest enough to know that she was jealous!

28

The next morning the sunny weather suddenly turned to scudding clouds and rain. There were two men working on the beach, their yellow waistcoats rainproof but wet, which made them gleam in the morning light. 'Bloody louts.' They were picking up crushed lager tins, Coca Cola tins, and they thrust them into the big black sacks they were carrying. A small handcart, also yellow, was parked above them on the promenade. 'The young are bloody louts,' he repeated, stopping for a moment to rub his unshaven chin, which made a rasping sound.

'Don't you be so sure it's always the young ones, Dave,' said the other man, putting a large, dress-size plastic bag into his sack with difficulty.

'What the hell's that?'

'Come off something.' He looked at it curiously. 'It's clean plastic, though. Come off some furniture, I expect.'

The other man spoke again. 'Well, as I was telling you, me and the wife came here one evening to see the rescue boat and helicopter doing their stuff. There were a lot of fat old white-haired ladies about. Two of them drank Coke, left the cans on the grass and walked away. Old buggers.' He picked up something else. 'Look at that for waste, half a bar of chocolate.'

'Shall we 'ave a bit?' asked the unshaven one.

'Nah . . . don't know where it's bin.'

They worked on, drawing nearer and nearer to the pier.

The morning brightened up, the rain stopped and just a few stray drops fell on their backs as they worked, heads down. They were about two feet away from the pier when they saw it: the tide was way out and large puddles lay in the depressions of sand. The legs of the pier were black, glistening with green weed. Here and there a newspaper or a magazine was caught in the struts of the pier, left there by retreating waves. A small, naked, plastic doll bobbed up and down in one of the puddles on its back, plastic legs in the air, eyes gazing heavenwards.

''Ere I'll have that for our Marlene, she loves dolls.' He dodged the struts of the pier, skirted the puddles and picked up the doll. He found a clean piece of newspaper in his sack, wrapped up the doll and pushed it into the large pocket of his yellow waistcoat. Then his eyes fell on the larger object lying half submerged in another shallow depression in the sand. He went over to it, bending down to get a better look . . . and then he straightened up quickly.

'Dave,' he yelled. 'Come over, there's a bloke here with a knife in his chest.'

Dave joined him, his black sack making a tinny sound as he carried it. 'Where?' His voice was disbelieving. 'You 'aving me on, winding me up?'

'No, I'm not.' He had drawn back, his usually brown, weatherbeaten face quite white. His pointing hand shook a little.

'Jesus, you're not wrong.' Not as squeamish as his partner, he set about moving the body to see it better. He pushed it with his foot.

The body was lying on its side, fully dressed, the eyes open, the knife protruding from the middle of the chest. None of the blade was visible but the black leather handle decorated with silver or chrome shone in the bleak sunlight.

Dave pushed the shoulder of the dead man and the body rolled on to its back. The wide eyes got to Dave a bit. 'Jesus, somebody had it in for him, mate.'

'Is he dead?'

'Oh no, 'e's not dead, 'e' just 'aving a kip. Go up to the nearest phone and get the police. I'll stay 'ere.'

Dave's mate, glad to get away from the scene, scrambled over the shingle, up the steps to the promenade. A telephone booth was almost at the top of the steps; it was a mercy it had not been vandalized. With a shaky hand he dialled 999.

'Fire or ambulance or police?'

'There's a body under the pier, miss.'

The voice at the other end remained matter of fact. 'Oh, that'll be the police. I'll put you through and to the ambulance.'

'Yes? What can I do for you, sir?' It was the police.

He repeated, 'There's a body under the pier.'

'Right, we'll be there. You stay with it.'

He came out, shut the booth door behind him and felt a bit better. 'Cor, I could do with a brandy,' he said and made for the steps that led down to the beach and Dave.

When he got there Dave was sitting back on his heels beside the body, peering at the dead face. 'I know him, it's Hebe.' He pointed. 'That pony tail and ear-ring. I'm not saying anything to the police, though.'

'What's 'is name?'

Dave shook his head. 'Dunno 'is other name but he's called Hebe. He runs, well used to run, those raves – you know, those parties up at the old garage.'

'Raves?'

'Yes. My kid wanted to go and I said she could and I'd call for her at eleven o'clock.'

'Did yer?' Dave's mate kept his eyes averted from the body.

'Yeah and I'm glad I did, a madhouse it was. He was by the bar, I remember him. I reckon it's him. Of course, he's changed.'

Dave's mate walked further away. 'Of course he's changed – he's bloody well dead, Dave.'

The police siren sounded, then another. 'Here they come, thank God. They'll ask us a few questions – sure to – then we can go home when they've taken the body away. But I'm not saying anything. If I do we'll be hours at the bloody station.'

In spite of the banging and yelling by the rapidly growing number of kids outside the large door of the rave venue it remained obstinately shut.

'What gives? Why is it shut?'

'For God's sake, I need a fix anyway. He promised some dope tonight and it's half eleven. He's always here at eleven on the dot.'

Another voice spoke. 'Reckon he's been picked up?'

'No. Hebe's no fool. He knows his way round the fuzz.'

They all waited, but even the bouncer didn't come. He was a big burly youth who Hebe paid to fling out anyone who got a bit over the top.

Then a girl arrived breathless and white-faced, her black hair made thick and bouncy by perming and washing. She could hardly speak. 'I ran, I ran all the way,' she puffed. 'It's on the late news. Found under the pier, pony tail and that gold ear-ring, drugs in his pocket, name not to be told until the next of kin . . . you know.' She stopped and leaned against a car, trying to get her breath back.

'It's Hebe, isn't it?' She managed to get it out with difficulty.

'What about the stuff he was bringing?'

'Of course it's Hebe.' It was a boy, tall, skinny, older than the others. 'The fuzz, they'll get on to this place. They'll know he runs it. We'd better scarper.'

The girl spoke. 'Know anyone who'll supply?'

'Nope, it's every man for himself now, kiddo.'

The scene cleared quickly of people and soon the closed and rather dirty doors were the only sign of Hebe's absence.

Not one of the ravers said, or obviously even thought, 'Poor Hebe, poor Mr Grant,' but only 'There will be a drug problem,' or 'Where the hell do I get a fix or an upper?' . . . or whatever. Those who only liked one E tablet while they were at the rave didn't give a damn about Hebe. 'Where to go for more dancing?' was their thought. 'Silly bugger to get himself drowned before the rave anyway,' muttered one boy as he and his mate slouched out into the night. They didn't know of the knife in the victim's chest. Anyway, what difference would it have made if they had? It was their own problem that concerned them, not some bloody pusher's death.

'Why didn't he drown himself after the bloody rave, for God's sake?' the voice continued. No one answered, and no one said, 'Poor Hebe.'

The notice in the paper, and it was a brief notice, did not reach Stella and Miles until the evening when they came in from sailing. It had been a wonderful day, the rain had disappeared and the fresh wind had been perfect. Miles was teaching Stella to sail and she loved it.

Back in their hotel Miles picked up the paper on the table. 'Oh dear, no *Telegraph*, only the *Portsmouth Evening News*. I'll ring room service.'

'Shall I shower first?' Stella called from the bathroom.

'No, darling, let's shower together. Oh, look at that . . .' His voice sounded quite incredulous.

'Look at what, darling?' Stella asked.

'That man you know, Hebe . . . it says Herbert Grant here, but it's him by the photograph.' He peered closer at the paper. 'Looks as if it was taken recently.'

Stella came out of the bathroom. 'What is it?' she asked.

'He's dead. Found under the pier this morning. He was murdered.'

Stella sat down with a thump on the bed; her face even under her tan had paled. 'I'm not sorry for him after what he did to you. But who could have killed him?'

'Sorry, darling, I didn't mean to shock you.' Miles came over to her.

'It's all right, Miles. I didn't know him very well anyway. It's just that . . .' She went back into the bathroom. She felt herself shaking. She turned on the shower then she got another reaction . . . relief . . . It was tremendous. Now no one knew her secret – no more blackmail, no more fear. 'He's dead, he's dead, he's dead,' she whispered.

Miles joined her and took her in his arms. 'Not a nice end,' he said, but Stella seemed to find it easy to accept the murder.

'He was nothing to me, Miles. I didn't like him much. He was a friend of Rick's, not mine,' she said and felt with joy his arms round her naked body. Life was wonderful, and again no one said, 'Poor Hebe.' Why should they? Stella thought. He was a drug-pusher, a stealer of children, a blackmailer. As she responded to her husband's caresses her heart lightened with new hope. No one now knew of her deception. Little Bruce slipped into her mind – Miles's child . . . Another Bruce perhaps, or a little girl, then she could start again, take great care of her baby with Miles to help her.

The shower smelled wonderful, the lovemaking was wonderful, everything was wonderful – and Hebe was dead.

29

Bill went up to London. He had wanted Agnes to come but had seen the sense in what she had said. 'Bill darling, this is a big day for you. You'll need all your concentration to cope with your agent and the film people.'

He admitted he did feel a bit nervous. However, he went round to her house early in the morning as she was going to take him to the catamaran. As they drove down Union Street a poster outside the newsagents read in large, handwritten capitals, MAN FOUND STABBED ON BEACH IN RYDE.

Agnes shivered.

'Are you cold, darling?' Bill asked. He had not noticed the poster.

'No, it's just your going away.'

'I'll be back this evening,' Bill said, kissing her cheek and putting his hand over hers on the steering wheel.

When he had gone Agnes went to a newsagent on the way home. Once there she read the paper she had bought. They were not disclosing much, not yet anyway. Just that a man had been found stabbed on the beach under the pier. Agnes's mind went not to Bruce but to the little boy found under the pier – Bruce was all right, she knew that, but that little boy . . . Stella would now think that she was safe. Well, so she was, because Agnes could never hurt Bill by telling him of his daughter's deception; she loved him far too much. Fate had caught up with her and for once the hidden knowledge which she always felt made her powerful was now no use to her at all.

When Bill returned from London that evening he was tired but elated. He couldn't stop talking about it all and Agnes listened.

'It's going to make quite a lot of money, darling. My agent was very good, I hardly had to say a word – in fact I felt totally at sea.' He sat down on the settee and he kept a firm hold on Agnes's hand. 'The contract should be signed in about a month – I thought it would take longer. I always thought film companies . . .' He talked on, not letting go of Agnes's hand.

She listened but only half heard, only half took it in, her mind was so preoccupied with thoughts of Hebe. She longed to hear the local news but did not like to interrupt Bill's flow of excited talk. She had switched on for the lunchtime news, but there had not been much about Hebe except that the murdered man was quite well known in the Ryde area; they said something about him running a rave club unlawfully and added that the man concerned may have got away to the mainland immediately.

Drugs were involved and the police were continuing their enquiries. When the news had finished she had switched off, satisfied.

That night the talk was mostly about the date of their marriage. Bill seemed so much more confident, so well able to handle the situation. 'Would you like to sell the two houses and get somewhere nearer the sea? Would you like that?'

That appealed to them both, setting up in a lovely house nearer the seashore.

'Where, darling? In Ryde?'

They were lying together, naked, their bodies close. She could hear and feel his heart thudding slowly and rhythmically. Agnes had never in her life felt so safe, so sheltered. How she prayed, longed, that nothing would happen to shatter this wonderful feeling. She so hoped not, prayed not.

'What about Bembridge or Yarmouth?' Bill went on.

'I don't mind, darling, as long as you're there.' She stirred in his arms, his head bent and he kissed her breast and then, after all, all thoughts of where they were to live and what they would do in the future melted away.

Two months later Agnes was alone in her sitting-room. Winter was in the air, the shrubs showed leafless arms and must soon be cut back. Agnes was pleased she had planted the winter pansy border – it glowed with colour – and at the bottom of the garden at the back of her house the bay tree remained obstinately green.

Yesterday's headlines are quickly forgotten. A war in one place, the world is stirred up, and another war dies down. Fresh atrocities drive interest away from the last. A shooting in London gave way in a day to a murdered child in a northern town. It was just a question of today's news being more violent, more bizarre. Agnes put the *Telegraph* down and picked up the local paper. The same applied – a child drowned under the pier had given way to a dramatic robbery in a building society in the middle of the Island. That had been pushed aside by the man in the sea with a knife in his chest – interesting reading, she felt with a little grimace. Today, an elderly woman mugged in Freshwater in broad daylight by two twelve-year-old boys who had beaten her up, blackened her eyes, knocked her down and broken her hip, and stolen her handbag with her pension in it. That occupied the headlines today.

It was Agnes's wedding day, twelve thirty at the registrar's office in Newport. She drank her early morning tea as she glanced through the papers. She felt calm, no nervousness, just happiness. She had arrived, reached her destination, that's what she thought.

Her house had been changed a little as Bill's had sold first. Maybe because the asking price had been a little less than hers. The furniture was to go into storage for the moment and the room next to her sitting-room had been turned into his 'office', as he called it. It pleased Agnes to see his word processor there, the much-missed waste-paper basket, his desk, his ashtrays.

Stella had insisted that Bill and Agnes should not meet that morning. 'Bad luck,' she had said. They, too, would come later in the morning, meet at the registrar's office and then stay the night in her house, just the one night, before returning to London.

Bill and she were off to Paris for a week. Agnes felt a trace of her calm giving way at the thought. She must go upstairs and start to get ready. Madge and Bernard Hillier were coming. The marriage was to be a very small affair, just as she and Bill wanted it.

So many problems had been sorted out – only one remained. Agnes folded the daily papers and put them on the side table on top of some magazines. She was always neat, always tidy, but uncharacteristically she left a magazine open on the settee.

The ceremony was short. The registrar was a woman, dark-suited, tall, neat hair, her cheeks pink and healthy. Disinterested but smiling, she married them. The ring slipped easily on to Agnes's finger; she was almost bemused by it. She had chosen a thin gold ring – the new thicker patterned ones had not pleased her although Bill had rather liked them. As it fitted on her finger she looked up at him.

'You may kiss the bride,' the registrar said and it was done.

Lunch followed. Madge and Bernard, Stella and Miles, six of them. Agnes began to taste and savour the feeling of being married, of being Mrs Turner, especially as Madge laughingly called her by her new title every few minutes.

Agnes noticed, and perhaps Stella did too – Agnes was not sure – Bill's change of attitude to his daughter. It was warmer. After the wedding he had taken Stella into his arms and given her a long, long hug. Perhaps Stella had thought it was emotion because of his wedding, but Agnes knew that this was not altogether the reason. Bill knew now she was really his daughter and that her marriage was a blessed event and not the horror, the incestuous thing, Bill had first thought.

The conversation at lunch was all happy with anticipation of good things to come. Their visit to Paris, their new house when they had eventually decided which of the two they preferred – the one in Bembridge or the one in Yarmouth.

Bill's agent had telephoned to say the film company were moving faster than usual and that the contract was being drawn up now and perhaps would be ready for signing on their return from Paris. Everything in their lives was blooming, like roses in summer. Agnes still prayed, yes literally prayed, that nothing would happen, no black spot to mar the beauty.

She had done what she had to to put things as right as she could. Whether what she had done would help or hinder she was not sure, but as Stella and Miles, Madge and Bernard waved their smiling goodbyes, the Island growing further and fainter in the weak misty sunshine, Agnes had a wonderful feeling of gratitude for her life – she was no longer half a person, she was whole.

Stella sat on the settee in what was now Bill and Agnes's house. Miles had driven Madge and Bernard to the ferry and it was late afternoon. Everything had gone well, Stella thought; Daddy was so happy and Agnes had looked charming, her white linen dress beautifully cut, so simple and, Stella guessed, so expensive.

She felt tired, emotionally drained for some reason. She leant back and picked up the *Hello!* magazine which lay open on the settee beside her. Then she saw it! On the bottom right-hand corner of the page there was a photograph a little larger than the others – a wedding, handsome kilted bridegroom, pretty bride in a charming dress, a flowered headdress framing her face, the veil falling cloud-like round her. Their arms were linked and they were standing just outside some church.

It was not the bride and bridegroom who captured Stella's eyes, but the small, also kilted, page standing beside them – brown eyes fixed with serious intentness on the camera lens. It was Bruce! A little taller, bigger? Had he grown? His hair, always curly, was cut a trifle shorter. Stella gazed at him for a long time. The caption underneath meant little to her: 'The marriage of Miss Sharon Macdonald to Charles Norton which took place on September 3rd, and their little page Mark.'

The picture was marked in the corner on the white surround by a cross made with a thick red felt-tipped pen. Of course, Stella knew at once it was Agnes! She got up unsteadily. On the small escritoire lay the pen, still uncovered. How long had Agnes known? Some time, Stella was sure, or she would not have left the cryptic message without a word, in a magazine weeks old.

It was as if a great weight had been lifted from her. Her son was not dead. He was alive. His name was not Bruce any more but Mark – Mark. He was safe and her lie had done nothing to hurt him; nor would she ever do anything to interfere in the life he now led. How it had happened, how he had got there, she didn't know, and she knew she would never try to find out.

Miles called from the hall. 'Back, darling! They got off safely – and guess what?'

Stella looked up as he came into the room. 'Guess what?' she asked. She still felt slightly dazed.

'The Hilliers have got a surprise wedding present for Bill and Agnes. A clumber spaniel, liver and white. Apparently he's not ready to leave his mother yet. I hope Agnes can handle a puppy. She doesn't know about it yet.'

He looked down at her and Stella looked up at him.

'Oh no need to worry, Miles dear. Agnes can handle anything.'

She stood up and kissed him, then picked up the magazine, closed it and put it on top of the newspapers.